To
ELSIE AND BERNARD
SANGSTER SIMMONDS

'Life is love, and without love there is no light nor life, but only darkness and weariness of soul.'

The Stolen March

1

Francesca sat on the low brocaded stool in front of her big triple mirror and crooned to herself as she delicately outlined a very lovely mouth with her lipstick.

It was a low, sweet, velvety sort of voice. It seemed to suit the particular type of beauty which the gleaming mirror reflected for her between two tall electric candles.

The maid who stood just behind her holding a fur coat with an enormous fox collar looked adoringly at the reflection of her young mistress, and listened with equal adoration to the murmuring voice. And after all, it wasn't to be wondered at if Mary, who had been in Francesca's service for three years, had learned to adore everything about her. Most people did. The big public included.

Francesca, the Girl with the Crooning Voice.' That was how she was described by her critics. London raved about her – and about Fane, the clever young man who composed so many of the catchy, crooning little songs which she sang, and who accompanied her on the stage.

They were billed together as: 'FANE AND FRANCESCA.' They had been an enormous

11

success ever since they had first appeared in one of the outstanding revues a year ago.

There was nothing very spectacular about them. Francesca, always in a black-and-white dress and white shoes, and with a sleek white topper which she wore at a rakish angle on her fair head. Fane in tails and white tie at the big ebony grand, and black velvet curtains with big white notes of music sewn upon them for a background. Effective! And particularly when Fane began to play and Francesca to sing.

It had been more than effective from Francesca's point of view. For not only was this a paying business concern, their strong combination, but a fount of personal happiness for them both. They were in love – quite madly in love. They were going to be married very soon. And perhaps it was that very love which inspired Fane to write such charming, sentimental songs, and Francesca to sing them so perfectly!

'What time is it, Mary?'

Francesca turned to her maid as she slid on a little diamond wristlet and fastened the jewelled strap. She looked affectionately at the watch. It glittered on the smooth ivory arm which tapered into a delicate wrist and slender smooth fingers with pointed coral nails. Francesca loved her watch, not because the diamonds were of value, but because Fane had given it to her to celebrate

12

their engagement a month ago. It had his name engraved on the tiny platinum back. And when he had first slid it on to her wrist he had kissed every finger on her hand and said between each kiss:

'I love you!'

She was quite certain that he loved her, but no more than she loved him. And that was the beautiful part of their affair. They were utterly necessary to each other. Inseparable in their work, their friendship ... everything.

Mary handed her mistress the coat.

'That was the bell, Miss. It will be Mr Fane.'

Francesca smiled and nodded. Yes, it would be Fane. He came every evening at six o'clock to take her out for a light meal, after which they went to The Quality Theatre – new and luxurious – where the revue 'STAND BY' was running, and in which they played considerable parts.

Francesca gave a last glance at her mirror. She was satisfied. She had reason to be. That slim, supple young body of hers in the apricot velvet dress which had a little cape to match, edged with Russian sable, was the envy of most women who knew her. Just as her clothes were enviable. Francesca kept to her black-and-white toilette for professional purposes, but outside the theatre she loved colours. Tonight she was wearing something very new and special because Fane was going to take her to supper and dance after the show.

Invariably she was tired, and after a sandwich and a drink she came back to her small flat and went to bed. But tonight they were celebrating. This was the first anniversary of the day when they had signed their contract together and started on the career which had developed along such magic lines for them both.

Francesca gave a little contented sigh and walked across the warm untidy bedroom, which was littered with clothes and smelt deliciously of perfumes. Long before she reached the drawing-room she knew that Fane would be in one of his excited, restless moods. He would be walking up and down the room, smoking, impatient for the sight of her.

Something seemed to grip her by the heart at the very thought of him ... her beloved lover, so inexpressibly dear and important to her. Fane, the temperamental composer, with his quick temper and swift engaging smile which won pardon for him whatever he did or said, and that wonderful touch on the piano keys! There was nobody in the world like Fane. And all this success and happiness was still so new to Francesca that she held her breath even now when she thought about it.

It did not seem so long ago that she was

unknown ... just nobody at all but Francesca Hale, who lived with a widowed mother in a Sussex cottage, and divided her time between singing the music which she so passionately loved and looking after her mother, who was almost always ill.

Then had come Mrs Hale's death, which had left Francesca alone in the world at the age of twenty-two. And after that, a studio party in Chelsea, given by a girl who had been at school with Francesca. To that party Fane had come, and had heard Francesca sing for the first time. Just one of her own crooning songs to a Spanish guitar which she could play. And before the end of that evening Fane had commandeered her in his egotistical and impetuous fashion, played song after song for her at the piano, and then asked her to call and see him in the morning and meet one of London's biggest theatrical producers. Her very name had inspired him, he told her. Why, the name of Francesca was meant to be linked with that of Fane, and her velvety, appealing voice was just what he needed for his songs.

Fane had been on the stage before. He had money of his own, and two or three years after he had come down from Oxford he was making a steady income by composing. He had influence with the theatrical magnates and he used it. Francesca was shy, but that could easily be remedied with a

15

little tuition and experience. He himself coached her, helped her, worked with her for weeks, and at the end of it she was what he wanted.

Then, after the nerve-shattering experience of a first performance, Francesca knew that everything was going to be all right. The public took her – like Fane's songs – straight to their hearts. And one of the things that pleased her most was that she had justified Fane's faith in her.

He had told her that he had no wish to eradicate entirely that shy and sensitive strain in her. That was what he most loved. That was why he had fallen in love with her, he had said. Because she was different from others on the stage. There was no hardness, no cynicism in the soft dark eyes of Francesca. They radiated kindness and generosity. Fine, brilliant eyes, exquisitely set in a pale oval face framed with the smooth shining hair which made such a contrast to the darkness of narrow brows and long, jet lashes.

Francesca found Fane just as she had anticipated, pacing the room. But he stopped when he saw her in her apricot velvet gown, standing in the doorway. He came towards her with that graceful, gliding walk which singled him out from other men. Francesca had never seen anyone walk just that way. He moved like a born dancer. Not very tall, slightly built, he was extraordinarily good-looking with hair almost as fair as her own, and long, heavy-lidded eyes of a curious cold grey. Students of physiognomy might have said that Fane Braber's eyes and lips were cruel. But Francesca had not discovered the cruelty. For her Fane was warm and tender and, as a lover, all that a woman desired.

'My sweet!' he said when he was close to her, and took her hands and kissed them each in turn. 'How adorable you look.'

'Do you like the new dress?'

'Terribly. What do you call it? ... tangerine? Peach?'

'No,' she laughed up at him, 'all wrong – it's apricot.'

He took her in his arms.

'And you smell lovely, and you're warm and beautiful, and oh ... rather like a ripe apricot from the South.'

'You say beautiful things, Fane darling.'

'Only to a beautiful girl.'

'London's full of beautiful girls.'

He drew her closer, and with a forefinger touched a shining curve of her hair which winged over both small ears and just showed the smoky-pearl earrings which she always wore.

'There isn't one lovely as you, Adorable.'

'And how many have you said *that* to?' she laughed again.

17

'My sweet, I don't think that I have ever heard you say a cynical thing before. It hurts, rather ... on this day of days, too!'

She linked both slender arms about his neck, reached on tiptoe and kissed his chin.

'Darling idiot, I was only teasing you. But I dare say you *have* paid compliments to other girls.'

'I dare say,' said Fane rather languidly, 'but I don't remember – I remember nothing but you.'

Francesca hummed under her breath.

'Most every day,
Most of every hour of every day
I'm thinking of you.'

He stopped the rest of the verse by kissing her on the lips, passionately.

'When you sing like that you drive me crazy.'

'Darling, aren't you tired of my voice yet?'

Flushed and starry-eyed she looked up at him.

'I never shall be.'

'I believe you love my voice more than you love me.'

'You and your voice are one and the same thing.'

'Not quite. I might lose my voice but there'd still be *me!*'

'Don't think of such horrors. Tonight we

are going to celebrate the day that we became partners.'

Francesca looked up at him a trifle wistfully. Fane hated any deep discussions, any philosophy. There were times when she would like to have talked to him about all kinds of things which were in her mind and heart. But she kept silent because she was afraid of boring him. He was so gay, and he loved gaiety in others. He skimmed over the surface of things, brilliantly. He adored her. She knew it. But was it not because her voice and her beauty appealed to him rather than because he realized that the real Francesca was his mate, essentially, integrally part of him?

'Just supposing,' she persisted, 'that I *did* lose my voice, would you go on loving me?'

'Sweet, I refuse to answer such foolishness. Don't be so depressing! Let's go along to "The Ivy" and have a spot of food before we go down to the theatre. The car's outside.'

She sighed and smiled. No use trying to make Fane say any more than that. He hated to be depressed! Well, bless him. She wasn't going to upset him. But there remained in her a remote desire to go deeper, to get nearer to him, spiritually closer. Hers was a deep, generous nature, passionate and sensitive. Fane had awakened all the real woman in her. Yet somehow she felt that it

19

was not the real woman that he wanted. Not the Francesca who was an idealist and who believed in love for love's sake and in sacrifice and the blinding beauty of love as the poets had seen it... *'The desire of the moth for the star.'* There had always been that poetic and idealistic quality in Francesca which had lifted her thoughts to the stars. But Fane persistently brought them earthwards.

He adored her success. The applause. The glowing criticisms of her artistry. He liked to be seen in public with her.

He liked to hold her, ardent and tremulous, in his arms and to watch the effect of his caresses upon her; liked to feel that she was very much under his spell and that she was his to command even when he knelt and kissed her small shoe to prove that he was her devoted lover. He was extravagant in all his methods. Yet every action was tinged with caution and personal vanity. Francesca had helped to make him famous. Yet somehow, skillfully, he managed to make her feel that he was mainly responsible for their success.

There were a dozen women in love with him, and a good many hundreds whom he would never know were 'Fane fans' after having listened to him play and sing with Francesca.

She was immensely proud of him and of their association. It was marvellous to feel that he belonged to her and that very soon they would be married, so much more completely united than they were now. It never entered her head to be jealous, because she trusted him implicitly. He was the more exacting of the two, but she adored him for his very jealousy when he showed it. He was terrified of losing her. He told her so, continually. And she liked him to feel like that. That was proof of his love.

She walked across the drawing-room and opened the long French windows which led on to a balcony overlooking the river. The April night was soft and warm. It was so clear that she could see all the hundreds of lights which glittered on the bridges and the shadowy buildings across the water, as far as the Tower.

Not so very long ago she had been living in a country cottage and imagining that she would never get used to London. Now she would not care to leave it. She was absolutely content in this small flat in Whitehall, high up, close to the roof, with an incredible view of the river; of smoke-grey house-tops, the church steeples, the tall stately monuments, and the grand old Abbey close by.

Big Ben rose proudly like a superb sentinel, showing her the time on its lighted face. Dear Big Ben ... she felt a personal affection for it and the friendly booming voice that chimed its hours! Then she turned and looked back at her room. That was beautiful, too; polished floor and soft blues and reds of old Persian rugs; her cherished Blüthner grand which her mother had bequeathed to her; two parchment-shaded lamps on Italian wrought-iron stands; many books, green chairs and sofa, green and gold cushions, and just one picture over the fireplace. An oil-painting of an Italian lake, brilliant blue water, silver olive trees and green mountains. Como, the birthplace of the Italian grandmother from whom Francesca had inherited her name and the velvet darkness of her eyes and brows.

Fane watched her small, expressive face with a tinge of amusement in his smile:

'What's the matter with you tonight, darling? You're all "fey"...'

She came back to him and rubbed her cheek against his sleeve.

'No – but just so happy that I don't feel that I'm in this world at all.'

'But you are, very much so.'

'Fane, when we are married, can't we have another flat in this building? I hate to leave the river.'

His brows contracted. A view was not so important to Fane as being right in the centre of things ... things that mattered to him. His own flat was in Piccadilly, close to the theatres; in the core of the world that he loved. So far, the arrangement was that both he and Francesca should move to a larger flat in his building. He intended that it should be so, but he did not press it tonight. He always got his own way, but gradually, subtly. He just kissed her finger-tips and murmured:

'Sure – we must talk it over.'

Sweet Francesca! What a wonderful thing it had been finding her! Duffeyne, their manager, had told him the other night that they had made a phenomenal hit with their piano and songs. So simple, but it just hit the mark. And so lucky that a girl who looked like Francesca, and who was so lovable, should have that perfect voice. Without that crooning voice Fane might never have come before the public eye in the way that he had so much wanted. Now his songs were in huge demand. Sung by Francesca, of course! They couldn't be separated. They had broadcast with considerable triumph a week ago. Tomorrow they were to make gramophone records together. This they had already done before, and these records were selling well.

'Don't forget, sweet, we're making that new record for H.M.V. at twelve o'clock tomorrow,' he reminded her.

She nodded.

'We're going to do *Nobody Knows*, aren't we?'

'Yes. I think it ought to record well.'

23

'Are we singing it tonight?'

'As an encore in the second act, yes.'

Francesca's rich, low voice lilted the words:

'Nobody knows how much I love you,
Nobody cares but you.'

Fane whistled with her, then suddenly pulled a small parcel wrapped in tissue-paper from his pocket.

'Good lord, I was forgetting this. For you, darling, a first anniversary present.'

Her eyes widened with pleasure as she opened the small case and found a brooch sparkling against the velvet. Emeralds and diamonds on a delicate platinum bar.

'Fane! How gorgeous, and how extravagant!'

His handsome face was tender as he pinned the brooch for her on to the apricot velvet just above the slight lovely curve of her breasts. Yes, it was extravagant. More expensive than he could really afford. He was making money, but it seemed to trickle like water through Fane's fingers. He was always in debt no matter how much he earned. He had been like that since he was a boy at Oxford – always overdrawn. Whatever he did must be done in the most lavish fashion. Just before Francesca had come on to the scene his finances had been in rather a serious way. Now, fortunately, they were making money together, so his accounts could run on. Everybody in London today knew 'Fane and Francesca.'

She raised a warm face with starry eyes to his.

'A million thanks for such a lovely present, and I've got one for you...' She drew a packet from her bag and pressed it into his hand. A set of black pearl studs. Of course he was enchanted with them, and insisted upon going into her bathroom and putting them on at once.

Then when he came back, there were long, ardent kisses, all their passionate love closing round Francesca's heart and body like a white flame. She had never thought it possible for anybody on earth to be as happy as she was tonight.

She was humming one of his songs, gaily, when he helped her into the beautiful blue and silver Bentley which was his latest extravagance. They drove through the warm spring night down St Martin's Lane toward 'The Ivy' where they were to have a short meal before the show.

2

At half-past six 'The Ivy' was almost deserted, because it was much too early for the usual diners. But Fane and Francesca came here for their lunch and this quick, early meal regularly. Later, after the theatre, they would go on to a night club for supper and dance, where there would be heaps of people who knew them; the usual cheery theatrical crowd.

Very often they had the little restaurant to themselves at half-past six, but tonight one table in the corner was occupied. Francesca, as she sat at her usual table, glanced at the couple who were quite close to them. Rather an unusual pair, she remarked to Fane. A big, dark-haired, brown-skinned man with a hard, bitter face, and a little old lady with snow-white hair, forget-me-not blue eyes, and a black velvet ribbon Victoria-wise round her neck.

'Isn't the old lady a darling?' Francesca whispered to Fane.

'M'm,' said Fane with a brief glance, and then returned to the menu. 'But the fellow looks decidedly unpleasant.'

'Until he speaks to her, and then his whole

face changes,' said Francesca. 'I think she must be his mother. He adores her.'

'Quaint child,' said Fane, 'you do notice such extraordinary things.'

At that instant the big, dark man beside the old lady caught Francesca's eye. She had a queer uncomfortable sensation that he was regarding her with hostility. He gave her a swift scornful look. And why? It wasn't customary for men to look at her like that. Francesca shivered a little and turned to Fane. She had a definite, intuitive feeling, either that she had met this man before or that she was going to meet him again.

The old lady was saying:

'Julian, my dear, did you notice that perfectly lovely child as she came in? I have never seen anything so sweet.'

The man called Julian gave a short laugh.

'They all look sweet, Mother mine. Like Dead Sea fruit ... beautiful without and ugly within.'

The old lady winced.

'Don't be too cynical, darling,' she said gently.

At once he took her hand and patted it.

'There, darling. Sorry! As a matter of fact I agree – the girl is beautiful. I wonder who she is...?'

A waiter, pouring some hock into his glass, volunteered the information.

'They're the famous couple, sir ... she

sings and he plays... 'Fane and Francesca' they're called. In that revue at The Quality Theatre.'

'Never heard of them,' said the man called Julian.

The old lady was quite excited. She had read about Fane and Francesca and had heard one of their records. But then she lived in England, and Julian was nearly always abroad.

'Francesca is a beautiful name,' she said. 'It's quite thrilling to be here and to see such a famous couple.'

Julian patted her hand again. He was glad that she was thrilled. His heart seemed to drop within him like a stone as he looked at her sweet ivory face. The only person in the world whom he loved and in whom he still believed. He had no use for women. The only girl whom he had cared for and married had left him for somebody with more money, two years ago. She had been fair – a little like that girl over there with the blonde hair and slim, lovely body in the apricot velvet dress. God, how he hated all women today! All except this precious mother, and she was dying. They had told him yesterday that she hadn't a month to live.

This morning he had arrived back from abroad in order to take her to a nursing-home. She would probably never come out of it alive. And tonight he was giving her a last treat. She wanted to dine out because she lived in a remote village in Devonshire and this was a tremendous thrill for her. They had come early because she must be in the home, in bed, before eight. She was in pain and she refused to let him see it. But he knew it. He suffered with her. He felt nothing but pain and bitterness tonight. And it was with that hostile expression that Julian Grey caught Francesca's eye, and then looked away again.

Somehow or other, although she never quite realized why, a shadow fell across Francesca's happiness from that moment onwards. She was glad to get away from 'The Ivy' and find herself in her dressing-room at The Quality. Busily making up her face, with the dresser waiting behind her ready to help her into her black-and-white frock, Francesca remembered the extraordinary-looking man and the white-haired old lady. She shivered even at the remembrance.

'I can't think why he looked at me like that,' she reflected.

And the memory disturbed her even when she was on the stage that night singing to an adoring public.

It was then, for no apparent reason, that she broke down for the first time. Not because she was nervous or had forgotten her words, but because her voice failed her. As she told people afterwards, it just 'died on her'! She noticed that she was becoming husky and cleared her throat several times. She became conscious of Fane's surprised and distressed face, and tried desperately to get out the notes, but the words simply would not come. She ended in a whisper.

Fortunately it was at the end of her performance, and it was to be hoped that the public imagined that the whispering was part of the turn. She and Fane, hand in hand, took several curtains.

Then she found herself back in her dressing-room staring at her reflection in the mirror, white as death under her make-up, clutching her throat with one small shaking hand.

Again she tried to sing, and could not. Only that husky whisper issued from her throat. She was forced to realize that her singing voice had vanished ... just vanished mysteriously in the middle of a song.

Through the mirror she caught sight of Fane's face, almost as white as her own. With a soft towel he was automatically rubbing off his greasepaint. His long blackened lashes made his features look almost girlishly beautiful. But his lips were a thin line.

'What's happened, darling?' he asked abruptly. 'Surely you can sing? It's absurd! What is it? Try again, now.'

She tried, and croaked.

'I can't!'

He turned, filled a glass with water and

handed it to her.

'There! Drink that.'

She gulped down the liquid and choked a little. 'I don't think water will be any good!'

'Try,' he persisted; 'try to sing again.'

She made another effort. A husky whisper issued from her throat. Then she burst into tears.

'I can't … I *can't* sing… I've been trying… I tried on the stage … you don't know how awful it was, I nearly died of nerves. I just couldn't sing and I can't now.'

Francesca's dresser, a fat, good-natured woman, came bundling forward.

'There, Miss, don't cry … 'ave another drink… I know a lady, Miss Muriel Markes … you've 'eard 'er name! She was in pantomime and 'er voice suddenly went, but it come back the next morning.'

'Oh, get away,' said Fane savagely. 'Leave us alone.'

The dresser walked out, muttering under her breath.

Francesca went on sobbing. She was frightened. More frightened than she had ever been in her life. It was a terrible feeling … not being able to sing when she tried. What would have happened if she had been in the middle of the act? It was a mercy that it was at the end of the performance, and Fane and Francesca did not appear until they took the final curtain with the rest of the company.

She felt Fane's hand on her shoulder.

'Don't cry! It will only make you worse. We must get you to a doctor at once.'

She turned to him, her face piteous, disfigured, tears and make-up blotched together. She caught his hand and clung to it with both her own.

'Fane, isn't it awful? What do you think has happened?'

'I don't know.'

'And you remember I was joking about it at the flat... I said, what would you do if I lost my voice?'

He moved uneasily.

'You haven't lost your voice. It's only a temporary thing, a sort of laryngitis.'

'But my throat doesn't feel particularly sore.'

'Does it hurt at all?'

She put her hand to her hot, damp forehead and pushed back a wave of thick shining hair.

'I had a little pain ... a very little one ... yesterday ... but it passed off. I didn't take any notice of it. I felt it again this morning early, when I swallowed. But it got better, and so I just thought I'd strained my throat a little through singing so much.'

'Good God, you ought to have told me or seen a doctor.'

Her velvety-brown eyes, swimming with

tears, beseeched him.

'But it didn't seem important. I mean, the pain didn't go on.'

'And then this,' he said, beginning to pace up and down her room. 'God, it's frightful!'

A moment's silence. Francesca tried, desperately, to use her voice, and only that frightening croak came forth. She shivered and hid her face in her hands again.

'I don't understand it.'

'Get dressed, and let's take you straight to a doctor ... there's no time to be lost.'

Duffeyne, the manager, came hurrying into Francesca's room. A fat, cheerful American with horn-rimmed glasses and twinkling eyes.

'Say, Francesca, what's happened to the vocal cords? I thought for a minute you were fooling on the stage, but they tell me your voice has gone.'

Fane answered for her:

'So it has. Something's wrong. I'm going to take her straight to the doctor.'

'But your final curtain?'

'We must cut it tonight, that's all. There's no time to be lost. If there is anything to be done, it must be done at once. Francesca's voice is more important than anything else.'

'Sure it is,' agreed Duffeyne, 'it's a gold mine! All right, cut the final curtain and take her along...' He turned to Francesca and patted her head... 'Don't worry, baby, it's just a touch of laryngitis, and a few days' rest will put you right.'

Francesca had been sunk in a deep well of despair, but hope revived in her. They all said it was laryngitis. That wasn't very serious. That could be cured with rest and care. It was just as she had thought, she had been using her voice too much.

She wiped her face and then laughed, a trifle hysterically.

'Sorry to be such a little fool, Fane, but it scared me, I tell you.'

'I bet it did. It scared me as much as it did you.'

She held out her hand to him.

'Oh, Fane darling...'

'Darling,' he said, took her in his arms, and gave her a little hug: 'Poor sweet! What a shame! And when we were going to celebrate, too. What a thing to happen on our anniversary.'

'Awful... Oh, *darling.*'

She clung to him, and hid her wet eyes against his shoulder.

He kissed the top of her head.

'Hurry and get dressed, my sweet, and I'll drive you straight to a throat specialist. I'll 'phone the doctor who attended me when I had 'flu last spring. He's a good fellow and will know the best person to take you to. I'll be back when I'm changed.'

He was all kindness and comfort and ten-

34

derness. Francesca, in the arms of her lover, had no fears ... knew no despair ... even this throat trouble seemed a trifling affair.

When Fane had gone, she called to her dresser breathlessly, and began to repair the damage which weeping had done to her face.

Twenty minutes later she did not look as though she had shed a tear. She was lovely and glowing again in the apricot velvet gown and fur coat. Fane, gay and optimistic, drove her in the Bentley to Wimpole Street, pouring out his news. His doctor had recommended Mr Trent-Conning. He was considered a most reliable throat specialist. He would have liked Francesca to see Sir Hugh Wynch. Wynch was marvellous. He had just flown to India and operated on the throat of a Maharajah. But he was abroad cruising on holiday. However, Trent-Conning was almost as good.

'The doc said it sounded like laryngitis when I explained what had happened,' said Fane. 'We'll get you right, darling, so don't despair any more.'

Francesca snuggled in her rich furs close to him and sighed:

'You're so sweet to me, darling. I can't be scared of anything when I'm with you. But I wish I hadn't joked tonight about you loving my voice more than you loved me.'

'Darling idiot!' he murmured.

But, as usual, he refused to be drawn into a discussion of that kind.

Then they were at Wimpole Street, and Francesca was sitting in a dark room, with her mouth open, and powerful lights were being splayed upon her throat. The small spatulate fingers of Mr Trent-Conning worked busily for a few moments. A low, quiet voice questioned her, closely. Then the examination was over.

Francesca was with Fane again, holding his arm, shivering a little with nerves as they stood together before the desk in Mr Trent-Conning's big consulting-room.

'It's laryngitis, isn't it?' asked Fane hopefully.

'He must know an awful lot about my throat now,' said Francesca, laughing a little hoarsely. 'He did lots of funny things and saw miles down my larynx!'

The surgeon looked at the notes which he had been making on a pad before him, tapped his pen on the blotter thoughtfully, and then glanced up at Francesca's lovely, questioning face:

'It isn't laryngitis,' he said.

Francesca felt her heart miss a beat.

'Then what is it?'

'Is it something worse?' demanded Fane.

'I wish I could say otherwise,' was Trent-Conning's reply, 'but I must be frank with you.'

Francesca felt Fane stiffen beside her, and because she knew that he was afraid now, she made a great effort to be brave, although her heart beat furiously.

'Please tell me.'

'It's a condition,' said Trent-Conning, 'known as "singer's nodules," which consists of little fibrous tumours growing on the vocal cords. These do appear at times quite suddenly, and it isn't unusual for them to grow without the sufferer noticing it for some time. Then without warning you lose the power to sing, although it may not affect the speaking voice at all. I remarked that you are husky tonight, but you say that you have a somewhat husky voice normally. Therefore, still less would you have noticed anything but the slight pain which you felt yesterday and this morning.'

Instinctively Francesca's fingers flew to her throat. Her eyes dilated, fixed themselves on the surgeon. He spoke so quietly and im-personally, as though he were delivering a lecture to a crowd rather than telling her, Francesca Hale, that something terrible was happening to her vocal cords.

'Singer's nodules' sounded absurd, even comic; but 'little fibrous tumours' sounded much worse, horrifying. She groped for Fane's fingers, and he pressed them in sympathy. She said:

'Well – what does it mean?'

'I'm afraid,' said Trent-Conning, 'you'll have to have an operation.'

'Oh, God!' said Fane.

And feeling rather sick, he sat down suddenly and stared at Francesca. He was very pale. He disliked anything to do with illness, and the thought of an operation unnerved him. It frightened Francesca, too. Although her knees were shaking, it was she who comforted Fane. She steadied her own nerves, realizing somehow that it was necessary to give him the moral support which she needed.

'It's all right, darling,' she said, 'don't look like that – I'll be all right – won't I...?'

She turned to Trent-Conning. He smiled and nodded at her in a kindly way.

'Of course you will.'

'And it isn't a serious operation, is it?'

'No, we'll have you right in a few weeks' time, I hope.'

Fane groaned.

'A few weeks, my God! That means months before you sing again.'

'But it might have been so much worse,' she said valiantly. 'I might *never* have been able to sing again.'

Trent-Conning looked from Fane's handsome egotistical face to the lovely one of the girl who was smiling at him, soothing him. He thought:

'What courageous creatures women are!

The man goes to bits, and it's her trouble! Poor pretty thing! I don't think I'll tell her that there is a chance that she *might* not sing again. I think we'll just operate and hope for the best.'

3

Francesca discovered that there is far too much leisure in which to think when one is lying in bed for a long time.

She did a great deal of thinking during the slow days and the many wakeful nights which seemed so endless while she was in the nursing-home. And they could not be particularly cheerful thoughts, no matter how brave or optimistic she was about the future. It can be so lonely in a nursing-home, in spite of the nice, attentive nurses and the friends who come to see one. There must inevitably be set visiting hours, and when those were past Francesca found that there was nothing much to look forward to except eating and sleeping and the interminable circle of thought.

The operation on her throat had been performed ten days ago – as far as she knew, quite successfully. Whenever she questioned Trent-Conning or her nurses, they told her that she was all right and 'doing well.'

The first forty-eight hours had been horrid. The pain had seemed awful, and she had had the terrifying sensation that she would never be able to use her voice again; that she would always speak in a whisper. There had been intermittent blessed periods of peace, the result of narcotics, then the pain and fear again.

Before a week was ended she was able to speak almost normally except for slight huskiness. Then the visitors came pouring in.

Fane, of course, was the first to come. Darling Fane! A little subdued and different, perhaps, from his gay, brilliant self; awkward beside that bed which was so stiff and white and straight, and in which Francesca lay drained of colour and shadowy-eyed, looking up at him with enormous eyes which begged for his tenderness. Tender he was, and most sympathetic; showered her with flowers and fruit, books and magazines. His were always the most extravagant bouquets. The little room with window overlooking Manchester Square had been a bower of flowers from the first day that Francesca entered the home. Three-quarters of them she had sent to a hospital.

'The Girl with the Crooning Voice' had an admiring public. Bouquets and messages streamed in from all quarters. That was very pleasant and flattering, and Francesca would not have been human if she had not been thrilled by her popularity. But it was only Fane's attentions which really counted; his particular flowers which were put beside her bed, and the moments when *he* came which compensated her for the pain and the long, lonely hours.

Only for 'moments' did he stay. Generally he rushed in, covered her hand with kisses, begged her to hurry up and get well, and rushed away again. There was always so much to be done. He spoke of his engagements, the rehearsals, the work which he was putting in on one of his new compositions. He had had to find a substitute for his Francesca: not an easy job, and, so he told her a hundred times, nobody could really replace her. But the show had to go on.

Duffeyne had discovered an American girl – Kay Wynton – who had just come over from the United States. She had one of those attractive Southern voices which could do justice to Fane's crooning melodies. She had been rushed into Francesca's place, and it was now 'Fane and Kay' who were billed together.

Impossible for Francesca not to be secretly wildly jealous, although not for worlds would she have shown Fane what lay in her heart. She told him that she was thankful that he had discovered a good substitute. She admired the photograph which he showed her of his new partner. Kay was a slim, vivacious, red-haired girl, all flaming curls and mischievous eyes and an impudent manner utterly different from the shy sensitiveness of Francesca. When she asked Fane, half in fun, half in earnest, if he preferred his new partner, he said:

'You bet your sweet life I don't, honey.'

That remark only half-consoled her. Already Fane had a slight American twang. He seemed to be absorbing some of the 'new partner's' personality.

The newspaper critics were kind. They deplored Francesca's sudden illness, and, as one paper said:

'The revue, "Stand By," is certainly standing by at the moment, waiting for "The Girl with the Crooning Voice" to come back.'

Then, on this bright May morning, she realized with a deep pang that they had originally fixed the 4th of this month for their marriage. It was to have taken place at the registrar's office on Saturday morning. They were going to drive in the Bentley up to Oxford for a brief week-end honeymoon in that adorable old Tudor inn, 'The Trout,' at Godstow. Fane wanted to show her his Oxford. And she wanted to see it through his eyes.

But of course those plans were cancelled.

Perhaps in her heart of hearts Francesca had hoped that Fane would suggest marrying her here, in the home, just so that they really belonged to each other for ever. But he had shown no inclination to do so. He had said:

'Let's wait till you're out of this beastly place and fit again, and then we'll get married and I'll take you away for a whole week. The show will have to get on without us.'

Well, Trent-Conning had told her that she could leave tomorrow. So perhaps her wedding wasn't so far off, after all. She tried not to be depressed. She believed the nurses who assured her that it was quite normal for people to be low-spirited after any operation.

Knowing how Fane shrank from illness or anything which was depressing, Francesca was particular gay when he came to see her today, just before lunch. She had been allowed to sit up in a chair for the last few days.

Today she sat in a chair with a rug over her knees, wholly dressed for the first time, wearing a new frock which had been sent for her approval from Hanover Square; a particularly charming silky thing; green and white, to delight Fane's beauty-loving eye.

The moment he came into the room she stood up and saw that he was pleased. Those cold grey eyes of his glowed in a way which told her, who knew him so intimately, that he was stirred by the sight of her. The excitement and anticipation of seeing him had brought a warm pink to her cheeks. The green dress with white organdie collar and big green bow made her look very young, and her skin was dazzling white, and the blonde hair almost of silver fairness.

'Darling!' said Fane; came towards her with his gliding walk and dropped flowers, magazines, chocolates in a heap on her lap: 'How marvellous to see you dressed and on your feet! And how adorable you look!'

Her heart-beats quickened. Tears of sheer weakness came into her eyes. Mutely she walked into his arms and clung to him while he kissed her. It was such a relief to feel the warmth of his embrace and the touch of his lips which never failed to stir her to the depths of her being.

When he released her she said:

'You shouldn't bring me more things, sweetheart, I have so much already.'

'Never enough for you,' he said, smiling as he glanced round the flower-filled bedroom. Then he caressed her with subtle, experienced fingers and added:

'Darling – you've grown thin.'

She took his hand and held it tightly between her small fingers.

'I'll soon get fat again. How are you? What have you been doing? Tell me everything...'

They sat down side by side near the window.

'Oh, I've been frantically busy,' said Fane, 'but it is more important to know about you. How *is* the throat?'

'Don't you think I'm speaking more clearly?'

'Definitely. But what about the singing?'

'They've forbidden me to try. But two doctors – Trent-Conning and a physician – are both examining me early tomorrow, and I'm to be told then when I can sing again.'

'It'll be super to get you back, sweetness,' he said with his most engaging smile.

'Oh, darling, have you really missed me? Isn't Kay Wynton as good as Francesca?'

'How could she be?'

'Easily.'

'Well, I want my Francesca back,' he said, and dropped a kiss on the top of her head. 'Kay is amusing and a good actress, but she doesn't get the applause you do.'

Francesca, woman-like, probed deeper.

'I don't mind about the applause, but I mean, do you want *me* back, because of *me?*' she asked wistfully.

'Of course I do.'

'It's the first of May today.'

'And you're queen of it, honey.'

She looked at him with passionate intensity.

'I was thinking of the 4th...'

'What about it?'

She was horrified because he had forgotten.

'Darling! ... we were to have been married...'

Fane put up a hand and smoothed his fair hair, which glistened with brilliantine.

'Of course! What a damned shame, darling. But it's only postponed.'

She wanted to be taken in his arms – to be allowed to rest there, caressed, comforted. But he plunged into details of his latest achievements. He had written a new melody. He had wanted new words for it, and Kay had supplied them. Clever little devil ... wrote very amusing lyrics ... most useful ... some firm had suggested that he and Kay should record together for the gramophone ... perhaps he would fix up a broadcast with Kay too ... he and Kay were thinking out a new colour scheme as a change from the black and white.

Kay .... Kay ... Kay!

Francesca listened, her gaze never leaving Fane's face. He chatted on in his gay, inconsequent, airy fashion. All froth, all on the surface, so typical of Fane who refused to be pinned down to one subject if he could avoid it, or to be serious about anything. And so much Kay! Try though she did to stifle the feeling, Francesca was healthily jealous this morning.

So Kay could write words! That was one thing she, Francesca, had never done. And those two were to record together! That devastated Francesca. She swallowed hard, cleared her throat, fingered that long slender neck of hers, and wondered when she would be able to sing again. Of course she *would* be able to sing later on. Kay was only a makeshift. Kay would have to drop out of it once Fane's Francesca was fit again.

Fane broke off in the middle of one of his long bright speeches, touched Francesca's cheek and said:

'You're very quiet, sweetness!'

She pulled herself together and smiled at him.

'Not really.'

'This is my new song,' he said, and murmured it for her:

'What's a man to do
When you look at him so charmingly
And smile at him disarmingly,
What's a man to do...

'And so on,' said Fane. 'Rather a good tune, isn't it?'

'Most intriguing, darling. Did Kay write the words?'

'Yes.'

And Francesca, with the hand of jealousy

47

gripping her very hard, smiled and said:

'Good for her.'

'I must fly,' said Fane.

'Oh, must you?' Her fingers twined about his hand, reluctant to let him go.

'Yep. Kay and I have got a rehearsal.'

It was all that Francesca could do not to burst into tears and say:

'Oh, don't go, don't go to her ... stay with me... I need you... I'm frightened ... frightened about my voice ... about Kay ... and about losing you, whom I love better than anything, anybody, in the world.'

But instead she whispered:

'Fane, you know I'm going home tomorrow afternoon?'

'Rather, darling! I'll be here at four to take you. And I want to bring Kay to see you, too.'

'I would like to meet her.'

'I expect you have got lots of other people running round, haven't you?'

She put his hand against her cheek and closed her eyes for a moment.

'I don't think anybody amuses me except you, and I don't want anybody but you.'

'Angel!' said Fane languidly.

Struggling against the inclination to weep, she added:

'Everybody's awfully kind. Duffeyne came yesterday, bless him. He's a dear. And heaps of them from the theatre have called.'

'What about that special admirer of yours … the gallant Captain Elliott?'

'Oh, he calls every day,' said Francesca with a little grimace.

'I should tell him to look you up at the flat sometime,' said Fane.

She made no answer, only felt those icy fingers of doubt and jealousy clutching her very heart again. Was it her imagination, or was Fane changing? A month ago he would have been riddled with jealousy if any man had called to see her every day. Jack Elliott was in the Air Force. She had met him at a dance six months ago. He was a nice boy and a persistent admirer. But she had granted him very few favours. Fane, without any real cause, had often remarked when Elliott's name was mentioned that 'he had better keep away unless he wants a bullet through him' … one of Fane's extravagant theatrical ways of expressing his love for her.

But today he suggested that she should have Captain Elliott to see her! Well, it would be foolish of her to misconstrue what was, no doubt, only his kindly desire that she should not be too much alone. She stamped on her fears and kissed him good-bye with her usual charming tenderness. He refused to let her get up, and wrapped the rug round her as though she were a baby.

When he reached the door she called his name in that slightly husky voice which still hurt just a little bit when she used it:

'Fane!'

He turned and smiled at her.

'Yes?'

'Do you love me?'

'Incredibly, darling. But hurry up and get fit. I hate the smell of anaesthetics and I loathe nursing-homes.'

'I'll be home tomorrow.'

'Then you can sing all my new songs.'

Her eyes were brilliant with unshed tears.

'That will be marvellous.'

'You'll have to stay quiet a bit before I take you away.'

'Yes, I will.'

He opened the door, looked out, and then put his head back into her room.

'Who's in the next room? I've just seen a tall, dark fellow go in.'

'Oh, Fane, it's so curious. That's the son of the old lady whom we saw at "The Ivy" that night when I broke down, do you remember?'

'Can't say I do.'

'Yes. You know … the sweet old lady with the white hair whom I pointed out to you, and you said the man was unpleasant. He had rather a bitter face. Well, by some coincidence, she's here, in this very home. Her name is Mrs Grey, and that's her only son, Julian. I've been in to see her several times and sat talking to her. The poor darling had

50

an operation, but she's never going to get well, and they say he simply adores her. I told you at "The Ivy" I thought so.'

'I remember now,' said Fane.

'It's rather pathetic. She loves me going to see her, but he takes care never to be there when I'm with her. I think he's a woman-hater!'

'You'd thrill even a woman-hater, darling,' said Fane. 'I adore you in green. *Auf wiedersehen!*'

So saying, he blew her a kiss and departed.

Francesca sat motionless for a moment after he had gone. She stared at the red roses which he had brought. Then the tears came – just flowing down her cheeks – and she was helpless to stop them. Fane had only stayed with her for a quarter of an hour and it had passed like a flash. He had been just the same as ever, charming and lover-like. Yet she was miserable and afraid. She did not know why, really.

A pleasant-faced young nurse came into the room.

'Well – well, Miss Hale, so your visitor's gone! I'm sure there are some more flowers to put into water, aren't there?'

Francesca nodded and pointed to the roses.

The nurse smelt them.

'M'm … how gorgeous! Aren't you lucky! I was telling matron I had never seen so many flowers in my life, and we've had a number of actresses and film stars here. And isn't your Mr Fane handsome? I saw him go out just now. My word! If he were my young man I'd be scared of losing him…'

Then she saw that she had said the wrong thing. Her patient was crying, fair head bowed, face hidden in her hands.

'Why, my *dear!* What's the matter? Nothing wrong, I hope.'

Francesca shook her head.

The nurse took her wrist and laid a professional finger on the pulse.

'Back to bed for lunch, I think. We'll have your temperature going up. Too much excitement, my dear, what with getting up and dressing and having your fiancé here.'

Francesca stopped crying and raised a flushed mutinous face. She said in a hoarse little voice:

'No. I'm not going back to bed, I hate it! I shall *never* get fit in bed. I've got to get well and be out of here by tomorrow; I've *got* to, I tell you.'

'So you will, my dear. But you must keep quiet and not upset yourself. This sort of thing won't do your voice any good!'

Francesca seized the nurse by the arm:

'Tell me, honestly, you *do* think I'll be able to sing again, quite soon, don't you? It's so terribly important that I should.'

'But of course. Now I'm going to send you

up a nice little lunch, and some of that champagne Mr Fane brought you. And if you're a good girl, you can stay up for a bit longer.'

Francesca leaned back against the cushions in her chair and closed her eyes. She felt spent, and ridiculously emotional. She told herself that it was just nerves and weakness, and that she must conquer it for Fane's sake as well as her own. As long as she could sing again in a few weeks' time, what did anything matter? Kay Wynton wouldn't matter. Fane and Francesca would work together again and they would be married. This wretched, miserable affair would be forgotten. It was just an experience. Life was like that. It sent you these dark, anxious moments. You had to face them and surmount your troubles to show what you were worth. You couldn't expect continuous and unbroken happiness. And she was wicked to grumble. These last two years of her young life had been so splendid, just teeming with success; crowned by Fane's love for her.

The nurse went out, gave the roses to a passing maid, and walked into the next room, where the atmosphere was very different. No lovely, popular young actress here, with her life only just beginning, but a frail old lady facing the end of things.

Mrs Grey was dying slowly of a painful malady. But the fleeting spring sunshine was as bright in her room as it had been in Francesca's, and there were almost as many flowers here. All supplied by her son. The nurse had seen many touching cases in her career, but this was one of the most moving. This big, blunt man's devotion to his dying mother was remarkable. He spent every possible moment with her. To the outsiders, even to the nursing staff he was a little grim and curt. He wasted no words. They realised that there was something tragic about Julian Grey, although they none of them knew his history. But his tenderness and devotion to the old lady never altered.

'I want her to have everything that money can buy to make her last days as perfect as possible,' he had told the nurses who attended Mrs Grey.

But it seemed that she wanted little save the presence of her son, who was the only person in the world who mattered to her; and he was her sole visitor because they were alone in the world, these two.

When the nurse came in, Julian was reading to his mother. As the nurse remarked to her colleagues that evening, Mr Grey had a very attractive, soothing voice, and was really a distinguished figure; so tall and powerfully built, and with a dark, arresting head and fine hazel eyes. A compelling face marred by the hardness of the lips and his somewhat bitter, censorious expression.

He closed the book from which he had been reading.

'Time for your lunch, Mother mine!'

The old lady, who might have been carved of ivory against her big white pillows, smiled at him.

'What time are you coming back, darling?'

'For tea with you.'

'Wouldn't you like to do something else for a change – go out for a drive – it must be so boring here in my room and…'

He broke in:

'There's nothing else I'd rather do than be here with you.'

She smiled happily.

'Julian, I believe the little actress next door, Francesca, is coming in to see me.'

'H'm!' said Julian Grey abruptly, 'then you had better tell me what time she will be with you and I'll drop in later.'

'Oh, but why do you avoid her? She is so very lovely, isn't she, nurse?'

'She is a darling,' said the nurse.

'And she's so much in love with her Fane,' said old Mrs Grey with a little sentimental sigh, 'she just lives for him. I think she's quite domesticated by nature, rather different from the ordinary modern girl, Julian.'

'They're all domesticated and faithful and sweet when they're in love,' said Julian Grey.

'Oh, darling!' his mother reproved him gently, 'don't be so bitter.'

'Sorry,' he said, and dropped a kiss on her hand.

'Francesca really is a dear child, and she's been so kind to me. Ever since she's been allowed up, she's dropped in to bring me some of her lovely flowers or show me her press notices or amuse me in some way.'

'I'm glad she's been nice to you, dearest,' he said.

'Won't you meet her today?'

He restrained the refusal which rose to his lips. If the dear little mother was thrilled by this baby-faced actress, let her enjoy herself, poor darling.

'I may find her here when I turn up,' was his non-committal reply.

'Poor little Miss Hale,' said the nurse who was shaking up Mrs Grey's pillows.

'Why poor?' said Julian, his dark brows curving ironically. 'She appears to be a most successful young lady.'

The nurse lowered her voice.

'But there may be a blow in store for her.'

'Oh, I hope not,' said Mrs Grey.

The nurse, relishing her gossip, added:

'The doctors are having a consultation to-morrow, you know. We haven't told her or her fiancé yet. But the operation wasn't such a success as they hoped for. Between ourselves, there's quite a doubt whether she will ever be able to sing again!'

4

With special permission from the matron, Francesca took her small portable gramophone into old Mrs Grey's room that afternoon when the old lady had wakened from her customary sleep.

'You must hear the record which Fane and I made for H.M.V. just before my illness,' Francesca told her; 'it's great fun.'

Mrs Grey was enchanted. In the midst of her pain and failing strength it was a great treat to her to have this pretty, vivacious child come with all her beauty and talent to bring sunshine into this room when Julian was absent.

'It must be so amusing for you to hear your own voice, my dear,' she said.

Francesca, winding up the gramophone, smiled and nodded.

'And even more wonderful to hear Fane on his piano.'

'Always Fane, my dear. What a lucky child you are to be so happily in love.'

'Yes, aren't I?'

And Francesca felt a quickening of her pulsebeats at the very memory of Fane and the last kiss which he had left, warm and eager, upon her lips. She felt better after her lunch and an hour's doze; stronger, less depressed. She was so very sure of Fane's love, and it was ridiculous for her to worry just because he had to be a great deal with his new partner. Jealousy was an ugly thing, she told herself, and must be stamped upon ruthlessly. Besides, it was uncomplimentary to her lover to doubt him for a single moment.

She sat beside the old lady's bed in the armchair with a rug over her knees, and together they listened to the record.

Mrs Grey's fading eyes turned to the girl and drank in the picture of her slender loveliness in the new green dress and of that expressive face with the dark-lashed eyes which suggested such depth and capacity for feeling. Those liquid eyes were eloquent during these few minutes while the disc revolved under the tiny needle which so miraculously reproduced her own voice. But Mrs Grey knew that it was not the haunting, crooning voice which brought that look to her face. It was the piano accompaniment. The thought of her lover. When the record ended Mrs Grey applauded the song.

'It is one of my best,' Francesca admitted. 'And doesn't Fane play perfectly?'

'Perfectly, my dear,' said the old lady tenderly. 'I am hoping that my son will meet you here this afternoon and then you must play the record to him.'

'I don't think he wants to meet me, does he?'

'My poor Julian certainly is not very sociable.'

'Do you know, that night at the restaurant where we first saw each other, I caught his eye, and he seemed to look at me as though – oh, as though I were quite obnoxious. I wonder why?'

Mrs Grey sighed.

'He is a little bitter, my dear. Life hasn't been too kind to him, and love didn't bring him the wonderful happiness it has brought you and your Fane.'

Francesca nodded.

'I rather guessed...'

'Yes! An unhappy marriage. My poor boy ... and he is one of the finest men in the world. Things just went awry and the affair warped his outlook. I wish it hadn't. I worry about him so much. He has nobody but me ... and I'm leaving him ... I could have gone quite happily if I had known that he had somebody who would love and take care of him. He isn't strong. He has to fight against both ill-health and disappointment. Sometimes I think there is a melancholic streak in him which frightens me. We never discuss his personal affairs, nowadays. But oh, my dear, a mother knows ... and I realize that Julian is an unhappy man. That's why I hate leaving him alone.'

Francesca, all sympathy, took one of the old lady's delicate hands and patted it.

'Poor you! But you mustn't worry too much.'

'I can't help worrying, child. It was all so sad...'

She began to tell Francesca the tragedy of her son's life. Three years ago, soon after he had inherited a considerable amount of money from his father, who had been a successful barrister, Julian had bought a house in Devonshire which suited his mother's health, and had settled there with her. At the age of twenty-eight he was a confirmed bachelor, and more interested in architecture than in women. As a boy he had meant to become an architect and had studied for it. With money behind him and no necessity to work, he still interested himself in buying derelict houses of historic value and restoring them. Their own house, Mrs Grey told Francesca, was a marvellous sixteenth-century manor which Julian had mostly perfectly redeemed to its 'former glory.'

Then *The* Woman had come into his life, but not at all the one his mother had hoped he would marry. Irene, six years younger than Julian, was just the opposite of all Mrs Grey's ideas, and not the type she had expected Julian to admire. As is so often the case, the quiet studious man was caught by an enchanting face and figure, swept off his feet in a passionate episode, and led into matrimony.

Because it was his nature to do so, Julian gave body, heart, mind and soul to this girl Irene, but she, Mrs Grey said, 'hadn't a brain in her head, and wasn't capable of loving anybody but herself.'

They had had eighteen months together, during which Julian had gone through the slow and painful process of discovering that he had made a mistake and that Irene was as shallow and selfish as she was beautiful. He had built his house of dreams on shifting sand.

He had hoped that a child would bring them together, but she had refused him even that. With the end in sight, he had taken her over to the States on a visit, hoping to hold her interest. There she had met an American who went crazy about her physical charms and who offered even a bigger income than Julian's.

'Julian came back from America alone,' Mrs Grey finished her story. 'Six months later they were divorced. He barely mentioned her name in our house, but I think it broke his heart so far as hearts can break! It hurt his vanity so badly. Can't you understand ... when a man as reserved and as deep as my boy gives his heart to a woman and makes her his wife, he expects her love and loyalty in return. It shook him to the foundations when Irene left him. It made a cynic of him. He went abroad, bought an old castle in the South of Spain and restored it. But he seems to have lost interest even in his architecture.'

'I think his affair would make any man cynical,' said Francesca. 'Only some take divorce more lightly, perhaps.'

'Julian never took it lightly, my dear. It just smashed up everything for him.'

'Do you think he still loved her after it was all over?'

'He is the faithful kind. But even he had to see her discrepancies in the end. I don't think he has anything but contempt for her now. He would not have minded so much if she had left him because she loved somebody else, but the American was unattractive and elderly – it was the money which interested her.'

'He must have a rotten opinion of women.'

'I'm afraid he has, although he tries not to let me see it because he knows it hurts me.' The old lady sighed deeply and then added:

'She was fair and a little like you to look at, my dear, only that her eyes were blue, and she was very different from you in character.'

'I hope so,' said Francesca with a little laugh.

'I can't imagine you either marrying your Fane for his money or deserting him for somebody else.'

Francesca thrilled to the thought of Fane. 'No, you're right.'

The old lady looked at the girl through a slight mist of tears. There was something about Francesca which she found irresistible. Something gentle and wistful which made her yearn over the girl. Despite her recent stage success and the full, exciting life she had led, Francesca seemed such a child; unspoiled and sensitive. Mrs Grey was almost afraid for her. She hoped that this Fane was worthy of her and would never let her down; never hurt her as Irene had hurt Julian.

It was queer, but once or twice since she had known Francesca she had wished that Julian had met *her* and given *her* all that he had given Irene three years ago. She could have loved this girl. Francesca would have been a devoted and faithful wife and the mother of Julian's children. She wanted children. She had said so.

'A foolish old woman's fancy,' Mrs Grey reflected, and lay back on her pillows and dozed for a few minutes with closed eyes.

Francesca sat still thinking over the story of Julian Grey's unfortunate marriage. Inevitably there sprang into her mind the thought:

63

'What would I do if Fane left *me* for somebody else? It would break *my* heart ... nothing else would seem worth while. Poor Julian! I understand...'

The door opened, and a big dark-haired man in grey flannels, carrying a couple of books, came quietly into the room.

Francesca stood up and faced him. Here was the great Julian himself! She had a queer, inexplicable sensation as she met his gaze. Although she had only seen him once before, she remembered him clearly. She had never quite forgotten the hostility of his expression when he had seen her at 'The Ivy.' She wondered at it then; now she was better able to understand. He disliked the very sight of her because she bore some slight resemblance to the wife who had run away from him, but for the sake of the old lady to whom she had become firmly attached, she greeted him with friendliness.

'How do you do,' she said, 'I'm Francesca Hale.'

He bowed. They did not shake hands. He glanced at the old lady in the bed.

'Is my mother asleep?'

'Just dozing.'

She saw his gaze turn to the gramophone on the floor.

'I've just been playing her my new record,' she explained. 'I'll get nurse to carry it back to my room.'

'Allow me,' he said with cold courtesy, put down his books, and lifted up the gramophone.

Francesca led the way into her own room. Julian's big presence seemed to fill it. He set the machine down on her table and glanced around. Not since Irene had left him in New York had he set foot in a room like this. The atmosphere was redolent not only of flowers, but of some delicate French perfume, and the room was filled with all the dainty, pretty fripperies of a pretty woman's toilette. A room, in fact, painfully reminiscent of the one which Julian had shared with his wife. God! How little he wanted to be reminded of her and all that agony of disillusion and shattered love. He wanted to rush out of here rudely and slam the door like a sulky schoolboy. But Francesca was framing the doorway, so for a moment he had to stand there looking at her under his dark, frowning brows.

She returned his gaze and told herself that he was like a great bear waiting to eat her up. How different people were! Could two men possibly be more different than Julian Grey and Fane Braber! Julian, black-haired, almost a giant, athletic, strong; and at the same time with the broad brow and searching eye of the intellectual. Fane, so fair, slight and graceful, essentially the musician, the artist!

Suddenly Julian Grey said:

'I must thank you for being so kind to my mother. She has often spoken of you, and it's good of you to have visited her.'

The unexpected praise brought a slight colour to her cheeks.

'Not at all. It wasn't good of me, because I loved doing it. I think your mother is an absolute darling.'

'Yes,' he said curtly.

'Is there no hope of her getting better?'

'None.'

'I am so very sorry...'

He stirred uneasily under the soft, sympathetic voice. Definitely attractive that slightly husky voice; undeniably lovely the velvet brown eyes raised to his. But he could never look at a fair, pretty woman without remembering Irene and how madly he had loved her; how insanely he had believed in the beauty of soul behind all the physical attractions. Poor blind fool! Today he would not be deceived by a pretty face and figure or a soft voice. He would want to know Francesca Hale much better before he would credit that she was the gentle and sincere creature that his mother believed her to be.

Nevertheless, he was grateful to anybody on earth who had been good to his mother. The frail old lady in the next room was the lodestar of his existence. When that star flickered out, he wondered what he would have left and what use it would be going on!

He forced himself to say.

'I hope *you* are better.'

'Oh, much,' she smiled and nodded. 'I am leaving the home tomorrow as soon as the doctors have made the final examination. I am to be told when I can sing again. I am dying to get back to work.'

'Of course… Now, if you'll excuse me … I must get back to my mother,' said Julian, moving toward the door.

She stood aside to let him pass.

'Goodbye, and thanks,' he added.

'Goodbye,' she said, with a half-amused smile as she looked after the broad back. And she thought, turning back to her room: 'What a queer personality! Poor Julian Grey! He was quite the wrong type to have had a wife like that girl, Irene. It's just soured his whole existence! And I'm sure he could be so nice; the very way he behaves to his mother shows how nice he could be!'

The nurse put Francesca to bed early that night. 'If you're going home tomorrow, you must have a good night's rest,' she said, as she removed all the flowers and tidied up.

Francesca agreed. She was still so weak that she was glad to lie down and shut her eyes. And depression seemed to roll away from her completely at the anticipation of tomorrow – of getting away from all the paraphernalia of the home, the atmosphere of illness, medicines, doctors and nurses. It would be marvellous to be back in her own pretty flat. Back to her view of those grey carved stone roof-tops and towers and archways; the flashing signs and lights dipping into the river; London on an April night. From her high balcony it looked like an Eastern city; jewelled and mysterious.

Back to old Mary, who was crazy with impatience to get her young mistress home again, and who looked after her as well as any nurse. And last, but not least, back to Fane, who could see her so much more often at the flat than in this nursing-home.

In a few days she would be strong. By the end of the month she would be singing again. And before that she would be Fane's wife. What else could she ask of life?

Before she slept that night, she was happier than she had been since her operation.

5

The two doctors had just finished making an examination of Francesca's throat. She sat in her room with a nurse beside her. She was dressed in the new green-and-white frock; all packed and ready to leave the home. She was as excited as a child and chatted gaily to the two men before they made the examination.

Trent-Conning had, as usual, been non-committal. The consultant-physician, Dr McAllis, was a blunt Scot who wasted no time and had frightened her somewhat by asking her to try to sing a few notes. The result had been a hoarse croak which had appalled her until Trent-Conning had said:

'All right, all right, Miss Hale. We are only just making a test. It's early days yet...'

And now the two men were talking together in lowered tones at the other end of her room; arguing a little, Francesca thought, as she watched them anxiously.

'Do tell me when I *shall* be able to sing,' she begged them.

Finally they came back to her. Trent-Conning seemed ill at ease, took out his watch, murmured that he had an important appointment, that he would leave Dr McAllis to talk to her, and hurried off. The nurse showed him out.

Francesca, alone with the physician, offered him a cigarette.

'Don't let's be too formal,' she said, with her disarming smile, 'it scares me. Do smoke!'

He took the cigarette.

'Thank you, I will.'

'And can I?'

'I shouldn't just yet. It may make you

cough, and you want to keep that throat quiet as long as you can.'

'Isn't it healed?'

'Practically.'

'Doesn't look good to you this morning?'

He lit the cigarette and avoided the answer. He was a capable doctor with a direct manner; a busy man who had no time for frills. On the other hand, he had rarely had a more difficult task than this one which faced him now. His profession forbade that he should give away a colleague. Even though he knew that 'someone had blundered' he must not say it. He must wrap the truth up in cotton wool. But it would not prevent him from giving this pretty young actress known as 'The Girl with the Crooning Voice' a hideous shock.

Francesca, looking at him, had a sudden sinking sensation; a premonition of disaster.

'Dr McAllis,' she said, 'will you please tell me the truth. You and Trent-Conning have been very mysterious this morning. What's the trouble? Hasn't my operation been a success after all?'

That paved the way for him.

'No, it hasn't been quite the success that we hoped for,' he said.

'You mean ... that my throat isn't ... isn't quite right yet?'

'I can't say that it is.'

Her heart was beating at a suffocating

70

speed. All the pink colour which excitement had painted in her cheeks ebbed slowly away.

'Will you please tell me exactly what it means – what you have found?'

'I wish that I could give you better news, Miss Hale. But it is no use beating about the bush. You must know sooner or later. Trent-Conning did his best ... he is a very able surgeon...' McAllis cleared his throat and frowned. To himself he was adding: 'But too damned erratic, and this has been one of his failures...'

Francesca put both hands to her pounding heart.

'Go on, please!'

'But it's just happened that things didn't turn out the way he hoped for.'

'You've said that already. What does it mean?'

'It means that it will be a long time before your singing voice is restored to you. To that I am bound to add that there is a grave doubt as to whether it will *ever* be restored.'

There! The truth was out, unpleasant though it was, and McAllis felt better for having done the job. But while he smoked hard he looked at the white, horrified young face of one of London's most popular revue 'stars' and hated himself for having brought that look into her eyes. She was such a child, and she seemed to him so much more gentle and unfitted for the life she led than

71

the usual run of actress whom he had come up against. It must be a hideous blow for her. After all, she relied on her voice for her living. It was like telling a professional boxer that he must lose his right hand.

Francesca shut her eyes. The blow which had been struck at her was indeed a 'knockout.' She felt stunned and sick. She heard McAllis say:

'Shall I ask nurse to bring you a little brandy?'

'No,' she said breathlessly, opened her eyes again, and looked at him piteously. 'I don't want brandy, but I want to know more. I just can't believe it ... are you sure ... *absolutely* sure?... Mr Trent-Conning assured me that when he had removed these "nodules" I would be all right.'

'I'm terribly sorry, Miss Hale. It just wasn't a success. He did his best, but operations are, at times, of no avail. The medical profession is by no means always infallible. I wish that it were.'

'But couldn't another operation be performed ... couldn't somebody else try...?'

'I'm afraid not. At this stage, anyhow, it would be quite impossible.'

Her lips twisted. She choked a little:

'Then later ... when it's healed ... couldn't I see Sir Hugh Wynch? He'll be back from abroad by now.'

'Sir Hugh's a fine surgeon, and you can,

by all means, consult him. But you must try to believe me. I know a good bit about these things, and I wouldn't tell you that it was hopeless if I thought that there was a shred of hope.'

'Then you don't think that there *is* a shred?'

'That's my opinion, and Trent-Conning, of course, shares it.'

'Oh!' said Francesca under her breath, '*Oh!*'

And suddenly the room seemed to grow black, and the face and figure of Dr McAllis grew blurred and then faded right out.

Her last sensation before she fainted was one of absolute despair.

'I'll never be able to sing again,' she said to herself. '*Never ... be able ... to sing ... again...*'

When she recovered consciousness she was lying on her bed, and the nurse was moistening her lips with brandy. She struggled back to her senses and, with reviving intelligence, the hateful truth stabbed her like a knife.

She sobbed weakly:

'I'll never ... be able to sing again.'

Then she saw that Fane was here in the room. He was standing at the window with his hands in his pockets, talking to Dr McAllis. She heard what he said:

'But, my God, it's terrible! I thought Trent-Conning was the best man we could

73

get hold of.'

McAllis's answer was blunt:

'So he is. But, as I explained to Miss Hale, every operation cannot be a success.'

'There are other men ... good God ... don't you see how important it is for her?'

'If I thought that there was any possibility of any other man effecting a cure, I'd tell you, Mr Braber, but I don't.'

'My God!' said Fane, once again, and turned to the bed.

Francesca pushed the nurse aside and sat up. She was still deadly white, and her fair silky hair was dishevelled. She looked at Fane with such agony in her eyes that even he, the supreme egotist, forgot himself and his own distress for a moment. He hurried towards her, seized her hands and pressed them tightly.

'Francesca, darling! This is frightful. Absolutely incredible!'

She clung to him, shivering violently.

'Dr McAllis says there's no hope – that it would be a waste of time going to other men now.'

'But you must go to them, of course. We must have every possible opinion.'

'He says it's no good,' she repeated, and leaning her head against his shoulder, sobbed like a broken-hearted child.

Dr McAllis and the nurse went out together. McAllis shook his head.

'A bad business,' he said.

'The poor little thing,' said the nurse. Then threw one of her bright professional smiles at Mr Grey, who was just coming up the stairs to see his mother. 'Good morning, Mr Grey.'

''Morning, nurse. How is my mother?'

'There's no change, Mr Grey.'

'Is she alone, or is Miss Hale with her?'

'No, Miss Hale is in her own room.' Then the nurse added in a confidential whisper: 'Poor child, it's so tragic. She and Mr Fane, her fiancé, have just been told ... that her throat operation wasn't a success, and they don't think she will ever be able to sing again.'

Julian looked at the closed doorway of Francesca's bedroom. Was it his imagination or did he hear the faint sound of sobbing? Never be able to sing again! That sounded bad. The girl earned her living with that voice of hers!

'Most unfortunate,' he said awkwardly, and passed on into his mother's room.

Francesca was clinging passionately to Fane; clinging as though she were terrified to let him go. Never in her life before had she needed the comfort of his arms more desperately. She was pouring out all her grief, her woe, her agony of mind. He was her lover, the man who was going to marry her, and to whom else could she turn in this hour if not to him?

'Fane, Fane,' she kept sobbing until her voice grew hoarse and faint, 'I've lost my voice ... lost it for ever ... I shan't be able to sing your songs any more... I shan't be able to go back into the revue. Don't you see what it means?... I shan't be able to do *anything*. I'm just ruined ... ruined...'

He comforted her as best he could. He covered her hair with kisses, he hugged her close to him and assured her that it wouldn't make any difference to him; that he would always love her and take care of her; and that if Trent-Conning had made a mistake, perhaps McAllis was also mistaken – they would see Wynch when he came back from abroad. They would go the length of Harley Street before they would give up hope.

She fastened hungrily on every word he said. But she went uncomforted. Somehow she believed that McAllis had spoken the truth. She had tried to sing. But the vocal cords failed. As an actress who relied on her singing, she was ruined. Her career was at an end. 'The Girl with the Crooning Voice' was 'out' – right out.

'*Crooning Voice*,' she sobbed against Fane's heart. 'Oh, God, what a farce! Fane, I can't bear it, I can't *bear* it.'

He went on kissing her, murmuring endearments. But he looked over her head with a queer uneasy expression in his eyes. This was a frightful business … he was beginning to pity himself now, as well as Francesca. Of course he was sorry for her, poor darling! It was frightful for her. But what about him? He had made her what she was, and they had achieved success together. And now he had lost his partner for good and all.

Of course Kay was damned good. What a mercy that Duffeyne had found Kay for him! The turn would become permanently 'Fane and Kay' from now onwards. *But there would still be Francesca!* They were supposed to be getting married at the end of this week. They had planned to work together, act together, do everything together. But – But now it would be all quite different. This was going to ruin everything! It was devilish luck on *him*. He hated illness, even shrank from little indispositions in people. Everything about him must be gay and glorious! It was going to be most depressing to have a wife with an incurable throat and a ruined voice.

'Don't cry any more, if you can help it, darling,' at length he said, and giving her a little hug, released her.

She sat with her face hidden in her hands. It seemed to her that there were no more tears left, so that she could not go on crying even if she wanted to. She was exhausted.

Fane began to walk up and down the room with his customary restlessness. He wanted a cigarette. He had been asked not to light one in Francesca's room lest the smoke should make her cough. That irritated him a little. He said;

'I came early to see if I could get you back this morning, because I've got an unexpected appointment soon after four. Is that all right?'

With an effort Francesca controlled herself. She got up and walked to her dressing-table. Her swollen eyes reflected a ravaged face. She disliked to think how Fane would react to such a picture! Her very adoration for him made her regain courage, and swiftly she applied lipstick, powder, rouge. When she turned back to Fane, she made a brave show of smiling.

'Yes. That'll be all right. Marvellous, in fact! I don't want to stay here a moment longer. Do take me along now, darling; Mary will look after me when I get back.'

He looked at her gloomily.

'It's tough luck, honey.'

She kept herself in hand and answered:

'I suppose it might be worse. I might be dead!'

'So might we all,' he said in the same gloomy voice.

She was determined to keep her control. With her chin in the air, she went on smiling.

'I might have lost my sight. Think how awful it would be to be blind.'

'I can think of nothing that I would prefer

at the moment,' he said. 'For the lord's sake. let's get to the flat and have a swift brandy.'

'Darling, don't make puns!'

She put her hand on his arm and looked up at him with her engaging smile. She wanted to be kissed, hugged, comforted. But Fane, who liked so much to be understood, rarely looked beneath the surface in others, and took it for granted that because Francesca had recovered her spirits so rapidly, she did not realize how serious this was for him as well as for her.

'Let's get out of here,' he said almost roughly. She turned from him, her heart beating very fast. She was in the very depths of despair. But nobody would have known it from the gay way in which she chatted to the nurse who came in to bid her goodbye and help her into the soft brown fur coat with the big fox collar, and closed and locked her dressing-bag.

'It'll be marvellous to see the big world again!' she said as she pulled a small green hat over her fair head and adjusted the little veil which stood out stiffly from the brim.

'Of course it will,' said the nurse, 'but mind you don't get cold, and that you keep very quiet for the next few days, my dear.'

'Fane will take care of me,' said Francesca.

'Of course,' he said.

But he was thinking:

'I want to take Kay to that cocktail-party

at the Cochranes' this afternoon.'

'Will you forgive me one moment, darling,' Francesca said to him, 'I must just say goodbye to Mrs Grey.'

'Hurry up, darling,' he said, frowning.

He went downstairs with the nurse who followed with Francesca's suitcase. Francesca knocked on Mrs Grey's door and tiptoed into the room. She paused as she saw Julian Grey sitting by the bedside. At once he stood up and bowed with his usual cold formality.

The old lady held out her hand.

'Dear child, come in. How delightful you look. But why the coat and hat? Are you going this morning? I thought it was to be this afternoon?'

Francesca glanced from the old lady to the man who stood rather stiffly to attention beside the bed.

'My plans have changed. Fane's got tied up at tea-time, so he's come to take me now.'

Mrs Grey held one of Francesca's small hands between her ivory fingers.

'Child, I hear rather grave news... I so hope it isn't true...'

Francesca swallowed hard. She dared not look at Julian now, and she had to keep a tight hold of herself as she answered:

'Yes, it's true. I've lost my voice.'

'But not for *ever?*'

'They tell me so... Dr McAllis and Mr Trent-Conning. I suppose I must believe them, even if I go for advice elsewhere. But it seems to me that they're right. I've tried and I know. I can't sing. I can't get out a note.'

'Oh, my dear!' said the old lady, shocked, and turned to her son: 'Julian, do you hear ... what a terrible thing!'

'Yes, indeed. I'm extremely sorry,' he said; 'please accept my very sincere sympathy, Miss Hale. I can only hope that things are not as bad as they seem.'

'Perhaps not, but I ... I don't think I shall sing again,' she said, and her voice cracked a little as she spoke.

He saw that the wide brown eyes behind the coquettish veil were brilliant and terrified, and that her face was puckered like that of a child who is about to cry.

The tragedy of his marriage and his experiences with Irene had hardened him; made him suspicious and cynical. But he would not have been human had he not softened at this moment towards Francesca Hale. She was brave, but he saw how strongly the thing had struck at the very foundations of her existence. He was not a musical man, and a sweet singing voice had no attractions for him personally, but he could realize all that it meant to her. And it meant a lot to her public, too. It really was a disaster.

'I do hope that you will find somebody who can cure you,' he said.

She had heard that gentle note in his voice only when he was speaking to his mother, and it both astonished and touched her. But she was so afraid of breaking down that she dared not say any more to him. She just leaned down, kissed Mrs Grey, murmured huskily that she would come and see her again soon and rushed out of the room.

Mrs Grey looked at the closed door and sighed deeply.

'Oh, Julian, I wish that hadn't happened. I'm fond of that child and I'm afraid for her.'

'I agree that it's rotten luck, but she has compensations. That fellow she's engaged to, she's very much in love with him, isn't she? He'll look after her.'

'I hope so, my dear.'

'Have you any reason to doubt it?'

'They've been partners, Julian, done everything together on the stage. And now she'll never be able to sing his songs again. From what I can gather, he's one of those clever young men who are wrapped up in their own pursuits. I wonder if he'll stand up to this blow?'

'Humph!' said Julian, and returned to the book he had been reading to his mother. But he had a curiously uneasy memory of

Francesca's eyes, big and frightened and bright with unshed tears through the transparent lace of her veil.

6

One week later, Francesca returned from a visit to her bank manager, took off her coat and hat and sat down in front of the electric fire which Mary had switched on in the drawing-room.

She was cold, not only because the May afternoon was wet, and a chilly little wind was blowing, making it difficult to remember that summer was close at hand, but because she was tired and nervy. That makes one feel cold.

Mary, faithful and devoted, and at one time housemaid to Francesca's mother, fussed over her young mistress as she would over a sick child.

Miss Francesca maintained that she was heaps better than when she left the nursing-home, and no doubt she was a bit stronger on her feet, but she looked what Mary called 'that pale and peaky,' her appetite was poor, and in spite of a brave front, her spirits were low. Mary saw so much more than other people. Saw Miss Francesca 'dollingup' with the rouge-pot and lipstick when Mr Fane was coming; saw the way she always laughed and tried to be gay to amuse him; and how cheerful she was with her other friends. But Mary also saw her at night when everybody had gone, sitting just as she was doing now, huddled up on the stool in front of her fire, staring at it with her big eyes, lonely and depressed. And wasn't it enough to make anybody depressed – losing that lovely voice which had been her fortune! Why, it was altering the whole of her life. Nobody knew better than Mary how Francesca's life had changed. And Mr Fane was changing, too. That worried the honest and faithful Mary so much that she, herself, was off her food and unlike her usual cheerful self. It would be the limit, in her opinion, the *very* limit, if Mr Fane let Miss Francesca down. But there he was, only rushing in at odd moments to see the poor lamb, and then rushing out again. And all the papers saying how beautifully that red-haired doll, Kay Wynton, was taking Miss Francesca's part. It was a downright shame.

'It's early yet, but what *you* want is a nice cup of tea,' Mary told Francesca, and hurried away to make it.

Francesca sat alone staring at her fire. She wanted a cigarette more than a cup of tea, but she was still not allowed to smoke, which was a great trial. It seemed to her that she was prevented from doing most things that she wanted to do; just because of that wretched throat. Physically she was stronger, but she could not stand late nights and parties even had she wished to indulge in them.

This had been a long week – even longer than the days in the nursing-home. Queer how astonishingly one's world could alter in a brief time. And how people could alter! When she had been fit and while that voice of hers had been charming the public, there had been a constant stream of visitors, telephone-calls, celebrations. And always Fane. Fane, her partner, her constant companion, her lover.

Now the flat was curiously quiet and empty. There was nothing much for people to ring up for beyond a few polite enquiries about her health. No parties for them to come to, and only a few loyal friends who really cared for her, who dropped in now and again to talk to her and offer their condolences.

Of course there was still Fane. But a Fane who frightened her, because *he* was not the same.

She could call him her lover – yes. He was still full of graceful flatteries, charming endearments, and *tendresse*. But for the first time since their love had existed they were living in separate worlds. He was the popular pianist and composer, in the thick of theatrical parties and excitements and work. And she was the girl *without* her crooning voice; a rather tired girl with only her lovely face and figure left to her, sitting at home, trying to get better.

Not very exciting for Fane, and nobody knew that better than Francesca! Perhaps that was why nowadays he did not stay very long – why he was always with Kay. That, too, was why he avoided the subject of their marriage.

'We can't think of anything like a honeymoon until you're absolutely fit,' was his sole comment on that important topic, and Francesca would have died rather than be the one to suggest that he should marry her at once and take her away.

This afternoon's interview with her bank manager had done nothing toward lifting her depression. She was faced with having to cut down expenses in every possible way, and without delay.

While she was Fane's partner, she had earned big money, and her future had seemed assured. But her contract had terminated automatically when her voice failed. She was no longer, as Duffeyne would put it, able to 'supply the goods.' They just cancelled the agreement between them, and Kay Wynton was in Francesca's place – permanently.

She had saved very little money. There had

been nothing to save for. It had never entered her head that any such disaster would befall her, added to which Fane was making money – big money – and she had presumed that he, as her husband, would supply all that she needed. Their combined salaries could have bought them anything within reason that they required.

Now she found herself with less than £300 in her deposit account and not another penny coming in. She could no longer afford to keep on this flat. Fortunately the lease was coming to an end. She had meant to persuade Fane to let her stay here because she adored the position and the view. Now, since the situation had so changed, she would not dream of asking Fane to keep the flat on for her. Tomorrow she would put it into agents' hands, and she would have to find some other kind of work. What could she do? With the loss of her voice she was without her most valuable asset. On the other hand, she still had her face and her figure. Perhaps she could get a job on the films? Or would they want her with a husky voice and a delicate throat? It was doubtful. Possibly she could get a mannequin's job. That wouldn't be well paid. And what a comedown for the famous Francesca to become a mannequin…!

Of course, in the depths of her mind lay the belief that Fane would not let her work.

He was going to marry her. There had been no talk of breaking their engagement just because her career as 'The Girl with the Crooning Voice' was ended.

Yet, inevitably there crept into her mind a horrid frightening little doubt about Fane and their marriage.

He had wanted her desperately a month ago. Did he still want her just as desperately now that she was like this?

That doubt had assailed her in the lonely watches of sleepless nights when she had faced what seemed the wreckage of a marvellous career. It had made her sick with fear. She had ended by shutting out that thought and saying to herself:

'No – *no,* it isn't true. He won't stop loving me, he *couldn't!* I mustn't doubt him. It's disloyal of me to allow a single doubt to enter my mind.'

She wished that she did not feel so tired these days; almost too tired to get up and walk across the room. But perhaps that feeling would pass. She had not had very long in which to recover her normal strength, and all this doubt and depression had been against a speedy recovery.

Yesterday had been a ghastly day. The famous throat specialist, Sir Hugh Wynch, had returned from his cruise and had seen her. She had gone to him offering up a passionate little prayer that he would give her hope. But he had sent her away with none. He had been noncommittal about Trent-Conning's operation. Kindly but definitely he had assured her that nothing could be done to restore that beautiful voice, and at the moment any further tampering with her throat might have disastrous results. He was sure that she did not want to lose even her speaking voice. He advised her to leave well alone.

She had come out of his consulting-room with a feeling that she was dying a little death all on her own. And nobody could share her pain or her fear. Not even Fane, who had been there to drive her home. All he had done was to curse Trent-Conning and rant about the whole affair.

He was coming to see her at five o'clock today; bringing his new partner with him. Up till now Francesca had not felt able to face Kay Wynton. But she could not go on saying that she felt too ill to meet anybody new. And Fane seemed anxious for her to know Kay. So now, at last, Kay was coming.

While she drank the tea which Mary had brought, Francesca tried to nerve herself for the ordeal. It was not going to be very stimulating for her to meet the woman who had taken her place. When Fane had made the appointment he had said:

'You're such a sport, darling, I know you won't begrudge Kay her success.'

She thought about those words a little bitterly. It wasn't that she begrudged Kay anything, and she wanted to be a 'sport.' But nobody could imagine how hard it was to face this thing gaily. It was almost too much to ask of any human being.

Yet when five o'clock came, and a somewhat disapproving Mary showed Mr Fane and Miss Wynton into the drawing-room, Francesca was gay enough. She had put on that green frock with the white collar and bow which Fane had liked... (She wouldn't be able to afford many more new dresses like that!) She had made her face up skilfully and pinned cream roses on her shoulder ... and she looked flushed and well, and very young and pretty, as Fane brought his new partner into the room.

'It's wonderful to meet you at last!' she said, smilingly held out a generous hand to Kay, and gave the other to Fane with a swift adoring look.

'How are you, honey?' Fane asked, and kissed her finger tips.

Kay took in Francesca's appearance in a single, critical, feminine glance, took in every detail of the room, and gave Francesca a limp hand.

'I'm just too thrilled to meet you,' she said.

She was quite charming and sympathetic. After all, she could afford to be. Never for one instant had she expected such a stroke of luck as the permanent destruction of Francesca's voice. From the moment Kay had stepped into Francesca's shoes she had wanted to stay there. She was already head over heels in love with Fane. But because she had climbed one stile, that did not say she could vault the next. Fane was her partner, but he was still Francesca's future husband. However, Kay had hopes. She knew men pretty thoroughly, and she was quite sure that Fane was not the type to settle down and devote himself to a failure!

Francesca offered her a cigarette.

'Say,' said Kay in her drawling American voice, 'won't it upset you any if I smoke?'

'Not at all,' said Francesca, and when Kay had taken one, handed the box to Fane.

Fane smiled at her gaily.

The new song's been a big success, honey. We sang it in the show last night and had four encores. Duffeyne says it's going to be a "wow".'

'Gee, it's a good number!' said Kay.

'You wrote the words, didn't you?' said Francesca. 'I think that's so clever of you.'

'She's a clever little devil,' said Fane.

'Who's a devil?' Kay replied in a cooing, baby voice, and pouted at him.

Francesca felt a little sick. Those two were looking at each other in such an intimate way … in the way that she and Fane had once looked, conscious of a close, a perfect understanding. Had she lost that? Was it all between Fane and his new partner now? Oh, but she was a little fool to be jealous. That wasn't being sporting. She pulled herself together and said:

'Kay, I must call you Kay ... do take off your hat and be at home.'

Kay took of the tiny grey cap which was perched so rakishly on her red head and shook out the mass of flaming curls which framed her impudent, pretty face. She was dressed with consummate art, all pearly-grey, to soften her brilliant colouring. A little military cape with silver buttons; a magnificent silver fox which she tossed with the cap on to a chair. She perched herself on the edge of the sofa and smoked, keeping her provocative gaze fixed upon Fane, who went straight to the piano and began to run his fingers over the keys.

He played the new song; Francesca watched him, two small cold hands clenched behind her back. He was very casual these days; there seemed none of that old, restless, burning impatience to be close to her, one with her. But she said:

'Do sing it, Kay. I've never heard you sing, you know.'

Kay adored showing off. And she had no great delicacy of feeling. She did not want to be gratuitously cruel, but she never paused to wonder whether it would hurt Francesca to have her altered position rammed at her. So she just took the cigarette from her reddened lips and crooned:

'*What's a man to do...*'

She sang it to the end. Fane, with his charming baritone, joined her in the last chorus. And Francesca listened, her cheeks very white under the make-up. She felt that dreadful sensation of utter misery which comes across someone who sees the gates of Heaven slowly shutting before their very eyes.

Kay had a good voice, seductive enough, even if it had not the same quality which Francesca's had possessed. But it was good, and it made Francesca realize of what little importance one is in the world. With all one's gifts, nobody was indispensable. There was always someone waiting to take one's place. She was being brought very much face to face with this truth today. And try as she would not to feel jealous, it was a singularly depressing experience listening to her successor.

Fane played the final chord, swung round on the stool and said:

'Beautiful! Do you approve, Francesca?'

She smiled and nodded:

'Grand! I congratulate you.'

Kay beamed at her.

'How perfectly sweet of you. But poor you!'

Francesca tilted her head. She felt a sudden longing to rush out of the room and burst into tears. She had to keep hold of herself. She said:

'Oh, it's bad luck. But these things happen!'

Fane, leaning against the mantelpiece, kicked the kerb gently with his heel:

'No more news, I suppose?'

'You mean about this,' said Francesca, and put her hand to her throat.

'Yes.'

'Nothing. Sir Hugh was so definite yesterday. I can see no use in spending money on further consultations.'

'I do think it's dreadful for you!' said Kay. But she was looking at the diamond wristlet which Francesca was wearing. Fane had given her that. Kay wondered how much it had cost.

'I must get rid of the rest of the lease of this flat,' said Francesca.

'But why?' asked Fane.

'No money, darling,' she said with a tight little smile. 'And none coming in.'

That was the moment when Fane should have told her that she need not worry because they were going to get married very soon. But he said nothing, merely frowned, examined the point of his cigarette and murmured:

'H'm.'

Francesca, growing more depressed every second, turned the conversation from herself and questioned Kay about the show and the future engagements. Kay was ready enough to oblige with plenty of information.

All smiles and dimples, and with little affected shakes of her red curls, she told Francesca about this thing and that. The revue was going strong ... her turn with Fane was most popular ... it was such a lucky thing that that black-and-white toilette suited her so well, but they were going to have a change, and arrange a more daring background and toilette very soon ... and they'd been asked to broadcast ... wasn't that fun?

'Do listen-in to us, won't you? And tell us how it sounds,' Kay begged Francesca in her sweetest voice.

Francesca answered:

'Of course I'll listen-in.'

Then Kay noticed the big photograph of Fane which stood beside a bowl of flowers on the table by the window. She pounced upon it.

'Ohh! ... scrumptious one of you, Faney. Kay wants one!'

'She shall have one,' he answered, laughing.

Somehow, Francesca had the vague recollection of a day when Fane had told her he detested women who talked 'baby talk.' But he seemed to like this lisping and cooing from Kay. Was everything changing? Was it just a fantasy of her mind or were all the old ideas and illusions being shattered one by one? She felt strangely detached and remote from these two, as though she were much older than both of them, although in fact she was younger than Kay Wynton. Perhaps it was because she was so tired. But she would have given everything in the world to find herself back in that other world: that gay, careless, rapturous world in which only Fane and herself had seemed to exist.

She wanted Kay to fade out of this room, and to feel Fane's arms around her, and hear him telling her that it was nearly time for her to get dressed and go with him to 'The Ivy' for their usual meal; then on to the theatre... She wanted, desperately, to find that all this bitter pain was only a nightmare which had an end.

But it was all real, and there was no awakening. The nightmare was just going on and on. Fane, embarrassed perhaps by the position with the two women, seated himself on the piano stool and started to play again. Kay sang a little louder this time, more confident of herself.

Francesca felt that she must get away out of the room, and away from the sound of the music, or she would lose her self-control. And for that she would never forgive herself. So she murmured an excuse about 'giving an order to Mary' and walked out quickly, closing the door behind her.

She walked straight into her bedroom, and stood there a moment in the centre of the room with her face hidden in her hands. She found herself talking aloud:

'God ... I don't think I can stand it... God, help me to keep my sense of humour ... but it isn't very funny ... it's *hellish*...'

And then she added:

'Fane darling, why don't you follow me and come and tell me that you haven't stopped loving me? I can bear anything if you will go on loving me. But if you stop – then there won't be anything left at all.'

There seemed no answer to that call. Fane did not follow her. The piano had ceased, and she could no longer hear music. But he was in there with Kay, and he seemed content to stay with her.

Francesca told herself that it was no earthly good standing here in this hysterical sort of way. After all, other people had catastrophes and faced up to them. She wasn't worth much if she couldn't get over things and behave better than this. She must go back and make herself agreeable to Kay; keep on smiling. The best way to drive Fane away from herself was to let him see what she was going through.

She thought desperately of some joke

someone had told her. Kay was the sort of girl to like a funny story. She would go in and tell it to them and make them both laugh – and laugh with them.

Fiercely she dabbed her nose with a powder-puff, put on some more colour on her lips, and returned to the drawing-room.

She opened the door and found Fane standing by the piano with Kay in his arms. They were locked in a passionate embrace which left nothing to the imagination.

They sprang apart as Francesca came in, but it was too late. The joke died on her lips, and something seemed to die in her at the same time. She no longer saw either of them very clearly. And because she was still far from well it was actual physical weakness which assailed her now. She felt her knees sagging under her. Quite quietly she closed the door and then fell into a little heap in the hall outside.

7

Before Francesca had opened the drawing-room door at that psychological moment, Fane had had a few minutes' struggle between his better self and his most selfish desires. While he had been playing, he watched

Kay. He had watched her altogether too much during this last month. She had begun to prey upon his senses with her red curls, her marvellous white skin, and that provocative way in which she looked at a man.

She was so utterly different from Francesca. Once he had thought that shy sensitiveness was the most alluring part about Francesca, but since his association with Kay he had swerved somewhat in his ideas. He had come to the conclusion that he liked someone a little more daring – and less adoring. It was the old story. A woman has only to be a shade more in love with a man than he is with her, and – ultimate result – he is bored.

Francesca while she had her voice, while their partnership was flourishing, and everybody else had wanted her, had seemed a prize worth having. Not so the Francesca of today. He knew that he was a cad. But he could not help himself. While he played Francesca's piano, there rushed across him the certain knowledge that he could not be true to her, could not marry her.

He stopped playing, sprang up from the piano, and caught Kay in his arms.

'What's a man to do, eh!' he said thickly. 'Well – the answer is just ... *this*...'

And he kissed her in the way in which she had wanted him to kiss her for a long time.

Kay knew that it was a risk ... that Francesca might come back at any moment … but what did that matter? The sooner she knew the better. It was bad luck, but she had had her chance, and there it was.

Kay curved an arm about Fane's neck and responded to his embrace with all the sensuality of which her nature was capable.

It was Fane who first realized that Francesca had come in, seen them, and gone out again. He released Kay and felt a wave of remorse.

'Oh, my God! That's torn things,' he said.

Kay stretched her arms above her head languorously and looked at him through heavy blackened lashes.

'Dar–*ling!*'

Fane's fair skin was scarlet, but the flame died out of his eyes, leaving them their usual cold grey.

'Hell!' he said under his breath.

'No,' said Kay, 'Heaven.'

'But you don't understand – Francesca saw us.'

'A little awkward, certainly.'

'Damned awkward.'

'It can't he helped.'

'No, I suppose not.'

'Say, perhaps you regret it and you'd rather I just put on my things and went?' said Kay, and let her red curly head droop effectively.

Fane scowled.

'No, why should you?'

'Say – I can't help being just crazy about you,' she whispered.

The flame rekindled in Fane's eyes.

'And I about you. There it is. These things happen, and one can't prevent them. I'd better go and tell her. Only it seems the wrong moment to turn her down.'

'Well, if you turn *me* down, I'll get straight back to the States, because I couldn't stand it,' said Kay.

He caught her hand and pressed it hard.

'Don't be absurd! You know I couldn't do without you. It was marvellous finding you, and I'm not going to lose you now. Wait a moment...'

He turned to the door and heard Mary, the maid, give a loud cry as he did so. She had just found her young mistress lying there in the hall in a dead faint.

The next few moments were spent in carrying Francesca to her bed and reviving her. She came back to her senses to find Fane standing beside her, his face gloomy and ashamed. She struggled a moment with the mists in her brain, then there rushed across her the torturing recollection of what she had seen – and of all that it implied.

She shut her eyes again tightly.

If only she could sink back into that blissful state of unconsciousness. She did not want to come back to this suffering. She had heard Fane tell Mary to go away and leave them. Mary, with brandy and sal volatile, retired, muttering to herself. Fane began:

'My dear, what can I say to you?'

She opened her eyes and looked up at him. Those large brown eyes held such pain, such reproach, that he looked away again hastily. Egotist though he was, he found this business very unhappy and disturbing.

She whispered:

'It doesn't matter.'

'But I'm afraid it does. You saw … I mean … Kay and I…'

'Don't bother,' she interrupted, 'there isn't anything that you need explain. I understand. I don't blame you.'

He kicked his toe against the floor.

'Damn it, you must blame me. I'm very much to blame, and I know it. I'm an absolute swine. But one can't account for human nature…'

'No.'

'But of course I'll stand by you, Francesca. I'll tell Kay…'

'No,' said Francesca and sat up suddenly, two red spots burning in her white cheeks. Her head went back with a proud gesture. 'You'll do nothing of the sort. Do you think I want to keep you now that I know you don't love me any more?'

'But, honey, I'm still very fond of you, and I always will be.'

'Thank you,' she broke in. She was shaking from head to foot. 'But just being "fond" isn't enough, is it? I thought you cared so much more than that! But now I know you don't. You've fallen in love with Kay. I repeat, I don't blame you. I'm not the slightest use to you any more and she is.'

Fane's handsome face went scarlet.

'That's not a pretty thing to say.'

She put her hand to her heart. It was beating so fast that it hurt her. She tried to laugh.

'Sorry! I quite agree. It wasn't a nice remark. Please go away before I say anything worse.'

'But, Francesca... I tell you, if you want me, I'll stand by you.'

'No, thank you. I can look after myself. And you need not think that I am going to harbour any bitterness against you; I won't. I've loved you with every drop of blood in my body, Fane. I've always thought first of your happiness. I want you to be happy now. I'd a thousand times rather that you married Kay if you think she's the right woman for you, than that you married me – just because you thought you ought to.'

'It's all so damned difficult. I never meant this to happen.'

'I'm sure you didn't.'

'Why should everything have gone wrong? Why should you have lost your voice?'

'I seem to be unlucky,' she said with a grim little laugh, 'and I'm losing much more than my voice...' Then that poor, husky little voice cracked. 'Please, *please* go away. I want to be alone.'

Fane shifted uneasily from one foot to the other. For an instant he stared down at the fair, charming head, the sight of which had once made his heart beat so much faster. He was immensely sorry for her, but what could he do? Where was the remedy, he asked himself. One could not command love. One just fell in love ... and out of it. Certainly, at a time like this, when Francesca was ill and in financial difficulties, a fellow had no right to let her down. He had not intended to do so until later on. It was just that unfortunate moment of passion with Kay Francesca had seen – and there it was!

With sudden compassion, he touched Francesca's bowed head.

'Darling, I'm so dreadfully sorry. I feel abject.'

She shivered under his touch. She bit her lower lip violently in the effort not to turn, throw herself into his arms and beseech him to stay with her. He said that he had never meant this to happen. Poor Fane! He had always been the complete egotist who put his own wishes before anybody else's. He could not change his nature. She had adored him, knowing what he was. She still loved him because she was not the type who loved lightly or could change with ease. That was the awful part of it. She knew that she was going to go on loving him whether he had behaved like a swine or not.

'What can I do?' he asked. 'I'll always be your friend. I'll help you ... you needn't worry about money...'

'Oh, please...' She looked up at him quickly, her face convulsed, 'don't dare talk to me about *money!*'

'But I want to be your friend...'

She clenched her hands and shut her eyes again. She wondered how much more of this she could stand. She could see nothing but the picture of Fane with Kay in his arms and that revealing kiss. And to have Fane standing here offering her friendship was worse than death. She had loved him as a woman loves the man whom she is going to marry. She could not even begin to contemplate mere friendship between them. She said, huskily:

'Please go away – *please!*'

He shrugged his shoulders. He began to feel a little aggrieved. After all, he had tried to be very nice and do what he could. She was being rather difficult. It eased the situation for him somewhat; made him feel a little less of a cad.

'I can only say I'm damned sorry, Francesca, and if you want me, for God's sake let me know – I'll always be there,' were his last words to her.

She uncovered her eyes and watched him move away from her across the bedroom. It was physical pain to see him go. Every line of that slim, graceful body was so dear and so familiar. His head was gleaming goldenly in the light which Mary had switched on near the dressing-table.

The triple mirror reflected him as he moved to the door with that indescribable gliding walk which singled him out from others. Francesca held her breath and put a clenched hand to her lips... He was going ... for good. Probably this was the last she would ever see of him. He was going to Kay and he would never come back. And she loved him. She had cared for nobody, wanted nobody but Fane, since the beginning of their love affair. She had lived for him; seen the world through his eyes. She had saturated herself and her existence with his personality. Of course she had loved him too much. She knew it now that it was too late. It doesn't pay to love any human being as much as that. Oh, how intolerable to watch him walking away, and to know that it was final!

He did not even turn back and look at her. The door closed behind him. Francesca lay down and turned her face to the pillow. There were no tears in her eyes. She felt dried up, utterly exhausted, and she asked herself what else life was going to take from her. The loss of her voice and the ruin of her career had seemed bad enough, but this parting from her lover and the knowledge that she was absolutely alone was too great an anguish for tears.

Mary came into the room, her homely face wooden, her lips a thin line. If ever she had felt like violence, she felt it now. She guessed precisely what had happened, and just now when she had let Mr Fane and Miss Wynton out of the flat, she would have liked to have smacked that young lady across her smirking, smug little face.

What had they done to Miss Francesca? The poor precious little lamb!

She hurried to the bedside.

'Oh, dearie me, what now? Are you feeling better, Miss, dear?'

Francesca nodded her head, but no words came out.

'Did you ought to have the doctor?'

The fair head was shaken vehemently. The last thing that Francesca wanted was a doctor fussing round her. What could he do? This was the sort of wound which doctors could not cure; the kind of agony for which they had no lasting anodyne.

'They've gone,' said Mary, sniffing. Nobody could have put more malice into the word 'they.'

'I just want to be alone for a bit, Mary,'

whispered Francesca.

'Sure, you're all right, Miss?'

'Yes.'

Shaking her head dubiously, Mary retired from the room.

Then Francesca lifted herself from the pillows and looked around her, a little wild-eyed and dishevelled.

Her gaze was caught and held by the small leather-framed photograph of Fane which stood on the table beside her bed. Fane in white tie and 'tails' seated at his piano, with his hands hovering over the keys. A favourite publicity likeness, and one which she had loved because it was signed *'Yours utterly'* (that was ironic now!) and because it was so reminiscent of their partnership. She stared at it almost with incredulity. Was it possible that she would never see him like that again, and that not only would she never sing to him, but everything was ended between them ... *everything...!*

Curiously enough, it was at that moment, when her agony was at its height, that she remembered Julian Grey – remembered all that his mother had told her about the wife who had broken his heart; the divorce which had shaken him to the foundations and made a cynic of him. That was why he was so grim and humourless, why all the colour seemed to have gone out of his life.

Well, now she – Francesca – could understand. But she faced a new terror. She, too, might become grim and a cynic. She didn't want that to happen. She didn't want this thing to crush her, destroy her completely.

She put her hands to her hot forehead and moaned a little.

'Oh, what can I do?' she whispered to herself.

And then Mary came back.

'Miss, there's a Mr Grey called and is asking to see you. I told him I thought you wasn't well enough to see anybody – is that right?'

Francesca pushed the hair back from her eyes.

Julian Grey! The very man of whom she had been thinking. How strange! Suddenly she felt a desire to see him – yes, him – of all people in the world.

'No,' she said breathlessly, 'don't let him go, Mary. Tell him that I'll see him – in a few moments.'

Somewhat surprised, Mary turned to comply with the order. Francesca dragged her tired and exhausted body off the bed and began to take off her crumpled dress.

8

Julian Grey stood at the window looking at Francesca's view. It was a particularly fine one, and this was the perfect hour to see it, when the sky was streaked with the tangerine glow of sunset, and in the fading light of the May afternoon the grey cupolas and sooty chimneytops had a strange dignity of their own. So clear was the atmosphere that Nelson on his monument was a sharp black silhouette against the sky, and in the distance, between the waving flags of the Embassies, lay the pearly traceries of tall buildings, half-misted. A wholly enchanting London. A new London to Julian, stirring in him all the architect, the lover of beauty. His tastes lay in the country rather than the town. But from Francesca's window he saw a splendid olden city, with a greatness not to be denied.

When Francesca entered the room Julian was ready with an enthusiastic word of praise about that view. His stern face had relaxed. He gave a faint, half-embarrassed smile as he greeted her.

'I have been admiring your roof-tops, Miss Hale. A grand sight! Good of you to see me.

Your maid was afraid that you weren't fit enough ... but I just called in with a message from my mother. Are you better?'

'I'm glad you came,' she said, 'please sit down.'

He took the chair which she indicated, and she sat opposite him. And now he saw that she was not the same Francesca whom he had last met in his mother's bedroom on the day of her departure from the home.

She had just been told, then, about the permanent loss of her voice. She had been trying not to show her bitter disappointment and her fear, and she had been brave and gay with his mother. But he had remembered long afterwards the haunted look in her eyes.

This was a ghost of that Francesca. A fragile ghost of a girl, white and thin, curiously frozen. She wore a black velvet dress with long, tight sleeves and a square-cut neck which showed the hollow in her throat. She had not bothered to put on any make-up. With the fair shining hair drawn behind her ears, and that pale expressionless face, she struck Julian as being an unreal figure; something out of a fairy tale – an ice maiden, a princess bewitched.

He could almost see her in his Spanish castle in that velvet dress, walking through the vaulted corridors, haunting the battlements, a forlorn, a lost Francesca! What had happened to her? He was interested; more interested than he had been in a woman for years. There was something about this girl unlike any other he had ever met. She roused his imagination, and he was not given to fantasies.

'I hope you are better,' he said.

Then Francesca smiled, a frozen little smile.

'No,' she said, 'at least, my throat is not better and never will be.'

'I'm sorry – it's frightfully bad luck.'

'Yes, it's bad luck.'

Francesca spoke quietly, and without emotion. She felt dried up of all emotion, strangely stunned. She held a box of cigarettes out to Julian.

'Won't you smoke?'

'But isn't it bad for your throat?'

'No. It doesn't matter now.'

He took the cigarette and lit it, then sat back, crossing his long legs.

'How is your mother?' she asked.

'Failing rapidly.'

Francesca nodded.

'Poor darling.'

'I dread losing her,' said Julian, 'she's all I have – but for her sake it's better. I don't want her to have any more pain.'

Again Francesca nodded. It would be nice not to have any more pain. She would like that. She felt that it would have been very pleasant had someone told her, just now, that she only had a few days in which to live, rather than that she had years and years more – without Fane.

'I understand how you feel,' she said, 'one hates to see anybody one loves suffering like that.'

'She's very brave.'

'I remember the nurse told me,' said Francesca, 'that people who realize they are dying are wonderfully brave.'

'Sometimes it takes more courage to go on living.'

Her lips curved dryly.

'Yesterday I would have thought that remark very cynical. Today I understand it.'

'Why should you have become a cynic? You appear to have so much ... in spite of the unfortunate loss of your voice.'

The wry little smile still hovered about her lips. It held his attention.

'The fact remains,' she added, 'that I have nothing.'

'I hope that isn't true.'

'I'm sure you must find it boring to discuss me.'

'On the contrary. It interests me to know what is happening to you. My mother has a great affection for you, and I'm grateful to you for your friendliness toward her. If I can be of any help ... I mean, if you care to talk to me as a friend...'

He stammered and stopped. It was so long since he had said anything so intimate to a woman. He had men friends to whom he talked, but since Irene had left him he had avoided the opposite sex like the plague. But he felt instinctively that this girl was in need of friendship, of some kind of help at this moment. And because of his mother's affection for her, alone, he was ready to offer her what he could. If she had a story to tell, he would listen to it. His own unhappy experience had taught him not to believe a word that any woman said; not to be attracted by a tear or a sigh, nor taken in by either beauty or charm. But there was something about Francesca which made him feel as he would feel about a sick or frightened child. Irene had made him suspicious of her sex but he was prepared to accept what Francesca had to say as the truth.

She looked so cold, so small and lost sitting there, staring at him with her big brown eyes. Quite gently he said:

'Tell me … have you some other trouble in addition to this throat?'

She was silent a moment. She was much too unhappy to feel flattered by the obvious change in his demeanour. He could be rude or polite, friendly or hostile, what did she care? But somehow she wanted to sit here and talk to him. He had suffered as she was suffering, perhaps in a worse way, because he had been married to Irene. She could imagine how frightful it would have been if she had been Fane's wife and he had left her for Kay.

In a detached way she noticed a great likeness between Julian Grey and his mother today. Perhaps because of the sympathetic expression. When she had first seen him at 'The Ivy,' the glance he had thrown her had been dark and disapproving. Today he was just the opposite. His eyes were like his mother's, light, almost forget-me-not blue; rather striking, with those dark brows and the blackness of his head. Possibly an Irish strain.

She said:

'I am coming to see your mother soon.'

'She sent me to ask you if you would visit her tomorrow.'

'I will. I'll come in the morning. And I want you to tell her something for me. It will make it less hard for me than if I had to tell her myself, first. She has been so sweet … so glad about my happiness … I am afraid it will upset her… But I can't keep it from her. I couldn't possibly act about it, so she'd better know at once.'

There was not even the trace of a break in Francesca's voice as she said those words 'my happiness.' But there was a look in her eyes that Julian did not care to see. It was not good to witness such naked pain in the eyes of any human being. And now, even before she told him, he knew. That fellow, that cad, Fane Braber, had let her down.

Francesca confirmed his suspicions in her next remark.

'Will you please tell your mother that my engagement is broken?'

He looked at her gravely, then studied the red point of his cigarette.

'That isn't very good news.'

'No – it's not good, is it? That's what I meant when I said that I had nothing now. You asked me why should I be cynical? I don't want to be, it's the one thing I dread. But it seems so difficult to accept these things philosophically and not change in oneself. I feel changed … here…' She put a clenched hand against her breast and her eyes looked wild and bright. 'All in a few moments. Fane's only just gone … he came to see me with the girl … the girl who has taken my place.'

'You mean his present partner on the stage?'

'Yes, Kay Wynton. She is going to be more than his partner. He's going to marry her. At least, at the moment he thinks that he will. But I'm beginning to wonder if he'll ever marry anybody.'

'Did you break with him?'

'No. It was he who changed. I don't change easily. He was the first person I was in love with, and I don't think I will ever stop loving him. I haven't stopped now. That's the worst of it.'

Julian sat still. The cigarette burned to ash in his fingers, fine grey ash which fell unheeded on to the carpet. He felt, suddenly, that the old wound in him was opening while he listened to this girl's curiously calm story. She told it so simply, without hysteria. It rang true. She put no false values on anything. She just said that this man was the first whom she had ever loved; that she would go on loving. That was the worst of it. Yes, he knew all about it. The old sore was there, in his soul. Although in a fashion he had now recovered from the blow which Irene had dealt him, the memory of her could still hurt. Not because he was in love with her any more. Desire, even affection, was dead. It was the memory of the pain she had caused him rather than the memory of love which hurt. The pain of losing her, of losing faith, of wounded pride.

He heard Francesca's small quiet voice:

'I feel nothing much tonight. I am sort of stunned. But I'm awfully afraid to wake up tomorrow... It'll be like my operation. They doped me so that I shouldn't feel the first sharpness of the pain. But when the dope wore off, it hurt badly, became gradually worse. That's what's going to happen to me now. This thing is going to get worse every hour, every day. Isn't it?'

She said the last words in a tortured voice. Her eyes beseeched him. He realized then that she knew his story, and that she was appealing to him to help her. He felt powerless to ease any of her agony. But he felt utter compassion for her. She swept away all the cynicism, the disbelief and suspicion of her sex which the last year had bred in him. He knew that this girl, at least, was not acting, not lying, not trying to make an effect. He was stirred not only by her misery, but by the echo of his own. He leaned forward and spoke to her earnestly:

'My dear child ... you do seem an absolute child to me... I wish I could say something, do something to help you. It's the very devil. I know. I've been through it. But I can only assure you that it gets better ... just as the pain in your throat gets better ... with time. I don't say it stops hurting altogether. These things go too deep. But there'll be a change. One's attitude towards life alters. Very often one's whole nature.'

'Yes,' she whispered, 'that's how I feel tonight ... that my whole nature is changing. That's what I'm afraid of.'

'But why afraid?'

'Because I don't want to be hard and cynical. I've always believed in romance and in love. I want to go on believing. Don't you see that it's losing faith that I'm most afraid of!'

118

'My dear, why worry about losing faith? It's much better not to believe in anybody; then you don't expect anything and you don't get let down.'

The colour suddenly flamed in her white cheeks.

'But that's so dreadful – not to have faith. It would kill me, I couldn't live like that.'

'You're wrong. It'll be the making of you. What has your romance done for you? Only what mine did for me. Made a fool of you. I was like a foolish boy when I married. I adored my wife. You've adored this man. It's fatal. Take it from me that you're a lot happier in being impervious to emotion of that kind. Nothing can hurt me now except the loss of my mother. But that's grief without bitterness. It's the natural law and order of things that an old lady should die. I shall suffer, but without anger. It's the angry kind of suffering that tears one to pieces. Resentment because of unnecessary, gratuitous cruelty. Why should one direct one's whole energy and emotion upon one human being, only to have that person desert you for somebody else who probably cares far less?'

Francesca clenched her hands in her lap.

'Yes. That's true! I know that Kay Wynton will never love Fane as I love him.'

Julian shrugged his shoulders. In the fast fading light his face looked sharpened and older.

'Well, I was certain that the man with whom my wife ran away only loved her for her beauty. And I loved her much more completely.'

'And must that be the end of love?' Francesca asked passionately, suddenly stirred from her apathy. 'Must all the beauty of one's romance, all the generosity and fineness of loving be swept away in a moment and leave one cynical and disbelieving for the rest of one's life?'

'I'm afraid that seems the end of it in most cases. I don't say there is no happiness in love. But there's very little.'

Francesca shivered and closed her eyes.

This man spoke from experience. He had known this bitterness, this torture. And like this he had come out of the fire. Yet he had been a man with interests, physical and mental vigour, money. If nothing seemed worth while to him except his mother, what hope had she? She, Francesca, who was left with nothing but the ruins of a life.

Julian got up, came closer to her and put a hand on her shoulder.

'My dear, I'm more sorry than I can say...' His voice was amazingly gentle, like his touch... 'but I beg you not to take it too hard. It isn't worth it. I grieved and brooded and made a mess of things for a long time after Irene left me. But you mustn't be like that. Just have a good time and try to forget it. And if it makes you hard, all the better.'

She looked up at him with great bitterness in her eyes. 'Do you really think I shall be a better character for being hard?'

He frowned uneasily. She made him a little dubious as to whether he was giving her the best advice. After all, as his mother had pointed out, the chief charm of this girl was her sweetness, her gentle nature, and her manner of loving. If that was all to change, would it not spoil something rare and worth keeping? Well, that swine, Fane Braber, had done the spoiling. How now was she to preserve her faith, and what would be the use of saving it, anyhow? Stubbornly Julian Grey told himself that it was best to eliminate romance, good for her as it had been good for him. And the sooner she grew hard the better – before she could be hurt again.

'You must have plenty of friends; you've got a lovely flat here, and you're young and … pretty…' He stumbled a little over those words. It was so long since he had allowed himself to pay a woman a compliment. 'There ought to be plenty of opportunities for you to enjoy life and not let this thing get you down,' he ended.

Then Francesca gave a queer little laugh.

'It isn't quite as simple as that. Even if I had all that you say it wouldn't make me stop wanting Fane. But you see I've lost my job as well as my voice, and I've never saved a penny because I thought I was going to be married and work with Fane for years. So I've got to get rid of this flat and find a job. That complicates things. Not that I would mind working. But it isn't easy to get a job these days, especially if you're not very strong.'

He looked at her in dismay. The money question had never struck him until now. He himself had always had money and never had to worry about it. It certainly complicated things for this poor pretty child if she was down and out financially as well as every other way.

'Oh, my dear!' he said. 'That does rather alter things – doesn't it?'

She got up, walked across the room and switched on a light, then returned to her seat. The room had been growing dark, and the gloom had depressed her. Now the room was flooded with soft light from three tall candlesticks on an Italian wrought-iron stand. But the gloom within her prevailed. She was going to lose all this ... her lovely room ... her lovely things. She would have to find a small bed-sitting-room somewhere. She could only take a few of her possessions. The rest she would have to sell for bread and butter. Mary would have to go, too. That would be a wrench. Mary looked after her like a mother.

Talking to Julian Grey had given her

temporary relief, but, after all, he was only a stranger. He meant nothing to her. Fane, who had meant everything, had gone, and was never coming back. How right she had been just now when she had told Julian that this pain grew worse every moment, every hour!

Julian said:

'Have you nobody you could go to? No relations who would look after you?'

'Heavens, no!' she said with a faint laugh. 'Except for a few cousins, I have nobody, and I wouldn't want to be a burden to relations, anyhow. Besides, I can look after myself. I shall get some sort of job – you'll see!'

He liked her courage. He liked her. He began to realize why his mother had grown fond of her in such a short time. And, God, how he admired courage ... people who did not whine when they were down. If Francesca had wept and moaned and flung herself upon his sympathy, he might have felt sorry for her and offered assistance in a small way. But this mute suffering, this quiet, brave acceptance of one smashing blow on top of another, roused all his admiration and respect.

'I would like you to know,' he said, 'that anything I can do I will... If you'll just let me know ... if you would look upon me as a friend.'

He broke off with a gesture of the hand.

She looked up at him, and now, for the first time, her eyes filled with tears.

'Thank you,' she whispered. 'It's kind of you. But you can't do anything.'

'I might be able to. You never know. Just remember, anyhow, that I will if I can.'

'Thank you,' she said again.

'You'll come and see my mother tomorrow?'

'Yes; I shall look forward to it. I'm so fond of her.'

'And she is of you,' he said gently.

The thought that this girl cared for his mother would in itself have endeared her to him. It made him realize what a different thing life might have been if Irene had been endowed with some of Francesca's qualities. While he had been so crazily in love with Irene he had idealized her and excused her for her shortcomings; tried not to notice her lack of consideration when his mother had been ill at the commencement of their marriage. Now he could see so plainly that Irene's besetting fault had been her utter selfishness. This girl, this Francesca, put others before herself.

Why, in God's name, had that fellow whom she loved deserted her? If Irene had loved him, Julian, like that ... *If!* Truly the ways of God and men were inexplicable.

On an impulse he said:

'Why don't you come out and have some dinner with me? It would do you good.'

'It's nice of you,' she said huskily, 'awfully nice, but I want to be quite alone if you don't mind.'

'Till tomorrow then,' he said.

When he had gone, Francesca half regretted her refusal of his invitation. After all, why not let somebody take her out and amuse her? Julian Grey no longer seemed to her an ogre. He was friendly and understanding, and she liked him.

There was Jack Elliott, too; he was very much in love with her and would marry her tomorrow if she gave him the chance. He had private means as well as his pay, and he was doing well in the Air Force. Why not take what he offered? But she didn't want him. She didn't want anybody except Fane. That was the curse of it. Knowing the weakness of his character, bitterly hurt though she was by his infidelity and desertion when she most needed him, she could not stop loving him.

Tonight she felt utterly alone ... more lonely than she had thought possible. She would not have believed it possible that anybody could plunge so quickly from the pinnacle of happiness to the depths of despair. Scarcely more than a month ago, at this time of night, she would have been on the stage at The Quality ... with Fane. Fane's partner,

Fane's future wife, 'The Girl with the Crooning Voice,' and with the world at her feet.

Francesca put two hands to her throat and stared, big-eyed, in a mirror which hung on the wall. She whispered:

'Fane ... darling ... darling, come back and say you didn't mean it. Tell me that it's all right. You must, oh, you *must!*'

Then suddenly her calm deserted her. She flung herself down on the sofa and broke into passionate, desperate weeping.

9

That night Francesca slept soundly. But it was a sleep of sheer exhaustion, and she felt tired and heavy-eyed when she awoke.

Scarcely had Mary laid her tea and letters beside the bed, when the telephone bell rang.

Francesca lay back on the pillows and lifted the receiver to her ear. Her face, pale and sharpened in the grey light of early morning, contracted with the sudden pain of remembrance. At this hour Fane used to ring her up every morning of her life ... that life which had only seemed to begin for her since they had become lovers. It used to be such a gay, lovely awakening. A big post with all the letters from 'Francesca fans' ... a joyous, bustling atmosphere with Mary fussing round, laying out her clothes for the day, and discussing her many engagements. And then Fane's voice saying:

'Good morning, my sweet!'

That would be followed by a long, absurd conversation full of the ridiculous jokes and endearments which only lovers know about and share. Fane saying silly, happy things like:

'Honey, won't it be swell when they get television going so I can see what I'm talking to!'

And her answer:

'Just as well you can't, my precious. I haven't powdered my nose, and it's shining.'

'I bet your eyes are, too.'

'No – they're closed. I'm sleepy.'

'I wish I were there!'

'Mr Braber, you're on the wrong line. This is your maiden aunt.'

'Good morning, Great-aunt Francesca, and 'Hello, children!' This is Uncle Fane of the B.B.C...'

And so on, followed by a duet of laughter. Childish, trivial, but oh so deliriously happy!

It made Francesca's heart break to think that it was all ended; that perhaps Fane, this very morning, would be telephoning to Kay.

It wouldn't be the same. Kay couldn't say the things that *she* had said. Perhaps she wouldn't make Fane laugh in the way he had laughed at *her.* But there would be other jokes. They would find new absurdities. All lovers did! It was always both the oldest and the newest thing in the world.

In a very tired little voice, Francesca said: 'Hello, who is it?'

She was altogether amazed when Fane's charming, familiar voice answered her:

'Hello, Francesca, is that you?'

The blood rushed to her face. The hand that held the receiver trembled, but there was no happiness in her eyes ... only fear. She was afraid to speak to Fane; afraid of suffering all over again as she had suffered yesterday. She was on the verge of hanging up the receiver without speaking when Fane's voice came through again:

'Are you there, Francesca?'

'Yes,' she said.

'My dear, I had to speak to you.'

'Why?'

'I've had you on my mind. It's worried me most of the night.'

Francesca laughed, an unhappy little laugh with an edge to it.

'You with a conscience? Surely not!'

'Don't be unkind to me. I know I deserve it, but I do so want us to be friends.'

If there had been television, he would have

seen on Francesca's face a look of cynicism which was altogether new! She was wondering why he could not allow this thing to die and be buried decently before he started to rake up the ghosts. It would hurt so much less if he would leave her alone. She did not want friendship for the moment. She was still too much in love with him. When a woman is in love with a man whom she has looked upon as her future husband, and for whom she has dreamed all her most cherished dreams, it is almost impossible for her to regard him in platonic light. It was cruel of Fane to do this. But of course Francesca understood. He was spoiled, and he liked to be gay and happy. What conscience he had was pricked by the thought that she was alone and suffering, and that he had let her down. He preferred to think that she was resigned and not grieving too much. He would like to go round the theatrical world and tell everybody that although he and Francesca had 'split,' it was a mutual affair and they were quite good friends.

'Hello. Are you still there, Francesca?'

'Yes. I'm here.'

'Well, can't we be friends?'

'I've no wish to be anything else, but I can't exactly change my whole outlook in an hour or a night.'

'It was brutal of me. I feel a swine, but...'

'Don't make any more apologies,' she broke

in wearily.

'These things do happen, no matter how much one tries to prevent them. Kay and I...'

'I understand,' Francesca broke in, and set her teeth.

'But I want to do something for you. We were always friends as well as lovers, surely?'

She closed her eyes.

'Yes.'

'We had some fine times together, my dear. Let's have some more, even if it's got to be different in a way.'

'Does Kay want you to be – friends with me?'

'Yes, of course,' he said eagerly, 'we would both like you to keep in touch with us.'

Francesca's lips twisted. He was egotistical and insensitive to an almost humorous degree. Could he not see what this meant to her? Oh, yes, she knew that in the theatrical world men and women played with love ... made engagements ... broke them ... married ... got divorces ... and lots of them saw each other again quite merrily, and it was all in the day's work. But somehow she couldn't feel like that. She would find it quite impossible while this agony was still so acute to 'keep in touch' with Fane and Kay ... watch them together ... witness their happiness ... and be lost and lonely, outside it all.

'You meant a hell of a lot to me, Francesca, and you always will,' came Fane's voice. 'The love part isn't really as important as the friendship, is it?'

'Why are you ringing me up to throw all these platitudes at me?'

'Francesca, you *aren't* being very friendly.'

'Oh, what do you expect? You meant everything to me ... everything in the world, and now you're trying to make me behave as though I don't care. Perhaps that would be a brave, modern thing to do... If I could sing, I'd start that Noël Coward song about *"let's look on love as a plaything"* ... He said something about *"there'll be no regretting love that didn't quite last"*...'

Her voice broke; the wild tears were burning her eyelids and her breast rose and fell with emotion. It was almost more than she could bear to talk to him like this; to realize how badly he had failed her, and how much she still adored...

'Francesca,' he said miserably. 'I hate you to feel like this. Honestly I do. Look here, rather than make you damned unhappy, I'll give up Kay. I'll...'

'You'll do nothing of the sort,' she interrupted. 'Don't be such a fool! You don't imagine, do you, that I'd let you do that, that I'd want you back under those conditions?'

'Then you must let me be friends with

you. You *must!*'

She knew that he was seeking his own happiness, his own peace of mind rather than hers. With great bitterness of soul she fought her own pain and comforted him.

'Very well. We'll be friends.'

'And you'll let me come and see you?'

'Later. Not now, please.'

'But what are you going to do? I'll help you find a job. I spoke to Duffeyne last night. He thinks you might get on in the films with your face and figure, in a part where you only have to do a little talking. He'll give you plenty of introductions.'

'Thank you. I shall be glad of them.'

'I'll do anything in the world that I can.'

'Thank you, Fane.'

'You'll still get some royalties on our records.'

'Yes, that will be a help.'

'I swear that I'm sorry it's all gone like this. I wish it hadn't.'

She swallowed hard. The palms of her hands were moist. She felt weak and helpless. The strain of his conversation affected her much more than any physical exertion could have done. It was so difficult not to lose control and tell him that she wanted him back at any price, because she could not do without him. She would gladly have shortened her life by years to hear him jest with her, laugh with her in the old sweet way … know that in an

132

hour or two he would be coming round for a rehearsal; that she would feel his arms close about her; know that all was well with her world.

He said:

'I suppose I'd better say goodbye.'

'Yes,' she whispered the word with difficulty.

'You'll be all right, won't you?'

'Yes.'

'Say something kind to me, Francesca.'

'I wish you every happiness...' Somehow she got out the words... 'Goodbye.'

Then she hung up the receiver. Spent, white, she lay with closed eyes, not moving for a long while. But the tears trickled slowly and painfully down her cheeks.

Later she was up and dressed and ready for action. There was much for her to do, serious alterations to be made in her life, and no time for brooding and grieving.

She interviewed the manager of this block of flats in which she lived and asked him to dispose of the remainder of her lease, as soon as he could. She would stay in her beloved flat until she had let it, and then she must find something much cheaper. Meanwhile, she would have to economise in every possible way. The most important thing was to get a job at once. She shrank from the idea of approaching Duffeyne. He had always been nice to her, but he was so closely concerned with Fane. She would be beholden to Fane if she took work through the American. She had other friends connected with the stage, and she would try them all before appealing to anyone at The Quality Theatre.

At twelve o'clock she went to the nursing-home to see old Mrs Grey. She was due at the Berkeley at one o'clock for lunch with Jack Elliott. It was an appointment which had been made days ago. She had turned down his invitations so often that for once she had consented to give him the pleasure of taking her out. Last night she had half decided to put him off, but this morning she had shrugged her shoulders and asked herself why ... why refuse anything that came her way?

There seemed so little left in life, and Jack Elliott was a charming boy, still a persistent admirer in spite of the fact that she had lost her voice and her job. That made her feel kindly towards him.

It added to her already depressed state of mind to enter that nursing-home wherein the first crushing blow had been dealt her by the doctor who had told her she would never sing again. But she wanted to see the dear old lady who had been so sweetly interested in her all the way along. And she was determined to keep a tight rein on her feelings. It would only distress Mrs Grey to see how badly she had been hit by her broken engagement. She rehearsed all the nonchalant, casual things she would say. She would be the unaffected 'modern' … just what Fane wanted her to be … and nobody on earth must know that deep down inside her she was a sick, miserable, shivering coward.

Julian Grey was with his mother when Francesca was shown into the room by the nurse.

Julian had been waiting for Francesca. She had been a great deal in his thoughts since he had seen her yesterday. In fact, he had been astonished by the persistent way in which her image haunted him. Such a sad, forsaken little image! He was as eager as his mother, now, to offer her friendship and all that it entailed.

This morning he saw a change in her. An outward change. She was gay and talkative. There was a pink flush on her cheeks; bright, fixed smile on her reddened lips; she had put on a grey tailored suit and a cherry and white spotted silk blouse with a big bow at the throat; a tiny cherry-coloured cap on her fair head; a little grey veil over her eyes. She was the chic, lovely, glowing Francesca of the stage. Quite different from the lost, lonely girl whom he had pictured wandering desolately through the arches of his Spanish castle.

She came to his mother's bedside with a large basket of fruit (which he knew she could ill afford), kissed her warmly and said:

'How lovely to see you again, dear Mrs Grey! I've missed you!'

The old lady held out her arms.

'And I've missed you, child. It's good to see you again.'

They embraced, and Julian, looking at the charming young figure as Francesca bent over the bed, wondered why he had ever been even mildly irritated by the idea of his mother's affection for this girl.

He knew, instinctively, that she had come with this simulated gaiety entirely to please the old lady. The flush on her face was artificial like the scarlet of her lips. Behind it all she was still the forsaken, heart-broken Francesca. When he had talked to her yesterday he had bowed before her courage. And once again he knew himself her admirer.

She shook hands with him with the same forced good spirits.

'Isn't it a marvellous morning? The sun's so lovely.'

'You've brought it in here with you, my dear,' said Mrs Grey. 'Hasn't she, Julian?'

Forty-eight hours ago he would have said 'yes' just to please his mother. This morning he answered to please himself.

'She certainly has.'

Then, perhaps, a look in Francesca's eyes betrayed the bitterness that lay at the back of that sunshine. But for only an instant.

Then it was gone, and she was smiling again. She sat down beside the bed and took one of Mrs Grey's hands in hers.

'How are you? Better?'

'I shall never be better, my dear.'

Francesca was silent an instant. Secretly, she was rather shocked by the old lady's appearance. She looked a good deal worse, and she was a bad colour. She seemed to have more pain, and the nurse had told Francesca she was failing rapidly. Francesca shrank from the thought of the inevitable end. It would be so awful for Julian. He had himself told her that he had nobody else in the world whom he cared about.

Julian left them together.

'You don't want all your visitors at once, darling,' he told his mother. Then to Francesca he added:

'May I take you out to lunch?'

'It's kind of you,' she said, 'but I've got an engagement.'

'Another time then.'

'Thank you so much.'

He shook hands with her again and gave her his grave, almost shy smile. He looked years younger when he smiled. Francesca was beginning to feel that Julian Grey was an essentially nice person. When he had gone, she turned to the old lady and said:

'I don't wonder you say all the nice things you do about your son.'

'Ah! So you're beginning to know my Julian?'

'Not very well just yet. But we had a long talk yesterday, and I think I understand him more than I did.'

'You thought him harsh and unfriendly, didn't you?'

'Well, he seemed so at first.'

'You see, my dear, he doesn't quite trust women. He's a little doubtful of them, especially when they're young and pretty. But you know why.'

Francesca turned her eyes to the window and looked through it blindly.

'Yes – I know why – now.'

'I feel I'm growing weaker, my dear. It isn't that I'm afraid to meet my Maker. I'm prepared for that. But I hate to leave my boy. He's so very much alone.'

Francesca pressed the old lady's hand in hers.

'He'll miss you horribly, dear Mrs Grey, but he'll be all right.'

'I hope so. But you don't know Julian as I do. Behind all that quiet strength of his he has a wild, sad streak. I don't know quite what it is, but he isn't leading a natural life. He's too solitary. I don't think Julian ought to live alone. He's fundamentally a passionate and affectionate man. He should have love in his life. If only Irene hadn't left him ... if only he had somebody with him now!'

Francesca quietened her down.

'You mustn't excite yourself. It isn't good for you. I'm sure your boy will be all right.'

'I wish you could look after him … that you were one of our family.'

Francesca gave a brief little laugh.

'Darling Mrs Grey … how sweet of you. But I can scarcely look after myself.'

The old lady looked at the lovely young face of the girl. Then she said:

'Dear me, I'd forgotten. Julian told me this morning … you've had a dreadful blow, my dear. I couldn't believe it, and yet I was afraid… I was always afraid because you loved your Fane so much…'

Francesca braced herself. She had come prepared for this, and she put an iron heel on the inclination to fling herself at Mrs Grey's bedside and burst into tears.

She said quite quietly:

'My engagement is broken. Fane didn't love me as much as I did him, you see.'

'My poor darling!'

'Oh, I'm – all right.'

'How could he, Francesca? You'd given him so much, and to leave you when you had lost everything else … how could he be so cruel?'

Francesca clenched a hand in her lap.

'He didn't mean to be. It just happened to come at the same time as my illness.'

'That other girl… I suppose he's interested in her now?'

'Yes.'

The old lady shook her head sadly. Her voice quivered with distress when she spoke again.

'I wish this hadn't happened to you, darling child. It makes me very grieved.'

'Please don't be, dear Mrs Grey; I'll get over it. I'm going to be very busy. I've got to find some work and cut down my expenses. I shall have heaps to do. I shan't have time to grieve for myself.'

She spoke cheerfully. She was smiling. The small fair head was held high, and the eyes through the little grey veil were hard and bright. But Mrs Grey was not deceived. She knew that this girl was hurt to the very soul. She could not have been more distressed had Francesca been her own child.

'Julian was quite worried about you,' she said. 'He wants to be your friend. He's such a rock to lean on. You'll let him be your friend, won't you?'

'Yes, of course.'

'He will be understanding. He's been through this sort of thing himself.'

'Yes, I know.'

'Why,' said the old lady sadly, 'must the reward of love – great love – be suffering?'

'It seems to have been so from all ages,' said Francesca with a twisted smile.

Mrs Grey nodded:

'And life is love. Do you know those words... "Life is love – and without love there is no light, nor life, but only darkness and weariness of soul"...?'

Mrs Grey was whispering the last few words. Francesca barely heard them. She saw that the old lady's eyes were closing. She was reacting to the dope which had been given to her in her medicine. The fingers holding Francesca's relaxed. She slept.

Francesca, no longer smiling, and with a look of intense sadness, stole from the room and shut the door behind her. She met the nurse in the passage.

'Mrs Grey seems to be sleeping. When she wakes give her my best love and tell her I'll come again soon.'

The nurse, with a professional eye scanning Francesca, was not deceived by the make-up. She said:

'My dear, you're not looking as well as you should. I think we'd better have you back here and nurse you up a bit!'

Francesca smiled.

'I'm all right.'

And that was what she told Jack Elliott when she met the young captain at the Berkeley Grill. But he, because he was in love with her, noticed the look of strain in her eyes and the sharpened outline of her face. When she said 'I'm all right,' he shook his head.

'I wonder!' he said.

He had only just heard at his club that the engagement between the beautiful Francesca and her recent partner had been broken. The news had shocked him. His admiration for Francesca was very wholehearted and never for an instant had he imagined that he would have a chance with her himself. But that had not prevented him from seeing her, in the revue in which she had been singing, at least a dozen times. Neither had it stopped him from calling continually with flowers and messages. He was young … as young as she was … and this was the first big passion of his life. He had been more interested in flying than in women until the hour when he had first seen Francesca on the stage, slim and alluring in her black-and-white evening dress, with that white topper on the side of her blonde head, sitting on Fane's piano, crooning in her inimitable fashion. And after that, there were photographs of her all over Elliott's room, and he was generally ragged about his 'girl friend' in the mess.

But things were a little more serious now. The boy's calf love was not quite an idle fancy. This was only the third time in his life that he had been granted an hour alone with her, and it bred in him a new ambition; he wanted to marry her.

While she had been engaged to Fane, she

had seemed as inaccessible as the stars. But now, he saw no reason why he should not offer her everything that he had in the world. He did so, at the end of the lunch. Francesca listened with a half tender, half cynical smile on her lips.

'My dear,' she said, 'it's charming of you, but – don't be absurd. You're only at the beginning of your career, and you're going to do wonderful things in the air, and the last thing you want is to be saddled with a wife.'

'It isn't so absurd,' he said; 'I've got a small income as well as my pay, and my guv'nor has a bit of money and a decent little place up in Scotland. I could offer you something.'

'You've offered me a great deal. And it's sweet of you. But I'm a wreck, and scarcely the wife for you.'

He hotly repudiated this.

'A wreck! You! Look at yourself in the glass.'

'Yes – I've still got a face of sorts, but I've lost my voice, and that was so much to me…'

She broke off; her under lip trembled. Jack Elliott leaned across the table and put a hand over hers.

'My God! It must be frightful for you. That lovely voice … your whole career gone smash. Why in Heaven's name did that partner of yours…?'

Francesca did not let him finish. Hastily

143

she drew her hand away and tried to laugh.

'Don't let's talk about that.'

'Well, won't you give me a chance?'

She shook her head at him. He was a good-looking boy; dark, thin, vital, with a brown, healthy skin and bright hazel eyes. A clean-minded, clean-living boy; enthusiastic about his job, about shooting and fishing and animals. She knew exactly the sort of life he would lead in 'the guv'nor's place up in Scotland.' But it was utterly impossible for her to imagine herself married to him. She could not even consider it. He was not her type; not her man. He was utterly different from Fane! Perhaps she was a fool to have loved Fane so much, and to care so badly still – in spite of what he had done to her. But there it was! One couldn't command love. One could only do what one's heart dictated and enjoy or suffer as the case might be.

'It's very dear of you to be so nice to me,' she told Jack Elliott huskily, 'but it's quite impossible. Please just go on being friends with me. It's friendship that I need.'

He was disappointed but undaunted.

'Of course I'm your friend, whenever you need me. But – I shall go on hoping.'

'Foolish of you.'

'What's life worth without hope?' he said, and lit a cigarette for her and one for himself.

Francesca let her glance wander round the room. Certainly, Jack was right. Life wasn't worth much without hope. And she had none – absolutely none!

She bowed mechanically to a couple who were just passing her table. The woman was Lady Wellington, who last Christmas had given a huge party in her house in Chelsea, and had paid 'Fane and Francesca' handsomely for helping to entertain her guests.

The sight of Lady Wellington brought back the memory of that night for Francesca. The excitement of it all; the thrill of working with Fane; the applause, the delicious gaiety, and that one thing she had treasured above the rest … Fane's word of praise.

Gone! Those wonderful days and nights. Gone for ever!

She was a fool to come to a place like this. She had far better stay at home rather than see anything of a world in which she used to move, and which henceforth would be barred to her. It was too painful.

'Do you mind if we go?' she asked Jack Elliott.

'Of course, if you wish…'

Driving back to Whitehall in a taxi, they passed the Quality Theatre. Francesca tautened in every muscle. Somehow her gaze was dragged to the advertisements. The names 'FANE AND KAY' flashed out at her. She felt an unspeakable anguish. Clos-

145

ing her eyes, she leaned back in the taxi, and fought for self-possession.

The boy beside her watched, horribly embarrassed, and powerless to help her.

When she had said goodbye to him, she went up to her flat, walked straight into the drawing-room, face flushed, lips compressed. She reached the radio-gramophone, switched on the electricity, and put on a record. For a moment she stood listening to it, trembling in every limb.

It was a fine recording of Fane at his piano. And then came her own voice ... like a ghost from the past ... sweet, crooning, seductive ... the voice that had charmed thousands in its day. She was singing a hot favourite of the moment:

'Can it be the Spring that seems to bring
The stars right into my room?
Oh, no, it isn't the Spring,
It's love in bloom!'

Francesca stared almost wildly at the gramophone from which that voice issued so miraculously. It was horrible, uncanny, *unbearable*. That was herself singing ... at the height of her success. Kay couldn't sing better than that ... couldn't sing as well. But today she, Francesca, couldn't sing at all! That lovely voice was dead ... *dead*.

Francesca burst into tears – tore the record

off the gramophone. The needle scratched across it. The voice blurred away discordantly. Then there was no sound in the flat except that of Francesca weeping.

10

The telephone bell rang sharply beside Francesca's bed.

She awoke with a start, and, drowsy eyed, lifted the instrument from the holder and put the receiver to her ear. With the other hand she switched on the light. Glancing at her travelling clock she saw that it was a quarter to twelve.

Who on earth could be telephoning to her at such an hour? Midnight would have been quite early for the old Francesca of the Quality Theatre, but these days she went to bed early, and today had been particularly tiring, because she had been hunting for cheap rooms, so she had retired shortly after ten.

'Hello!' she said.

'Hello! Is that Miss Hale?'

She recognized the voice as that of Julian Grey. And she knew before he told her that this call was connected with his mother.

'You must forgive me for disturbing you at

this hour,' came Julian's voice. 'I'm afraid you were asleep...'

'That doesn't matter – what is it?'

'My mother ... I'm afraid it's the end ... and she asked to see you, otherwise I wouldn't have troubled you.'

'Oh, what does that matter?' broke in Francesca. 'I'll come at once.'

She took ten minutes to throw on a few clothes and find a coat. She paid only scant attention to her face. A comb through her hair, a quick sponge with cold water, a dab of powder, and she was wide awake and ready.

Then she was in a taxi driving to the nursing-home. This was the first day of June, and it was a peculiarly warm, windless night. But she shivered a little. She dreaded what lay before her. She had had so much to bear lately that she shrank from a painful scene at a deathbed. On the other hand, nothing on earth would have induced her to refuse to go to the old lady. There had been a warm bond of sympathy and friendship between herself and Mrs Grey ever since they had first met. And then there was Julian, who had been so very kind. She would like to do what she could to help him. This was going to be a great grief for him in spite of the fact that he had known for some time now that the end was coming.

While the taxi jolted through the streets

toward Manchester Square, Francesca remembered a dozen kindnesses from Julian Grey these last two weeks. He had come regularly to see her, and she had seen him whenever she visited his mother. Once or twice he had taken her out – insisted on giving her a little dinner somewhere, or making her accompany him to a cinema, anything rather than that she should sit at home alone every night and brood over her troubles.

She could not say that any of the evenings with him had been gay, or anything approaching it. He was a grave, reticent man who found it difficult to break through his reserve, and his rather quaint, old-fashioned conventionality.

Since that first night when they had talked together ... the painful and unforgettable evening on which Fane had broken with her ... Julian had not spoken of himself or his own past troubles. Each time she left him she thought about him with some perplexity; could not make up her mind whether he was being nice to her because he really liked her or only because his mother wished him to be her friend. But in her present mood he was the only person whom Francesca cared to see with any regularity.

Jack Elliott, young, enthusiastic, and hotly in love, was no use to her just now when she was on the very rack of love, tortured and despairing. The one or two other of her old theatrical friends who tried to be kind only succeeded in reminding her of her lost happiness. Everything – everybody – who reminded her of Fane could only hurt her.

It was almost a relief to be with Julian Grey. He was so impersonal. Music, art, any subject appealing to the senses struck at a vulnerable spot in her. She wanted to avoid them. And Julian had dry, practical things to say, and a certain almost brutal cynicism which fitted in with her present state of mind. He was hard, perhaps he would help to harden her. She needed it, God knew! She was so damnably soft; still so full of the romance which Fane had tried to murder in her; still wanting him back, day and night, with all her pride in tatters and nothing left but a heart that ached perpetually, and a wild desire for the old love ... the life which had meant love ... with Fane.

The taxi drew up in front of the nursing-home. Francesca stepped out and paid her fare. From the next-door house there issued a party of four, two girls and two men in evening-dress, laughing and talking. They made a rush for Francesca's taxi.

Francesca heard one of the girls say:

'It's been a gorgeous evening ... marvellous fun!'

Then the door of the home was opened to her and Francesca passed in. She thought how queer it was. There, next door, there had been a party... 'A gorgeous evening – marvellous fun' ... that girl had described it. Here in this quiet dim place an old lady was dying. That was life! Laughter, vitality, happiness, and hand-in-hand with these things, pain and sorrow and the Shadows.

She found herself in Mrs Grey's familiar bedroom. She felt that death was hovering here even when she entered. It was so very quiet. The flowers had been cleared away. There was a dim whiteness, a single shaded lamp beside the bed, and Julian sitting there, holding both his mother's hands in his. On the other side of the bed stood a night nurse and the doctor who had been hastily summoned.

Julian turned to Francesca. His face looked grey and tired. He whispered:

'Come in ... so good of you ... she's been asking to see you...'

The doctor and nurse moved away. Everything had been done that was in their power. There was nothing more for them to do. And Mr Grey had said that he would like to be alone with his mother as soon as Miss Hale came. So they went away and left Mrs Grey with her son, and with the girl whom she said she loved as she would have loved her own daughter.

Francesca took off her coat and sat down on the other side of the bed. The old lady,

waxen in colour and breathing with difficulty, opened her eyes, saw the girl and
smiled. She drew one of her hands from
Julian's and gave it to Francesca.

'My dear ... I wanted to see you ... is it
very late?'

Francesca bent over her:

'No, no, not at all, dear Mrs Grey.'

Mrs Grey smiled.

'Doesn't she look pretty, Julian? I like that
green-and-white dress. Don't you?'

'Very much, darling,' said Julian, and his
voice was the most tender thing Francesca
had ever heard. So different from the curt
voice of the Julian whom other people knew.

'And you've done your hair differently,'
whispered Mrs Grey. 'I like it like that ...
don't you, Julian?'

Poor Julian, thought Francesca. How em-
barrassing for him to have these questions
put to him! But he did not appear to mind.
He assured his mother that he liked Francesca's hair as it was tonight. Francesca
imagined it must look awful; she had barely
had time to do it. But Julian, manlike, did
not notice the details. He only felt some
slight compunction for having dragged the
girl from her bed at such an hour, when she
was still far from well. Perhaps it was this
dim light which made her face look so very
white and thin and painted such bruises
under eyes. But she really did look a little

ghost, he thought.

Mrs Grey said:

'Francesca ... will you be all right?'

'How do you mean?' Francesca asked, and pressed the frail little hand gently.

'I mean ... I hate leaving you like this ... you've had so much to bear ... and Julian ... I'm worried about him ... if only you and he ... oh dear ... I suppose it's no good me wishing any such thing...'

Francesca knit her brows and glanced at Julian.

'What does she mean?'

'Julian, tell her what I want,' whispered the old lady.

'Mother darling, I really don't think...'

'Oh, Julian! I should be so disappointed!'

The old lady's voice quavered, and a big tear rolled down one ivory cheek. Immediately Julian wiped it away with his handkerchief and touched her forehead with his lips.

'There – darling, very well – if she agrees and if you wish it.'

Francesca, utterly perplexed, looked at Julian again.

'What does she mean?'

He stood up and moved across to the window.

'Come here just one moment, I want to say something to you...'

She joined him, wondering. For an instant he pulled up the blind and stood there –

frowning out at the quiet, starlit night. Then he said in an undertone:

'I hope you don't mind, but my mother has a notion in her head ... rather an absurd one, poor darling, but you know ... dying people get these fancies ... and several times lately she has expressed the wish that you and I...' He paused, frowning harder, then suddenly turned those very blue penetrating eyes of his upon her. 'Well, the fact of the matter is, my mother would like to think that you and I might get married after she is dead.'

The shock of that brought the hot colour flaming to Francesca's face and throat. She gave a nervous little laugh.

'Of course ... that's impossible...'

He had not for an instant imagined that she would say anything else. He agreed with her.

'But you see, it's just an old lady's dying fancy. She's had it on her mind for a long time that I'm lonely and in need of a wife although I've assured her that I never want to marry again. And she's so fond of you. These things which have been happening to you lately have also preyed on her mind. You can understand ... she has a romantic heart, and she thinks it would be wonderful if you and I should console each other.'

He finished with a short gesture of the hand. There was not the vestige of feeling on his face as he explained the situation rapidly under his breath. The colour ebbed away from Francesca's cheeks. She looked white and tired again. She said:

'I quite understand.'

'Will you do something for her ... only for her...? Will you let her think that it *is* possible...?'

Francesca put a hand to her throat.

'But how?'

'Only for now ... perhaps a few minutes ... she can't last longer than that ... they've given oxygen ... and it isn't any use. The poor darling won't be here to see what happens tomorrow. But I'd like her to die happy. Will you act a part with me before she goes?'

Francesca nodded:

'I see. You want me to pretend?'

'That we're going to get married, yes.'

'Very well.'

'If you're sure you don't mind,' he said in an apologetic voice.

'I don't mind anything.'

'My dear child, you know that this means nothing and I'm your friend.'

'Yes, I know.'

'You would be doing me a great service if you could help me make my mother's last moments happy.'

She looked up at him and thought what a queer person he was. Even at a moment like this he was stiff and unbending, finding expression difficult. A cynic, from whom life had stripped all sex-emotion ... trying rather pathetically to stage a romance for the mother who was the only being on earth whom he still loved.

'Just tell me what you want me to do,' she said, 'and I'll do it.'

'Thanks. Thanks. Then we'll just go back and tell her, that we're going to – er – look after each other. Don't you – er – agree?'

He was stammering – obviously uneasy about playing this role, and Francesca was suddenly sorry for him. Life was going to be empty for him tomorrow. And it was easier for her than for him to play a part. She was used to the stage, but he was a man who would find artifice and pretence difficult.

'Don't worry,' she whispered, 'we'll manage it somehow.'

They returned to the bedside. Mrs Grey was panting. Her eyes, now glazing, but still that marvellous blue which she had bequeathed to her son, were anguished.

'Julian,' she said in a scarcely audible voice.

He bent over her.

'I'm here, dearest.'

'Don't ... want you ... be alone ... when I'm gone...'

'I won't be, dear. I've got Francesca.'

It was the first time he had used her Christian name. It sounded strange from his lips. Francesca felt that the whole thing was strange and unreal. But she played up to him as she had promised to do.

'Yes, Mrs Grey. I'll look after Julian, I promise.'

The old lady looked from her son to the girl.

'Then will you both ... is my wish to be granted...?'

'Yes, yes, darling,' said Julian, 'Francesca and I will get married and we'll look after each other.'

A look of incredible happiness came over the face of the dying woman.

'How truly wonderful! God is indeed good. Francesca, my darling ... will you really look after my boy? Can you love him ... a little ... in spite of what life has done to you?'

Francesca answered:

'Yes. Of course I can.'

'Truly wonderful...' Mrs Grey repeated. 'Julian ... how happy you've made me... I shall go in peace ... if you two dear children...'

She broke off, struggling for breath. Julian, his face contracting, watched the change that came over her face.

'Shall I fetch the nurse?' whispered Francesca.

'No, it's no use.'

The old lady opened her eyes again.

'My two dear ones ... you will comfort each other... I'm so glad. Francesca will make you such a good little wife, Julian.'

Francesca dared not look at Julian. She felt almost hypocritical. She hated deceiving the old lady. But Julian lied without blushing now. His one thought was for his mother. At all costs she must die in peace.

'We'll both be very happy, darling,' he said.

'Take Francesca in your arms, Julian. I would like to see you kiss her ... once...'

Francesca went hot, then cold. This was a little more than she had bargained for. It was becoming fantastic. But Julian was going doggedly through his part. He held out a hand to her.

'Will you?' he whispered.

She kept her promise to him. She walked into the circle of his arm and for a moment was drawn close to him. He was so very tall and big, and she was so small, her fair, shining head only reached his shoulder. She felt half afraid and her slim body stiffened. It was altogether a peculiar experience. And then she saw the apology in his eyes, and she gave him a faint smile.

That smile did more to upset Julian Grey than anything else. There was something so helpless and so sweet in it. He had always thought Francesca a gentle creature. And now he knew how amazingly soft and fragrant and little she was in his arms. The first woman he had touched since Irene had left him. For him too it was a curious experience and a fantastic one.

He bent his head and kissed her lightly. To her the kiss meant nothing – no more than an embrace on the stage from a fellow-actor would have done. But it was something more to Julian. He was both astonished and dismayed to discover how it affected him. Her lips were like velvet and very sweet, and the whole contact with her became, suddenly, a devastating thing. The hardened cynic, impervious to women's wiles, vanished. In his place stood the intense passionate boy who had loved Irene so madly.

He knew that as he had loved Irene, so he could love this girl, Francesca Hale. That knowledge, and the surging of all the old emotions through body and mind, terrified him. He let Francesca go, his heart racing. His face was like granite, betraying nothing of the flame which that brief embrace had lit within him.

'Thank you,' he said under his breath.

Then Francesca's gaze fell on the old lady, and she gave a low cry.

'Your mother...'

Julian looked. The old lady might have been asleep, but he knew that she was dead. There was the most perfect smile of peace, of quietude, on that ivory face. Even while a

159

wave of sorrow at his loss swept over him, he was glad that she looked like that. She was finished with pain and with sorrow. She would no longer worry about him. And he was profoundly glad that he had played that part with Francesca; brought such a look to that beloved face.

'Will you fetch the nurse, Francesca?' he said huskily.

Now that the strain was over and it was all ended, Francesca was in tears. She went downstairs to the waiting-room, and sat there crying quietly until Julian joined her. His own eyes were red-rimmed and weary, but he smiled at her.

'You must let me take you home,' he said.

She wiped her eyes.

'Have you … is everything…?' She broke off, stammering.

'I've done everything that's necessary,' he nodded.

She stood up, tidying her hair. She made no attempt to powder her nose. Looking at the small pale face disfigured by grief, Julian was immensely drawn to her. It was dear of her to care like this about his mother.

'You have been splendid,' he said. 'I can never tell you how grateful I am.'

'I did nothing.'

'So much more than you realise. My mother died happy and you helped towards that happiness.'

'That means quite a lot to me. But it seemed very little to do.'

'It was a lot. You said so much to comfort her.'

Francesca gave a wry smile.

'I promised to marry you, didn't I?'

He coloured like a boy.

'Yes, but of course it was all just acting…' He cleared his throat. 'I mean, it wasn't serious.'

'Of course not.'

'It was acting a lie … but I don't feel very guilty … I mean, it made her happy because she always wanted to feel that I was going to marry again … she hated the thought of leaving me alone. And she won't know now. Some people think the dead know what happens, but I don't feel that is so.'

'Neither do I,' Francesca agreed with him.

'But I'd like to feel I could do something for you… My mother was anxious that you should be taken care of.'

'Nobody can do anything for me,' said Francesca, turning from him.

He looked at her, strangely. Obviously the kiss, the embrace which had taken place between them upstairs beside that deathbed, had left no impression upon her at all. In him, however, remembrance was alive. He was astonished at himself, but he experienced an intense longing to take her in his arms again, this very moment, and hold her close. It was a long time since he had allowed such sensations to take possession of him. He could only suppose that it was emotional reaction after his mother's death. But the cynic in him was being annihilated tonight. He was once more a normal man with natural impulses, ready to admit that there was nothing more devastating than the soft lips and arms of a beautiful, sympathetic woman; nothing more desirable for a tired head than the soft pillow of a kind young breast.

Francesca knew nothing of these thoughts, and he was not prepared to convey them to her other than by a very gentle attitude toward her. He helped her into her coat.

'I feel you ought to have something to drink, some hot coffee or something. You got out of bed to come here. You're shivering ... are you cold?'

'No – I'm not cold. I'm just nervy.'

'Poor child!'

'Oh, I'll be all right. I don't want anything ... just take me home, if you will.'

He glanced at his watch.

'Lord, it's getting on for two o'clock. I had no idea it was so late. No wonder you're exhausted.'

They walked together into the quiet street. Julian hailed a passing taxi at the corner, helped Francesca into it, and gave the driver the address in Whitehall.

Once she was in that taxi Francesca realized how incredibly tired she was. She
leaned back with closed eyes. She put up a
hand and stroked her throat. It hurt a little.
Julian was quick to notice this action.

'Are you in any pain?'

'Only a little. Nothing to worry about. My
throat always hurts when I'm over-tired.'

'I hope it hasn't done you any harm coming out like this.'

'Of course not.'

She opened her eyes and looked at him.
She remembered his sorrow, his loss, and
impulsively put out a hand to him.

'Poor Julian.'

The friendly gesture and the soft huskiness of her voice unnerved him. In silence
he gripped the small cold fingers and held
them tightly with his own.

She thought:

'Poor old thing, he's dreadfully upset. He
adored his mother. He's rather like a small
boy who wants a little sympathy.'

And on top of that thought came another:

'What a couple we are! A pair of derelicts
… his wife has left him, his mother has died
– he has nobody. And Fane's left me and
I've got nobody.'

She let him hold her hand until they
reached the block of flats wherein she lived.
By that time she was almost stupefied with
fatigue and could not even think. He bade

her goodbye, stammering his gratitude again. She said:

'Don't … it was nothing … I was glad to be able to help.'

'I'll ring you up,' he said, 'I want to keep in touch with you.'

She nodded.

'Yes, do.'

'Good night, Francesca.'

'Good night, Julian.'

They parted – no longer strangers – but friends with a common bond of grief, of sympathy.

But although Julian's thoughts of her, that dawn, were vital with the memory of their single embrace, Francesca had forgotten it.

11

Two weeks after Mrs Grey's death, Francesca sub-let her flat, unfurnished. She had not yet found a cheaper place to go to, so she decided to store her few things which she was keeping. Some of her possessions which she called 'luxuries' she decided to sell. Amongst these was her beautiful piano. She sold that well, and was thankful to find that Blüthners had a good second-hand value. But she felt that she died a little death when the men came to remove the instrument.

So vanished one of the biggest links with the joyous past. The Blüthner was so closely connected with Fane. He, more than anybody else, had played it. Played it for pleasure, composing for her, entertaining her. Played it when they were working together. Her most vivid recollection of Fane was of him sitting at her piano.

She stood on her balcony that June morning and looked down at the big van into which the instrument was being lifted. Her lips were set and her eyes were hard and bright. But she felt as though a knife were being turned in her heart, and there leapt to her mind an odd line from a poem she had learned at school:

'O Death in Life, the days that are no more!'

Unbearable to think that Fane would never play that piano again, and that never more would she see him sitting at it here in her room, smiling at her with those gay, handsome eyes of his, pausing, perhaps, just to murmur:

'Good tune, eh, sweet? Come and kiss me...'

So humiliating to think that she could still suffer at the memory of him when he had treated her badly.

But that was what love was – one went on loving no matter how much one was hurt. Pride didn't come into it ... not when one really loved! She wouldn't whine to him, send for him, let him know what she suffered – like that she could be proud. But all the time her heart seemed to be breaking. She missed him and their past companionship intolerably.

The Blüthner was driven away, and Francesca turned from the balcony and the warm June sunshine back into a room which looked much larger and very empty. Mary came in and announced that a Mr Parsons had called to see her. Parsons was a dealer coming to make Francesca an offer for some Bristol glass and Spode china which had belonged to her mother. It was hateful to have to part with these things, but she needed the money. She was going to need every penny, soon. There was no hope yet of another job materializing.

Very soon, she thought, there wouldn't be anything else left for Life to take from her ... at least nothing that she cared about. Even Mary was going. Mary didn't want to go – she had wept profusely and continuously ever since Francesca had given her notice. But she had her living to earn, and if Miss Francesca could not afford even a small wage, Mary was forced to seek another situation. She had declared to Francesca that life wouldn't be the same to her in a new place. She had been in the family so long. Francesca tried to cheer her up by saying:

'Maybe one day I can have you back ... when things get better.'

But when she thought about it, Francesca told herself she should have said: '*If* things get better.' There seemed precious little chance of it.

She had a bad half-hour with Mr Parsons. It wasn't fun having to sell your most treasured possessions for a third of their worth, which was what she seemed to be doing. Altogether, it was a bad day, commencing with the loss of her beloved piano.

At tea-time she entertained a girl who had been on the stage with her, by name Peggy Lawton. Peggy, a radiant blonde, a dancer in the revue at the Quality, had been one of her best friends until Fane had entirely monopolized Francesca after their engagement. Indeed, now that the engagement was broken Francesca was feeling the draught so far as her other friends were concerned. She realized how much she had given up for Fane. She neglected most of her associates in order to give all her spare time to him.

Peggy, however, was still friendly and anxious to give Francesca all the stage gossip – not very tactfully! Francesca heard far too much about Fane and Kay. Peggy brought up those two names repeatedly. She meant well. She thought it would interest Francesca to know a few details. So Francesca had to sit like a little stone image, not moving a muscle, while Peggy informed her how well 'Fane and Kay' were getting on together.

Peggy ended by expressing sympathy.

'Of course, darling, we *all* say that Fane treated you rottenly. But he's a genius in his way, and I suppose one has to excuse geniuses because they're all crazy. But I do think it was unpardonable of him to rat on you just when you most needed him...'

That was where Francesca interrupted. With two little red spots on both cheekbones, she said:

'I'd rather not discuss Fane, please, Peggy.'

Peggy looked at her with limpid eyes, pulled a flapjack from her bag – examined her face – and busied herself with lipstick and powder.

'I've got such a divine new shade of rouge,' she said, and thus tided over an awkward moment.

And Francesca sat and thought of the days when she and Peggy used to meet in her dressing-room at the Quality Theatre and hold cheerful, frothy conversations about make-up and clothes and lots of things which had been important then, but now – how trivial they seemed! She would have given anything to be that other Francesca who had had nothing to do but to laugh and sing and dance and love... Life had meant love. She felt dead without it ... body and mind torn with suffering. Her imagination was only too vivid; it was so easy for her to picture Fane rushing along in his brilliant, careless fashion, taking Kay with him on the brimming tide of new inspiration, new success ... new love! And it was that last thought that hurt Francesca more cruelly than the rest.

She was glad when Peggy went. The good-natured Peggy hugged and kissed her and tried to persuade her to go on with her to a cocktail party. But Francesca declined:

'I honestly don't feel like it. I haven't got the party spirit at the moment.'

'Darling, you mustn't brood!'

Francesca smiled and shook her head.

'It isn't that. I'm just not very fit or inclined for a party.'

But in her heart she knew that she had turned down the invitation mainly because she did not want to risk meeting Fane. It was much better that she should not see him. Neither did she wish to find herself in the old crowd as an object of pity. That would be more than she could endure.

So Peggy went off without her, quite genuinely distressed about her friend. She expressed her opinions to a good many of the people whom she met at the party, which was being given by a stage favourite of the movement. Everybody there had known Francesca. They all sympathized. They all thought it terribly 'tough luck' that she should have lost her voice, her job, and her lover all at the same time. And they all declared that they must take her out, try to amuse her, do something for her. Most of them censured Fane. But the moment that Fane arrived at the party with Kay at his side, the general feeling altered. Pity for Francesca remained, but it was submerged in a wave of enthusiasm for the attractive, successful composer and pianist. Kay, too, was successful, amusing, and very pretty, and it was easy enough to find excuses for Fane, because, after all, poor Francesca *was* a wreck these days.

Peggy, however, hot on Francesca's side, found time to jab at Fane with her tongue when he greeted her.

'What have you been doing with yourself, Peg?' he asked, with his charming smile.

She shot him a resentful look:

'I've been having tea with Francesca.'

Fane's smile vanished. His lids dropped. He took a gold case from his pocket, and tapped a cigarette thoughtfully upon it.

'Oh! How is she?'

'Rotten.'

'You mean – not well?'

'Not particularly well, but it's more mental

than anything. You haven't done much to lighten her load, have you?'

He stared at her. He was not used to criticism. He spoke more coldly:

'My dear Peggy – you don't understand the position.'

'What is there to understand?' she flashed, 'except that you chucked her for Kay just when she most needed you.'

The cigarette in Fane's fingers remained unlighted.

'Aren't you being a little crude?'

'Sorry – but I've just come away from her, and I can't forget the look in her eyes. The poor kid's *broken*.'

A look of pain came into Fane's handsome eyes.

'My dear Peggy, you may not believe me, but I hate to think of her suffering. I loathe the whole business – I'd give anything for it not to have happened. It's just unfortunate that Kay and I … I mean … that it all happened in connection with Francesca's throat trouble…'

He broke off with a gesture of his slender hand.

Peggy sighed impatiently.

'Oh, well there it is…'

'It's tragic,' said Fane. 'The thought of Francesca haunts me – but what can I do?'

'Nothing, I suppose. She's lost her voice, and you've got a new partner, and I suppose it's essential that you should be in love with her.'

Fane went quite pale.

'How cruel you're being to me.'

'I can only think how cruel you've been to her,' said Peggy, and walked away, realizing that she had probably lost Fane's friendship. But she told herself she was glad she had 'got it off her chest.'

Fane stood alone for a moment, ruffled, even upset by the things which had just been said to him. He glanced across the room and saw Kay talking to Phillip Arnott, a dramatic critic of considerable importance. Kay was looking her best in black which showed up the marvellous whiteness of her skin and the redness of her hair. Moodily Fane stared at her. He was in love with Kay ... they were doing well together in the revue ... but she wasn't really what Francesca had been in the old days ... she hadn't quite that magnetism which Francesca had exercised over her audience; that subtle, stirring quality which belonged to such women as Marlene Dietrich or Katharine Hepburn. Francesca had looked a little like Katharine; he had often told her so. And she had been sweet and soothing to love rather than wickedly exciting – like Kay.

It was tragic – that was what he had just told Peggy, and he had meant it. Everything had gone wrong. He couldn't bear sickness and depression; for Fane so much of Francesca's allure had vanished once her voice and her radiant health had deserted her. So he had ceased to love her and allowed himself to be fascinated by Kay. He decided that he would ring Francesca up tomorrow and try to do something for her. He didn't want her to be broken or miserable. The thought of her troubled him for the rest of the evening, and made him singularly out of countenance with himself and the world in general. And if there was one person he disliked now it was Peggy Lawton for having brought him face to face with the realization of his own cruelty.

That same evening, Julian Grey called at the flat in Whitehall to see Francesca.

He found her alone, sitting on the sofa going through her jewel-case.

She had a smile for him when he entered.

'Hello, Julian. Come in. I'm sorting odds and ends – seeing what valuables I have to raise money on.'

'My dear child!' he said in a shocked voice.

'Sit down,' she said, 'and have a cigarette.'

He lit the cigarette but remained standing in front of her, staring down at her with his penetrating blue eyes. She looked up at him, still faintly smiling. She was, as usual, tired, and it had been a bad day, what with one thing and another. But she was pleased to see

Julian. He called regularly every evening to see her and nobody could have been kinder than he since his mother's death. After the funeral he had had to go down to Devonshire to settle up affairs, and as soon as he came back he had showered Francesca with kindnesses. It was almost as though he had made up his mind not to allow the once popular revue artist to miss all the tributes to which she had been accustomed. He sent masses of flowers. He never came without a box of chocolates or some books which he thought would amuse her.

He had established himself firmly as her friend, and she accepted him as such, and was grateful for what he offered.

She was beginning to know him quite well, and she had wondered many times why his wife had left him. He was a fine man to look at, and he was by no means a bore. Perhaps he was a little on the quiet side, but that was because he was studious. She soon discovered that Julian had brains above the average, and was a fount of knowledge. And he had a dry wit – a certain cynical humour which amused her.

She, herself, was no longer frightened of growing hard and cynical. She wanted to become both. It was better. One did not suffer so much that way. Or was that a fallacy? Did the hardened cynics suffer more than most people under the crust? It was difficult to tell. Her own pain was still so acute she could not judge what was to become of her psychologically.

She only knew that Julian had come into her life at the right time. He was the one person to whom she could talk and in whom she could confide, and whom she could see often. Other men, like Jack Elliott, made love to her. Julian did not believe in love after his own bitter experience. His outlook fitted in with her present mood.

She realized, too, that there was something pathetic about Julian. He was a lonely man, despite his money and his varied interests. That melancholy streak of which his mother had spoken to her was often apparent in his long silences, the difficulty which he found at times to rise above his own depression. She found herself wanting to help him – she who needed help so badly herself! But she felt that it was almost a religious duty, because she had promised his mother at her deathbed that she would look after him. He, too, had promised to look after her. And on that common ground they met. Otherwise, Francesca felt that they were as far apart as the poles, for she was never really in sympathy with Julian, never really alone with him. Fane walked, continuously, a charming, cruel, devastating ghost at her side.

Julian, curiously intuitive, knew this and whilst he regarded such enduring love in a cynical light, where Francesca herself was concerned he was entirely without cynicism.

He had been fully occupied with his mother's affairs lately, and on the day of her funeral had been so acutely conscious of her loss that he had not had much time in which to think about Francesca. But when he did turn his mind to her, it was with tenderness. Nevermore was she to seem the 'heartless blonde,' the 'gay coquette,' the 'mercenary, spoiled revue star' which he had thought her when they first met. Not because she appeared particularly to deserve such epithets, but because all women had seemed so after his disillusionment in Irene.

He knew the real Francesca now. He had even held her, sweet, soft, kindly in his embrace. That was unforgettable. Whenever he saw her he remembered their kiss with a strange leaping of the blood and half-laughed at himself because since Irene left him he had been a recluse and left women out of his reckoning. He had no right to be thrilled like a raw boy with a pretty woman in his arms.

Yet the more he saw of Francesca, the more vivid grew the memory of her arms and her lips. It almost frightened him. And the more he saw of her courage in the teeth of disaster the more he admired her. He wanted to help her now not only because it had been his mother's wish, but because it was his own.

He grew to dislike the mere thought of Fane Braber. One night he went alone to the revue at the Quality Theatre just for the purpose of seeing more of this man whom Francesca had loved so completely, and who still had such a devastating influence upon her. Every time Fane appeared on the stage Julian disliked him more. The man was a cad, an arrogant, rather effeminate cad. Handsome, yes ... moved well ... played the piano flawlessly in his fashion ... but he was not worth Francesca's tears, Julian told himself. Who could account for the taste of women? They seemed to care most for the blackguards and the cads.

Fane's new partner left Julian cold. She was amusing and pretty in a fashion, but he recognized in her a quality which he had discovered in Irene after they had lived together. A hard, mean streak. He knew that girl Kay would let any man down for another with more money. But not so Francesca.

Unconsciously he was beginning to idealise this girl whom his mother had loved; he who boasted that he had learned the folly of idealizing any woman, and who had sworn never to let another enter his mind or his heart.

Fate played funny tricks upon people. And this was going to be an odd jest ... Julian Grey falling in love for the second time in his life with a woman who was in love with somebody else!

He was trying not to admit even to himself that he loved Francesca. But there was an undeniable hunger deep down in him nowadays, which was for her. He was really only happy when he was with her. And he regarded with dread the prospect of seeing less of her in the future than he was doing now.

Still less attractive was the possibility that she might meet and marry another man. Not that that really came into it at the moment, because she was still so hopelessly in love with Fane.

This evening as he watched her – small, rather pathetic – huddled over the treasures which she was going to dispose of because she wanted money, he knew beyond all doubt that he was absurdly, wildly in love with her. He was not going to tell her so and drive her away from him, however. But there was a plan in his mind so enthralling that he dared not think too much about it in case she turned it down. It lurked there in his consciousness. He moved cautiously. He must not do or say anything to make her draw away from him in the way she had withdrawn from Jack Elliott, because the young airman had rushed to her with a passionate love which was the last thing on earth that she wanted under the circumstances. Julian knew how distasteful passion would be to her. He would have loathed to have had any woman hanging round his neck after his wife had left him when he was still raw and bleeding from that episode.

Francesca had grown to trust him, confide in him, and accept his friendship. And that was an attitude which he had no wish to alter, whatever happened.

'Will you forgive me for not being changed?' Francesca said after a long silence between them.

'Of course,' he said and added: 'I like you in that...'

Flattery did not come easy to a man of his temperament; yet he wanted to let her know that he was very satisfied with her appearance, and she recognized the fact and smiled at him. He was really rather sweet, poor old Julian, and 'that' was nothing but a blue linen smock with big pockets which she used to wear when she lived in the country with her mother. It was a relic of the old cottage days. She wouldn't have dreamed of letting Fane see her in such an attire, and with her hair a little untidy and her face flushed and unpowdered. But Julian didn't seem to mind – it was really very comforting. And such a singular proof of her attitude towards life at the moment – this not really caring what she looked like.

Had she but known it, she looked particularly charming in that linen smock with a slight flush on her cheeks. She had been far too pale lately. To Julian she seemed a mere child except for the intense sadness and weariness in her eyes.

He found himself apologizing for his dinner-jacket.

'I only changed because I thought perhaps you might like to come out, somewhere...'

'Thanks, Julian, you're a dear – but I couldn't move. I'm dead tired.'

'What have you been doing?'

'Selling up the old home.'

'But why ... what do you mean...?'

'Don't you notice any difference?' she asked, waving her hand around the room.

He looked around him. He had really only been conscious of her presence. But now he saw that the room was much larger and had a forlorn air.

'Good Lord! – the piano...'

'Yes, and my Queen Anne table; and to-morrow they are fetching some of the glass and these two Persian rugs. A dealer with a marvellous hooked nose and the most expressive gestures of the hand came and bid for them, and he is sending for them in the morning. Personally, I thought he did me down a bit, but he's offered quite a fair price, and I want the cash.'

Without waiting for Julian's comment, she began to give an imitation of the Jew. She did it well, and with laughter. But Julian listened to the husky little voice, an indignation growing in his soul, which burst forth when she had finished.

'It's outrageous.'

'What is?'

'That you should have to sell your things.'

'Lots of other people have had to do it, and I'm lucky to have assets which are worth something.'

He shook his head speechlessly. It seemed to him wonderful that she should make a joke of things. Yet she seemed to be parting with all that she most loved. She was teaching him a lesson. He was beginning to see how the brave accept a calamity. He had been a coward after Irene had gone. He found nothing to joke about; had just sunk into a sullen apathy, and had been filled with a hatred of everybody and everything in the world except his mother. This child made him ashamed of himself.

'I hate to think of you having to do this,' he said, his brows contracting. 'And you really mustn't sell these few jewels...'

'Oh, but I must,' said Francesca.

She lifted a locket and handed it to him.

'This was my mother. I won't sell this.'

He looked at the miniature. It was a very sweet face, with Francesca's grave, beautiful brows and tender mouth.

'She's like you,' he said.

'She was a very lovely person. Lovelier than

181

I shall ever be. We were very happy together in our cottage.'

'Isn't it a pity, in a way, that you didn't stay there! Somehow I don't think that you were ever made for stage life.'

Francesca put down the case, stood up, and with her hands in the pockets of her smock, walked across to the window and looked out at the glittering lights of her beloved London.

'You're wrong. I adored the country but I've adored London too, and stage life. Not necessarily the people. But the excitement of achieving something. That's what life means ... achievement. And if you have no hope of that, it's dreadful – futile!'

He glanced at the back of her fair young head.

'I agree with you that achievement is the great *élan* of existence,' he said. 'I feel that way myself. I like to do things. That's why I find old houses and restore them. It's good to do something worth doing.'

She turned to him with a half-smile.

'You don't think success on the stage a very worthy sort of achievement?'

'I don't really know anything about it.'

'But you don't like it.'

He made a little gesture with his hand.

'I wouldn't choose a stage career for myself. I couldn't begin to do anything in front of an audience.'

182

'No. You're the sort of man who does a lot behind the scenes.'

'That's dull, eh?' he laughed.

'Very often it's the power behind the scenes that is responsible for all the success. The very core of things, so to speak. The actors are, after all, only the puppets.'

'But I'm not decrying the actor. His is a great art. I just say I wouldn't choose it for myself, and I don't somehow feel that it suits you.'

'In a way it didn't,' she said wistfully. 'And yet I was, in my fashion, a success.'

'You certainly were.'

She dug her hands deeper into her pockets. Her lips twisted.

'The greater the success, the greater the fall.'

'You mustn't dwell on that.'

'I don't unless I can help it, but sometimes, Julian, I just long to go back.'

'Naturally you do, my dear.'

'If only my voice recovered – if only a miracle restored it...'

'You'd go straight back, eh?'

'Yes, I think I would.'

'And no doubt Braber would be damned glad to have the chance of getting you back,' Julian said with a queer, rough note in his voice.

He regretted the remark as soon as he had made it, because he saw the agonizing colour scorch her face and throat. Then she shrugged her shoulders.

'Who knows? But I dare say he finds my successor even more inspiring as a partner than he found me.'

'Well, I can't stand the woman,' he muttered.

That made her smile again. There was something of the schoolboy about this big, strong, studious man, which belied all his harshness.

'So you've seen the show? I didn't know.'

'Yes – I dropped in one night.'

'Fane's good – isn't he?'

'Yes…' Julian refused to meet Francesca's eyes. He knew what she would see in them.

'But didn't you like Kay's voice?'

'No – not as much as yours.'

Francesca's nostrils quivered. Her slender hands were quivering too. There was a wry little smile on her lips. She was feminine enough, human enough, to appreciate the comparison which he made in her favour. Then she said:

'But you've never heard me.'

'Yes, I have. You played a record to my mother once.'

'I've still got those records, and I can't part with them. Yet sometimes I want to *smash* them. I play them, and it's uncanny … it drives me mad… I know I *am* better than Kay. And to think that it's all gone –

184

dead – except for those records.'

She sat down suddenly on the sofa, and put her hands to her eyes.

Then Julian threw discretion to the winds. He could not bear to see her there, breaking down suddenly after she had been so gallant, and so gay. He walked to the sofa, sat down beside her, and took her hand in his.

'My dear,' he said, 'my poor dear...'

She pressed a clenched hand against her trembling lips.

'Damn, damn, *damn!* If you knew how I hate feeling this way, but I can't seem to fight it down.'

'It takes time, my dear. I assure you you'll get over it.'

'Are you so sure?' she asked, and looked up at him with burning eyes. 'I remember I asked you once before and you said that it would get easier, but it doesn't seem to.'

'But you haven't had time. It's all very recent, and this sort of thing makes it worse. This selling your things, and leaving your nice home. What you want is a complete change of scene – of life. After my divorce I went to Spain. It was a totally different atmosphere, and that helped. I'd like you to go away ... right away from London and everything connected with your old life.'

'I'd like it too. But there isn't a dog's chance. I've got to find a job. And as soon as

185

I start work and stop moaning, I'll be better.'

'You've never moaned. You've been splendid.'

The fervour in his voice astonished her – and made her suddenly aware of him rather than of herself. He was holding her hand tightly, and his face was alight with an enthusiasm which she had never seen there before. How amazingly blue his eyes were … almost as blue as gentians. They made her feel a trifle uncomfortable. She drew her hand away.

'Wouldn't you like a drink? I believe there is a spot of something left, in spite of my penury,' she laughed.

'No, thank you. But listen, Francesca… There is a chance for you to go abroad – if you'll take it.'

'How?'

'It's like this,' he said. 'I've been thinking a great deal about you, and I'll confess that on more than one occasion I've wished that what we told my mother was true. Well, why not let us make it true, Francesca?'

12

Francesca stared at Julian. Her heart-beats quickened a little with nervousness, rather than with emotion, because this big, strange man was sitting there beside her proposing marriage as calmly as though it were an event of no great importance.

'You see,' went on Julian, 'it seems to me so ridiculous for us not to let the thing materialize. It all began out of a wish to make my mother happy before she died. Now I see no reason why we shouldn't do as she asked – try to make each other happy. Do you think that would be possible? I have money, and nobody on earth to spend it on, and I'd love to look after you, Francesca. And perhaps you could look after me a little, eh?'

He gave his faint smile, which made the stern face curiously young and attractive. Francesca went on staring at him, as though the idea fascinated rather than frightened her now. He put the thing so prosaically. She could not shy from it as she would have done from a passionate protestation of love. Then she gave an embarrassed little laugh and shook her head.

'My dear Julian, of course it's impossible.'

He had expected her to say that at first, so he was neither disappointed nor daunted. He had made up his mind to marry this girl, and when Julian Grey made up his mind to do a thing he generally did it. Not by the slightest sign or word did he intend showing that he was in love with her. Neither would he make any demands upon her. That was going to put a pretty heavy strain upon him – he knew it – but he was prepared to stick it out. He wanted her with him; there was an almost fraternal quality mingled with the passion; something that made him want to take care of her very tenderly because he was frail and sad and forlorn, and because she had been through a hell which he understood. He believed he could make things easier for her. It would be intolerable to him to see her sell her possessions and face poverty as well as the loss of the one man she had loved.

'Francesca,' he said, 'it isn't really impossible, my dear. It's quite simple. I'm asking you to marry me.'

'But why? Why should you want to marry me? I'm a wreck, and...'

'Not such a wreck as all that,' he broke in, smiling. 'And I seem to remember you telling me that young Elliott proposed to you the other day.'

'A silly boy's infatuation.'

He would like to have told her that his was no infatuation, but the deep, growing passion of a man who had been through the mill and knew what he was about. But he kept a check upon himself and said:

'I'm very fond of you. My mother loved you, and I would like to do for you what she might have done had she lived.'

'You're sorry for me!' The words flashed out with swift pride.

He shook his head.

'No. I'm not asking you marry me because of that. I've been sorry for plenty of women, but I haven't wanted to live with them for the rest of my life.'

'But why? Honestly ... I don't understand,' she said in a helpless voice. 'I don't really understand why you want this when you aren't in love with me.'

He looked away from her.

'Would you want any man to be in love with you just now?'

'Definitely not. There can never be anybody for me but Fane.'

He wanted to argue against that; to tell her that he had once said those words about Irene. And yet here he was much more in love with her, Francesca, than he had ever been with his wife.

'I quite understand how you feel about Fane,' he said, 'and I'm not asking you to be in love with me. I only want you to marry me and let me take care of you. You can put it the other way as well … I want *you* to look after *me*. I find it damned lonely at times. I don't make friends easily, you know that.'

She drew a deep breath and was silent a moment. Then she said:

'You mean this is just a friendly proposition?'

'Yes. Plenty of people have married for companionship.'

'And has it worked?'

'Yes – in some cases.'

'And supposing it didn't in ours? Supposing, for instance, either of us wanted our freedom?'

'Then we can quit. We can arrange a divorce. But I don't see why it shouldn't work.'

'You take my breath away. I've never thought of marrying … I mean … I have never loved or wanted to marry anybody but Fane, and when he went out of my life, I just felt it was the end of everything.'

'So did I when Irene left me.'

'Why, yes! You, the cynic, Julian! You who've always scoffed at sentiment and said it was the best thing to become hard and not care for anybody! How can *you* want to marry again?'

He lit a cigarette, which he smoked uneasily for a second. He felt that he was being made to eat his own words. But he was not going to betray any of the sentiments he felt about this girl. He realised that one single hint from him that he was passionately in love with her would spoil the whole thing. At length he said:

'You're quite right. I wouldn't want – that sort of marriage. Neither would you. We are good friends. But as our particular laws compel us to tie the matrimonial knot before we're allowed to travel together or be constant companions, marriage is the only solution – if we want to be together. I decided that I want to be with you … now it's for you to make up your mind as to whether you want to be with me or not. Of course you may find me a complete bore. The idea of living under the same roof with me probably fills you with horror.'

He was smiling again – making it very easy for her. She had to smile back.

'I don't find you a bore,' she said.

'Then why not marry me, Francesca? I can give you most things that you want. I'll take you abroad. I want you to get fit again. Instead of having a career as a singer, perhaps it would amuse you a little to take on the job of running my home and that sort of thing.'

'Give me a cigarette,' she said.

He lit one for her. She only took one or two breaths of it, then began to cough, and threw it away.

'Oh, damn my throat,' she said wearily.

'Perhaps,' said Julian, with a long look at her, 'we might find somebody on our travels who could cure you.'

At once her cheeks were burning, and her eyes wide and bright.

'My God! If *that* were possible.'

'You never know.'

'But if I could ever sing again...'

'You'd want to throw up the dull task of looking after me and go back to the stage, eh?'

She did not answer. But he knew from her expression what flashed through her mind. She was thinking that if ever that voice of hers came back she would have another chance with Fane. Yes, she was still hopelessly in love with that cad who had let her down. Wasn't that the way of women – of the world in general?

Then the light seemed to die from her eyes and the colour from her face. She was limp, lifeless again.

'My voice will never come back, and if it did ... and I wanted to go back to the old life ... it wouldn't be fair on you...'

'I'm willing to take the risk.'

'But it's none of it fair on you. I've got nothing to give... I'm all frozen up ... and you're such a dear. You ought to find a wife who'd have everything to give you in return for your generosity.'

192

'Your psychology is all wrong, child. Would you want a husband who would give you everything? Or do you, like myself, just want friendship? Someone to care about, and that rather nice warm feeling that you're with a person who thinks of you and minds whether you live or die.'

Her brows contracted. She put up a hand and smoothed back her hair with an anxious little movement.

'Oh, I don't know. It sounds very attractive… I mean, *of course* it would be wonderful in lots of ways, but marriage…'

'Don't let the word scare you off, my dear. I swear that we'll live together as friends, and I think you can trust me not to break my word.'

She looked up into his eyes. There was no passion in them, only a great kindliness – and pleading. He wanted her because she was lonely and he had grown fond of her. She realized that he depended upon her acceptance of his offer – for his own sake. That touched her. She wouldn't want to accept mere pity from any man.

He began to talk to her, to tell her in his low quiet voice all that they could do together. Later in the year he would like to take her to Spain to see his castle. But now it would be too hot. The country was burnt up and not so beautiful at this time of the year. But Italy would be lovely; Como, for instance. He knew the lakes well. He would find a villa for her near Bellaggio. It was one of the most exquisite spots in Europe. She would have peace and sunshine, the snow-capped mountains, the dreaming, sun-drenched water. She would love Italy. Surely her name suggested that she must love it. And what about that picture over the mantelpiece? That was Como. He was sure of it.

Francesca found herself sitting up, talking with a tinge of excitement.

'Yes, it *is* Como. It's my grandmother's birthplace.'

'You're a quarter Italian and yet haven't seen your lovely Italy! We must put that right at once,' he smiled at her.

'I've heard so much about it from my mother.'

'Wouldn't you like to go?'

'I'd adore it – I've always wanted to see the lakes – but...'

'There need be no "buts," my dear. If you'll just trust yourself with me, I think I could make you happy.'

On a sudden impulse she held out both hands to him, her eyes full of tears.

'You're such a dear, Julian, and you're so terribly good to me! I don't know why.'

He held the small hands tightly. He would like then to have told her that it was because he loved her. He found it astonishingly difficult not to catch her to his heart and cover that wistful young face of hers with kisses. But he just said:

'I'm very fond of you. And if you like me enough to accept me as a constant companion...'

'Must I decide tonight?'

'No. Think it over if you wish...'

She looked away a moment. Instinctively her gaze wandered to the space in which the piano used to stand. A great aching pain seemed to grip her whole mind and heart and body with the memory of Fane. She couldn't love any man but Fane. She could never go through marriage in the true sense of the word with anybody but Fane. But he was irrevocably lost to her, and Julian was offering to make the way easy, as well as trying to gain a little happiness in his own life, through her. Why hesitate? She'd be a fool... Nothing lay in front of her but hard work (if she could find it) – disappointment – the awful feeling of having fallen from the stars. Why not accept Julian's offer and let everything else go to the winds? Her pain bred in her a strange recklessness tonight. And suddenly she turned to Julian and said:

'What's the use of thinking it over? I know my own mind tonight as much as I shall know it in the morning. I don't honestly think it is fair on you, but if you really *want* me to do this thing – I will.'

Julian's face flushed. The hard hammering of his heart warned him then that he would be taking on a singularly hard task if he married this girl and remained a platonic friend to her. But having once made up his mind to achieve an object, it was not in his nature to draw back at the first fence. He gave her hands a hard squeeze and then dropped them and stood up.

'That's grand. I can't tell you how glad I am. And I think if my mother could know, she would be very happy, too. It seems to make things better for me knowing that we didn't just fool her before she died.'

Francesca did not answer. Her tears were falling thickly. She tried to wipe them away, but they went on flowing. Perhaps it was because of Fane, or perhaps because she was so tired, or maybe it was a kind of relief because she knew that she had nothing more to worry about. Julian would give her all that she had ever had, and more, and she wouldn't be lonely. No, that wasn't true. Julian's companionship couldn't stop her from feeling terribly alone. Fane had been her other half, and without him she would be incomplete for the rest of her life.

If only she could love Julian! If only this proposal of his meant something more than just a way out...

'My dear,' she said brokenly, 'are you sure you won't regret it? After all, the thing isn't one-sided. It's from your point of view as well as mine.'

'From my point of view it will be a big success. I can't tell you how much it will mean to me to have your companionship. I dreaded going away alone.'

'Then I suppose I needn't be afraid?'

'No, you needn't be afraid,' he said. He came and stood beside her and stroked her hair gently for a moment. 'Now put away your jewel-case. You're not going to have to sell anything more. Let's talk over what we're going to do. I see no object in waiting, do you? How about a special licence and getting married next week? I'll wire to some friends of mine at Bellaggio, and we'll see if we can get a villa. What you need is a long rest in the sunshine.'

Francesca dried her tears.

'I must polish up my Italian... I used to speak a little.'

'That's grand. And perhaps we might rout out some of the relations in Como?'

'I don't think so. I believe they're all dead.'

'Well, at least you'll feel at home in Italy.'

The feeling of pain and weariness in Francesca slowly gave place to interest and a touch of excitement.

'Yes, and I've always longed to see it.'

'There's no sense in waiting, is there? Shall we get married next week?'

How strange that sounded! Getting

married … to Julian Grey! Then she remembered what a tragedy his first marriage had been and how completely that other girl, Irene, had shattered his illusions. God knows she could be sorry for anybody who was disillusioned in love. She knew what it meant. She felt suddenly a warm and friendly feeling for him.

'I'll marry you whenever you wish. And I'll try and make a good show of it for you.'

'You make a fine show of anything,' he said. 'Now tell me what sort of honeymoon you'd like…' He made haste to add: 'We'll give it that meretricious name. Shall we go by train or take a car – I've just bought a new Bentley – and drive through France and Switzerland, to the lakes?'

'That sounds marvellous!' she said.

He sat down beside her again, and they spent the next hour discussing plans.

Much later Francesca found herself in bed with the table-lamp still burning, her brain working so busily that she could not begin to settle down to sleep. With hands crossed behind her head, she stared round the shadowy room and tried to get it into her head that she had promised to marry Julian Grey.

It was the last position in the world in which she had expected to find herself. Earlier this evening she had faced quite a different prospect, and not such an attractive one. After all, it was more pleasant to consider that she was going to Italy for a long rest. It would be lovely to drive through France and Switzerland in the new Bentley which Julian had just bought. (Why must it have been a Bentley – just to remind her of Fane and that blue and silver car of his in which she had driven so often!) There must always be the ghost of Fane haunting her.

But no. She refused to let it haunt her any more. She was going to try to be happy with Julian. He was the greatest dear on earth. She felt complete confidence in him. He was so understanding, and he never made any demands. He never would – she knew it. And he didn't seem to want anything but friendship himself, so she need feel no compunction. She wondered what Fane would say when he heard she was getting married. He would hear it quickly enough through Peggy or somebody like that.

What did it matter what Fane thought?

Francesca tossed restlessly from side to side. She felt feverish and over-excited. She wondered if she would ever sleep tonight, and oh God, if only she could stop thinking about Fane!

The telephone bell rang.

The noise made her start ... it had been so still, so silent in her room. She raised herself on her elbow and put the instrument to her ear. Before she said the word 'Hello' she knew who it was… It was past twelve o'clock. Only one person in London would ring her up at this hour of the night. Then came that remembered, devastating voice.

'Is that you, Francesca?'

After the first wild leaping of her heart, she went stone cold. It was an icy little voice which answered him.

'Yes, Fane.'

'Can I talk to you for a few minutes, or is it too late? Have I woken you up?'

'No – I was awake.'

'I've had you on my mind all day.'

Her lips curled a little.

'Surely not!'

'Yes – I have. Ever since I talked to Peggy Lawton. God! How I hate that woman!'

'What's Peggy done?'

'Made me feel a swine.'

'That shouldn't trouble you.'

'You're very bitter, aren't you, darling?'

The 'darling' made her wince. It was so slick from Fane.

'What have you rung me up about?' she asked.

'I want to know how you are.'

'Quite well, thank you.'

'You sound terribly formal. I suppose I deserve it.'

'Aren't you spoilt! Fane… Do you expect me to be awfully affectionate?'

'You mean you don't love me any more?'

Something in her leaped again – but she trod it down with a merciless heel.

'Why should I? You don't love me any more.'

'I shall always love you.'

'Fane, dear, you're such a wonderful actor, and you say things so easily! You must forgive me if I don't take you seriously.'

'Perhaps you won't believe me when I tell you that I cared a lot more about you than I shall ever do about Kay.'

'You're a gorgeous cad, my dear!'

'I dare say I am – but that's the truth.'

'I'm sure you were very devoted to me as long as I was "The Girl with the Crooning Voice."'

'Straight from the shoulder, but I deserve it.'

She grew suddenly angry. Why did he want to ring her up and tear her to pieces like this? What was the use of all this humility, this remorse?

'You're going to marry Kay, aren't you?' she said. Her voice was growing hoarse, which always happened when she was overwrought. 'Kay can be everything to you that I can't be, and that's that.'

'I wish to God it hadn't all happened,' he groaned.

'My dear Fane, would you like me to suppose that if my voice miraculously returned, you'd chuck Kay and welcome me back with

201

open arms?'

'I know I'd give a whole lot to have you back.'

'Plus the voice,' she said brutally. Her own pain was making her brutal.

'Well … I've got to have a partner, haven't I? Are you going to tell me that you wouldn't like things to be as they were?'

She shut her eyes. She was breathing quickly. Then she said:

'They never will be. I'm going to be married next week…'

'Good God!' Fane's voice sounded thunder-struck: *'Married!'*

'Yes.'

'It hasn't taken you long…' he began, then changed his mind and said: 'Who's the lucky man?'

'Julian Grey.'

'Grey … Grey…? Who the devil…?'

'The man with the old mother who was in the room next to mine at the nursing-home.'

'Oh, now I know! Good Lord – *that* man! That great sulky-looking bear…!'

Francesca stiffened. There came upon her a sudden desire to defend Julian.

'He isn't a bear, and he doesn't look sulky. He's terribly kind.'

'Oh well, if you like him…'

'I do.'

'Obviously, since you're going to marry

him. When did this happen?'

'This evening.'

'I see. So it's goodbye for ever to our little Francesca. The old crowd will see her no more.'

'Quite so. I'm going abroad.'

'And are you in love with him?'

'You have no right to ask that.'

'You aren't,' he said roughly. 'I bet you aren't... I'll stake my life that he won't be your lover as I was...'

She felt the colour scorch her face and throat, then die away. She had the agonizing feeling that Fane was there, crushing her in his arms, claiming her lips with the old tempestuous passion. He was right – terribly right. Julian could never be her lover as *he* had been. Julian wasn't her lover at all. She felt that she could not bear any more of this conversation. She said:

'Please forgive me if I say … goodbye!'

'Francesca … wait…'

'No. Goodbye,' she replied, and hung up the receiver.

Then she switched off her table-lamp and lay very still in the dark for a long while, without moving.

The telephone bell rang again – and again. Fane wasn't going to let her go easily. Cruel, heartless Fane! Selfish, demanding to the end – wanting her back just because he had lost her. Angry, jealous because he thought

203

she wasn't grieving for him, and remorseful because he had left her alone. He didn't know what he wanted. He was like a spoiled child with a toy which he had broken and discarded and wanted again when he had time to remember it.

The bell went on ringing. It drove her mad. She took the instrument off the stand and laid it on the table. There was a muffled burr-burr – then another burr-burr. It continued for several minutes. Then it ceased...

13

One week later there began for Francesca a new life, a queer and not unexciting phase which for want of a better name might be called a honeymoon.

She was married to Julian in a West End registrar's office one fine June morning, after which they drove in Julian's Bentley to Dover and embarked for the wedding trip which was to take them through France and Switzerland to Lake Como.

Julian had fixed everything to his satisfaction. He was a man of action, and within two days of Francesca's acceptance of him he had been in touch over the wire with his friends at Bellaggio. From them he rented for six weeks one of the loveliest villas on the lake. There he intended that Francesca should have all the sunlight and peace and beauty that she needed, and it would be his happiness to see her growing better and losing all those signs of strain and exhaustion which marked her when they sailed from England on their wedding day.

Francesca could not have said that she felt actually happy as she leaned over the rails beside her husband, watching the white cliffs of Dover recede while the boat ploughed through the blue-grey waters across the Channel.

She was not a woman in love, neither was this tall bronzed man supposed to be in love with her. No, it was no love match – only a friendly arrangement. And that could not mean fulfillment for any woman; could not begin to bring her the ecstasy for which she had hoped and of which she had dreamed; all that might have been hers had she married Fane and carried out their wonderful plans.

She tried to banish the remembrance of Fane, and when Julian took her arm with a brotherly gesture and asked her if she was all right, she answered:

'I'm fine. It's a grand morning.'

'And you're a grand girl.'

Then she laughed at him.

'You've been reading *Farewell to Arms*.'

Julian actually blushed like a schoolboy caught out in some mischief. But he had to admit that he had read Hemingway's immortal love story recently, and that it appealed to him very much.

'I love it too,' said Francesca; 'they must have had great fun together, Cat and her lover.'

They both changed the conversation, because it didn't seem quite the right thing to discuss a passionate love story when they were embarking upon a purely platonic adventure.

Julian had been abroad many times. But to Francesca this travelling was all new and interesting. He was as pleased as any boy to watch her reactions to everything, and to mark her intense appreciation of what she saw that day.

He was a fine driver. With Fane, motoring had meant a good many thrills and hair-breadth escapes. With Julian it was steady going. That was really symbolic of their companionship. All the thrills with Fane … and the calm security with Julian. How ironic it was, Francesca reflected, that life arranged things so that one craved for the thrills!

They got through the Customs and the somewhat boring process of taking the car off the boat, and then began the journey in brilliant sunshine towards Boulogne.

Francesca was amused by everything. The busy, bustling town, the crowded cafés, the Continental atmosphere which was so different from an English environment.

'I'm going to like France,' she said.

'You're going to like Italy much more,' Julian told her.

'Ah!' said Francesca, 'Italy really means something; that's because I'm part Italian, I suppose.'

They covered over a hundred and fifty miles that day. As the Bentley raced smoothly down the long sinuous road toward Abbeville, Julian, who knew the route by heart, was able to point out all the scenes which were of special interest. At times there was nothing to be seen but flat, green pastureland. But they skirted the dark shadow of the forest of Crecy, which Francesca found beautiful, and during the afternoon they broke the journey at Amiens, which carried with it such history of the Great War, that war which had shattered the world, while Julian was still a boy at his public school and Francesca in her nursery.

Winding through the pleasant wooded countryside, it was hard for either of them to believe that this had been the scene of so much fighting, and that so many of the little towns and churches had been destroyed and then rebuilt.

Julian was determined to reach Compiègne and make that the resting-place for the first night of the journey, so he drove for the last few hours in darkness. Francesca was not tired, she assured him. It was rather nice to sit back in the luxurious car, wrapped in her fur coat and a rug and watch the stars come out and the French countryside grow mysterious and beautiful in the shadows. She was quite glad, however, when at last the twinkling lights of Compiègne welcomed them and they came down a winding hill, then curved round the fort into the Rue de Soissons.

They stopped at the Hôtel Joyeuse, a fine modern building which had been erected out of the ruins of a fourteenth-century inn, and provided plenty of matter for Julian's conversation. Expert as he was on archaeology, he was a fine companion on a journey of this sort, and Francesca enjoyed everything that he had to tell her.

He squeezed her hand in a friendly way as he helped her out of the car.

'Not too tired?'

'Not really. I've loved it all.'

But somehow it seemed unreal as she stood beside Julian and watched him enter their names in the book as Mr and Mrs Julian Grey. Such a short while ago she had been Francesca Hale – just Francesca to everybody on the stage – and here she was on the night of her wedding in a French hotel, with a fat little proprietor bowing and effusive, welcoming *'Monsieur et Madame.'* It was almost fantastic.

The Hôtel 'Joyeuse' was a lovely name, anyhow, and whether she felt joyful or not she meant to banish the old griefs this evening for Julian's sake if not for her own. He had been so good to her.

It had been very easy and happy, after all, the feeling between them during the journey today, and on the whole Francesca decided that she had made a wise move in marrying Julian. The longer she was with him, the more he proved himself to be a good companion. He was really not as quiet and studious as he had first appeared. A good deal of that was shyness on his part, which, when it wore off, revealed plenty of humour which Francesca appreciated. She could never have stood being continually in the company of a man who lacked a sense of humour.

He was so attentive, too. He seemed to understand exactly what she needed; when she wished to be amused – when she preferred to be left alone. He was ever tactful; made none of the blunders that an over-enthusiastic boy might have made. There was much in favour of marriage with a man who had already had experience, Francesca told herself. Julian Grey had certainly benefited from some of the lessons taught him by his first wife.

Francesca felt more contented than she had been for long weeks while she dressed for dinner in the ornate, typically French bedroom that night.

She was tired after the long drive, but there was some colour in her cheeks – the result of the Channel-crossing on a smooth sea in the warm sun. She was satisfied with her reflection in the long cheval mirror when she had finished her toilet. The dress was almost bridal in effect – parchment satin, with a short little velvet coat which had long tight-fitting sleeves. It made her skin and her golden hair look extraordinarily fair, and in contrast her eyes were of velvet darkness.

A trifle wistfully she looked at this vision of herself. Peggy Lawton had helped her choose the dress. Dear old Peggy! She had been so glad about this marriage, so thankful that Francesca had decided to take what the gods offered. Better than moping about, Peggy had said. And why not have a decent trousseau, even if she had to spend her last penny on it? Julian was a rich man, and she would not have to worry any more about that. And so Francesca had been led into spending nearly every penny of her savings. It had not taken much to persuade her, because she had no wish to wear any of the old dresses that reminded her so painfully of the past. Dresses, for instance, which Fane had liked, and which she had always worn for him She tried not to think about Fane this evening, but inevitably the thought crept into her mind:

'How thrilled I would be if *he* were here with me!'

But it was Julian who was dressing in that room which was separated from hers by a bathroom. Julian, who was neither lover nor husband, save in the eyes of the world. Dear Julian, who was kind and understanding, but whose presence could not make her heart beat one fraction faster than normal speed.

What a pity it was! But despite the pity, and the desire for Fane which nagged persistently, she was glad that she had married Julian. She intended to try to enjoy her new life.

When Julian came through the bathroom, knocked on the door and was admitted, he was a little unprepared for the loveliness which awaited him. Francesca was a poet's or painter's dream in that parchment-satin frock which outlined the slender figure and flared in rich, graceful folds from the narrow hips. He looked at her in silence a moment. This lovely creature was his wife, and this was their wedding night, and he was to behave casually, like a friend! God! He had taken a load upon his shoulders which he might not be able to carry very successfully. But of course he *must;* he couldn't break down, whatever happened. It was up to him to keep his part of the contract. After all, he was not supposed to be in love with Francesca and the sooner he remembered that fact, the better.

'You look very charming,' he said.

The compliment sounded to Francesca polite and friendly – and nothing more. She smiled back at him. She was not embarrassed. After all, there was nothing to feel shy about. They were really like two friends travelling together. A light-hearted mood fell upon her. It wasn't going to be fair on Julian if she moped around and sighed for Fane, so she would be as nice to him as he deserved.

'You're looking very smart yourself,' she said.

And she meant that, because Julian was the type that wore a well-cut dinner-jacket to advantage. The stiff whiteness of collar and shirt made his skin look very brown, and of course those eyes of his were ridiculously blue and recalled always his mother's.

'That reminds me,' said Julian hastily; 'I've got something for you – wait...'

He vanished through the bathroom. Francesca sighed. He really ought not to give her anything more. He had been much too generous already. And she glanced with feminine appreciation at the beautiful summer ermine coat lying on the bed. It had been his chief wedding present to her. But there had been so many others; all his mother's beautiful jewels and her lovely new travelling-case of Moroccan leather with its nice green cover and gold fittings.

Julian returned with a small box and a spray of pink roses.

'I thought you'd like to wear these,' he said, and pushed them awkwardly into her hand.

The box contained a narrow diamond and sapphire bar. Francesca looked at it almost in dismay. She was not crazy, like some women, about jewellery, and although this was an exquisite thing, she was just as pleased with the roses.

'Oh, Julian, how nice of you, but you really mustn't go on doing this! I've got far too many things already!'

'Don't you like it?'

'It's lovely – but you're just throwing money away.'

'No, I'm spending it on my wife – which I like to do.'

'You're very generous, my dear.'

He smiled down at her, fingering his tie.

'It gives me a lot of pleasure.'

'I wouldn't like to begrudge you that.'

The softness of her eyes went to his head a little. He turned away and began to pace her room restlessly.

'Let's go down and feed,' he said.

She pinned the roses on her shoulder with the new diamond brooch.

'I look the complete bride!' she said.

'I'd better find a white carnation for myself,' he said.

She took his arm in a friendly way as they walked downstairs together. There came into Julian's mind the memory of his wedding night with Irene. They had spent that night in London, and he had given her flowers and a jewel. It was instinctive in him to do these things. Irene had been in love with him then, ready for and responsive to his embraces. But she had gone wild with delight about the jewel and forgotten to wear her flowers. Women were different. Every marriage was different, and this fair, lovely creature who had taken Irene's place wanted no caresses, and had none to give. She was 'frozen up,' she had said, but for that fellow Braber she would have been fire rather than ice. Julian loathed the thought of Fane Braber.

During dinner, cooked by a famous French chef, and chosen especially for Francesca, there was one unfortunate incident. The sort of thing that was bound to happen and which cast a blight over what was otherwise a very pleasant evening.

The Hôtel Joyeuse was a popular place in the summer months.

There was an American band in the oak-panelled dining-room. The conductor chose as one of his numbers a song which 'Fane and Francesca' had made famous a year go. It was called 'Broken Hearted.' The moment the first bars were played, Francesca, who had been talking to Julian about an Alsatian dog which she used to have when she lived with her mother, sat up straight and listened, every nerve in her body quivering.

One of the saxophonists was singing through a microphone:

'Broken-hearted...
Me and my man have just parted,
He didn't care,
It wasn't fair,
And so we had to say goodbye.'

Francesca shut her eyes tightly. But that couldn't banish the vision of herself with the rakish white topper on her head and her black-and-white dress, sitting on Fane's piano crooning:

'He made me crazy about him...
Made me so I couldn't do without him,
Called me all his own,
Then left me here alone,
So now there's nothing but – goodbye!'

Silly, tawdry words, trivial enough, and yet they got home, dug deep down, hurt just where they could hurt most. The song had always met with a roar of applause when Francesca had sung it. She hadn't understood, then, what agony could lie behind every word of it. Now it tore her to pieces.

'Made me crazy about him…
Made me so I couldn't do without him.'

Those two lines drummed through her mind. She opened her eyes and looked straight at Julian. He was horrified at the anguish which he saw written in them. He half rose, and leaned towards her.

'Child, what's wrong? Are you all right?'

Then the music ceased, and during the applause Francesca recovered herself. She gulped down a glass of wine.

'Yes – I'm all right. Good tune that, isn't it?'

'Was it? I wasn't listening very intently.'

'I used to sing it,' she said through her teeth. 'The music was written by a girl called Daphne French – a friend of Fane's. She's written a lot of stuff which is pretty good. I expect Kay will be singing some of it.'

Then Julian understood. He sat down and was silent. He wanted to say so much, but there was nothing to be said that could help her. Poor little thing … it was just her luck … and his … that this should have hap-

216

pened tonight. They might have chosen any other song but one *she* used to sing.

Francesca twirled the stem of her wineglass between slender fingers that shook slightly. Then she gave him a wry smile.

'I'm a damn fool, Julian.'

'Far from it. Entirely natural.'

'You do understand? You're wonderful.'

'You'd just like to get up on this table and show that idiot in the orchestra how to sing the song, wouldn't you?'

'Yes,' she said, and sat brooding, brows drawn together. Then suddenly she said:

'Would it affect you, Julian, if you saw or heard something that reminded you absolutely of Irene?'

'Not a bit. I'm afraid I've grown hard as a rock about her. She doesn't matter any more. If she walked through the room now, I'd only look at her with faint curiosity.'

'How marvellous it must be to get to that pitch.'

'You'll get to it yourself,' he said, and added, 'I hope.'

And he wondered what she would have said if he had told her, then, that not only had he forgotten how much he had once cared for Irene and how badly she had hurt him, but that today he was wholly and entirely in love with another woman? And that woman – his newly-made wife. Madly, badly in love, and jealous as hell of that fellow

Fane, and of the fact that the song could bring such a look into Francesca's eyes.

He made her go to bed early.

'You look tired, and we've got another hundred and fifty miles to do tomorrow,' he said.

'What a nice, thoughtful man you are!' she said. 'No wonder that sweet mother of yours was so fond of her son.'

Praise from Francesca always pleased him greatly, but he was afraid of it – of too much sweetness from her. He left her outside the door of her room. Like a brother, he dropped a quick kiss on her forehead and said:

'Good night. Sleep well.'

'Good night,' she said, 'and thank you a thousand times for everything.'

Then she was in her room, and a plump, smiling *femme de chambre* helped her to undress, turned on her bath, and fussed about the room chattering like a magpie.

Francesca took her bath, then, conscious of real fatigue, sent the woman out and was glad to be alone. She lay on top of her bed for a moment, relaxed and physically content after lying in the hot water which had been scented with bath crystals, the kind she always used to use, and had given up since her disaster. It was pleasant to be able to indulge in these little luxuries again. She loved that perfume – *'Vol-de-nuit.'* It was Guerlain's, and one of her favourites. She was altogether luxurious tonight. The delicate apricot-tinted nightgown and the chiffon velvet wrapper with its ostrich feathers were a fitting choice for any bride.

But it was all such a farce. There was no Fane to come in and take her in his arms and tell her that she was lovely and meant for love. She was just a dead thing for whom there would be no more loving.

Then she thought of Julian. How was he feeling? He had been married before. Behind his reserve, his hardness, he was a passionate and affectionate man. This must be rather hard on him. He was not in love with her, but he found her beautiful and attractive; he had told her so many times. Perhaps he would have liked this marriage to be a real thing. The physical side meant more to men than to women, even when they were not in love. Francesca was not an ignorant prude, and she had talked about these things with Fane. She began to wonder for the first time if Julian was making a sacrifice just because he imagined that she wished to be left alone.

The idea worried her increasingly as the moments went by. She was a generous person, sensitive to the feelings of others. Being still in love with Fane, it was altogether distasteful to her to even consider physical union with another man. On the other hand, she despised women who took everything and gave nothing in return. They had made a bargain, and she was quite sure that Julian would stand by it. But the more she thought about it, the more the thing troubled her from his point of view.

It must have meant hell for that man to have his wife leave him in the way that Irene had done, and all these ensuing months he had been lonely and hurt. God! Didn't she know how hurt one could be! Wasn't it a little selfish of her to expect him to keep an unnatural bargain of this kind?

She could not reconcile herself to the idea and settle down to sleep until she had discussed it with him. That was her way. It might be difficult to be frank, and it was going against all her inclinations to alter the conditions on which they had married, but what did it matter? Nothing mattered very much any more. Julian was doing everything in his power to build happiness for her, and she felt she owed it to his dead mother, and to him, to do likewise for Julian.

She slid bare feet into apricot-coloured mules, and without further hesitation walked through the bathroom and knocked on the door of Julian's room.

Julian was not yet undressed. Still in his dinner-jacket, he was standing at the open French windows, looking out at the spires of the church of St Jacques, which rose darkly against the opalescence of the sky. The night was so beautiful that it made him reluctant to move away from the scene on which he gazed. He was thinking about Francesca; wondering if any man had set himself a harder task than his. It was so difficult not to walk through those communicating doors and tell her that he loved her. What a terrible thing this unrequited love could be! Perhaps she was suffering like this, for Fane, poor unhappy child! Why must there be so much sorrow and pain in such a beautiful and romantic world?

He turned from the window, to look for his cigarette case. He was smoking too much, he knew it – but his nerves were on edge, and smoking helped. He was beginning to wonder whether Fate singled him out especially for this kind of torment. It wasn't really so long ago that he had loved and married Irene, only to see her slipping away from him farther every day, and realize that she had never really loved him at all.

Well, Irene had let him down badly. But he couldn't blame anybody but himself for his suffering now. He had deliberately chosen to marry a girl with whom he was in love, knowing that he might never hold her in his arms. And the whole thing was worth while if he could make her a little happier.

He was completely astonished when the door opened and Francesca appeared on the threshold. He gave one look at the fair charming head and the slender figure which looked almost too fragile in the silken wrapper, then took it for granted that she must be feeling ill. He hurried towards her.

'My dear! Are you all right? Is it your throat?'

She shook her head. Her heart was beating rather fast. Now that she was here and fully conscious of her mission she was completely embarrassed.

'No, my throat's all right. Nothing's really wrong, but...'

'But what?'

He lit his cigarette. He needed it. His heart was hammering so at the sight of her. Francesca in her apricot-coloured wrapper was such a very lovely sight – she would appeal to any man, even if he were not in love with her.

'Are you after one of these?' he asked, and handed her his cigarette case.

She shook her head. For a moment she played with the delicate fronds of ostrich feather about her wrists. Then, with eyelids fluttering nervously, she said:

'Julian, I'm not sure that this business is fair.'

'What business?'

'Our marriage.'

'Not fair to whom – to you?'

'No, to you.'

'But why not?'

She made a gesture with her hand and looked away from him.

'I may be silly, but I've been worrying...'

'But why?' he asked, mystified. 'Why shouldn't it be fair to me? I thought we had had all that out long ago. You've made me tremendously happy by marrying me today.'

Now she turned her gaze to him earnestly. 'Are you sure I have?'

He put down his cigarette and took one of her hands in a warm, reassuring grasp.

'Why, my dear, there's no earthly need for you to think that I'm not satisfied. I am. The shoe's on the other foot. *I've* been worrying about *you* – afraid that you're not happy, that you might get fed up with me.'

'No, you've been so frightfully good to me.'

'You must try to understand how much it means to me to have you to look after and do things for. It isn't much fun living alone, and after Irene went I became morose and self-centred – a regular recluse. That isn't good for any man. You can't imagine how much happier and better I'm feeling now that I've got you.'

'Yes, but – you see, Irene *was* a wife to you, and I...'

'Well – you're the most charming companion that a man could wish for.'

Then, with cheeks burning, she blurted out what lay in her mind.

'I'm not flattering myself that you regard me as – as you did your first wife… I know you were in love with her … but I do try to see things from every point of view … and I know human nature … and I haven't much respect for women who take everything and give nothing. In other words, if you feel that I … if you…'

And then she stammered and broke off, completely at a loss for further words.

Only then did Julian realize her meaning. His heart gave a great jerk and then went on pounding. The lines of his face seemed to grow harder, even his eyes. Now he understood why she had come into his room. She was offering everything. Not because she loved him, but because that was her nature. She was generous – generous to the core. He was completely overcome and unable to answer her for a minute or two. Then he said, under his breath:

'You dear! What an absolute dear you are, Francesca.'

Red to the roots of her hair, she caught his gaze, then gave a self-conscious little laugh.

'I just had to come and say it – it was worrying me.'

'I wonder how many women would have done the same.'

'Oh, I don't know…'

'But I do.'

And he was remembering Irene now. Irene

who had been ready to melt into his arms during their honeymoon, because she had been infatuated with him then, and later had made every excuse to bar him from her room because she had been bored, and the rich American in New York was making her a better offer.

He wondered now, when he looked at Francesca tonight, how he had ever been so blind as to think that other selfish, treacherous woman worth loving. She was trying to make it easy for him, ready to make some return for what he was giving her. But although she knew it not, she was making the thing a hundred times more difficult for him. He wanted, badly, to trade on her generosity and take her in his arms there and then. The mere thought of her surrender was ecstasy in itself. But he was not going to do it. He was not going to accept any such sacrifice. She was still in love with Fane. And a woman in love with one man must inevitably suffer purgatory in the arms of somebody else.

Unconsciously he quoted Hemingway again.

'You're a fine girl, a grand girl, Francesca.'

'I'm not really.'

'Well, I think you are, and I shall never be able to tell you how much I admire and thank you for coming to me like this. I'm quite shattered by it, my dear. But I'm not going to ask for anything but your friendship. There isn't a man alive who wouldn't want to snatch at so much sweetness, but I want you to believe that you need not worry about me. I'm just perfectly happy as things stand – so long as *you're* happy.'

The look of relief which crossed her face, unconsciously, did much to console Julian for all that he was denying himself. He knew perfectly well that she must have come in here in fear and trembling lest he should accept her offer. And then he would have lost her friendship, and her confidence. He didn't want that. Above all things, he wanted to promote the feeling of ease and peace which she had had today. He would sooner have denied himself anything than shatter that very peace which he wished to bring to her. She had been through hell enough.

'Well, if you really feel satisfied with our friendship,' she said, 'I shan't worry.'

'Then that's fine. We understand each other,' he said.

He was smiling. And she was no longer embarrassed or afraid. She just looked at him and took it for granted that Julian felt as she did. Sex had no real appeal, since without complete love on both sides it could mean nothing. She felt almost happy. And she wanted him to be so. Impulsively she held out both hands to him.

'We ought to make a good job of this,

oughtn't we?'

'We will,' he said.

For a moment he put his arms around her and held her close, but only for a moment. He could not trust himself longer. She must never know that with every word he was saying he was locking himself out of a heaven which he most ardently desired. His lips touched her hair.

'Bless you,' he murmured.

She put up a hand and patted his cheek.

'Dear, kind Julian.'

Then she went quickly from the room and shut the door behind her.

For a moment he stared at that shut door, and the muscles of his face were working.

'I suppose I'm a damned fool,' he thought. 'I know I said what she wanted me to say – but – oh, damn and blast that fellow Fane!'

14

There were two very outstanding thoughts in Francesca's mind that next morning while she took her *café et croisson* sitting up in bed with Julian in a dressing-gown at a table beside her.

One was that she was glad that she and Julian could have this nice pleasant companionship without having to feel at all embarrassed by such an intimate meal. And the other – a not unnatural and purely feminine reaction to the incident of last night – a faint surprise that Julian was not interested in her as a woman. Not that she really wished him to be while she still suffered from the pangs of a hopeless passion for Fane; and neither was she really piqued – for she was not as vain as most women – but she was normal enough to be conscious of her attractions for men.

She knew that a good many of her past admirers could not have accepted her quite as calmly and prosaically as this. Julian's apparent indifference to her charms gave her food for thought, and also made her wonder how she would have felt had he acted quite differently and taken all that she had offered.

I should have hated it, she told herself.

But looking at Julian, a nice enough sight in his blue silk dressing-gown which just showed a column of strong brown throat, and with the sun slanting through the French windows making his eyes a brilliant blue, she could not add that she would also have hated *him*. It would be very hard to hate this Julian whom she had thought in the beginning a hard, cynical, sulky creature, and who had proved himself quite the reverse.

He looked after her as though she were a baby; buttered her roll, poured out her coffee, fussed over her until she laughingly protested.

'You're as bad as Mary ... she waited on me hand and foot. Really, Julian, you must let me do something for myself!'

'Well, you can turn on your own bath,' he laughed.

'I expect the *femme de chambre* will do that! Isn't it a lovely day?'

'Grand! We ought to reach Neufchâteau tonight. Do you feel you can stand another hundred and fifty miles?'

'Easily. It's great fun.'

She gave a little sigh, stretched her arms above her head, and lay back on her pillow.

Julian turned from the disturbing vision of her, and went rather hastily to his room to dress. She was such a bewitching person. Too bewitching for his peace of mind. However, he was enchanted with his position as her protector and companion, even while he wanted so desperately to be her lover.

The second day of their marriage was for Francesca as interesting and successful as the first. Even more so because she was more certain of Julian. The old life in London, the stage, even Fane, seemed a long, long way away now. The old pain nagged on, but there were new sights to see, and fresh adventure is an amazing anodyne for sorrow.

The weather held good, and it was wonderful driving through the forest of Compiègne to Soissons and through the lovely green valley of the River Vesle to Reims, where they stopped for lunch.

Here, Julian declared, she would have to use all her force to drag him away, because there was so much here to be seen that he enjoyed – so much that he wanted to show her. And they had only time to pay a flying visit to the famous cathedral, the most royal, most noble in France, which had been so shattered in the War. They had many more miles to do, so they must pass on, and leave sight-seeing to another time.

They took the old Roman road to Nettancourt, and paused once more for a rest and some tea at Ligney-en-Barrois. From there they followed the beautiful Ornain valley to Gondrecourt, and finished the day's journey at Neufchâteau.

That night they retired early, and there were no misgivings or anxieties on either side. They were both healthy, pleasantly tired, and glad to say good night and go to sleep.

The third day took them through the wooded countryside on the outskirts of the Vosges, where they were soon to come within sight of the Jura Mountains. Here, Francesca became really thrilled. Switzerland was in sight, and tomorrow they would reach the Italy of her forefathers. It was wonderful scenery all the way after they passed through the French-Swiss customs, left the magnificent forest of Hard, and began the sinuous ascent through the valley of the Ergolz.

Somehow, for Francesca, Switzerland had always conjured up visions of snow, winter sports, skiing and icy peaks. Certainly there remained the perpetual snows rising into infinity above her, but this was Switzerland in June; a country of rich green pastures, lovely little toy villages nestling at the foot of the mountains, and all the brilliant colour of wild flowers which made Francesca gasp with pleasure.

'One could never live long enough to stay long enough in all the places one wanted to see,' she told Julian. 'I'm getting quite dazed with everything.'

Her pleasure brought him great satisfaction. What with all the driving, and the hours he spent explaining everything and answering her innumerable questions, he had no time to brood over the missing link between himself and this young wife of his. Neither had he any opportunity to relax into the old feeling of melancholia and gloom. He was alive again, and this was a much more absorbing union than the one he had had with Irene. That had been so purely physical. He realized now that he and Irene had had nothing in common. She had never been a good traveller. The purely aesthetic appreciation of scenery bored her. She wanted to go to fashionable resorts and be amused in crowds.

But Francesca was speechless with emotion at the sight of a mountain-side starred with flowers, or a crystal torrent gushing over the rocks, or the dark splendour of a forest cutting against the clarity of the summer sky. And these were the things that he, too, loved, and needed for his soul's good. That journey sealed one bond between them which nothing could destroy – a mutual love of nature and the glories of earth and sky and sea.

They spent that night at Lucerne in an hotel overlooking the lovely blue waters of the lake.

There, once again, these two were brought face to face with their own peculiar torment. For Julian it was almost unbearable to look out of his window at the shining lake, steeped in moonlight, glittering like onyx, feel the pure sweet air blow against his face, and know that Francesca was divided from him only by a wall. More than anything in the world he wanted to have her here with him in his arms, and fulfil the glory of such a night. But feelings such as these had to be fought down, and he mastered them.

And Francesca looked long and earnestly into the beauty of the night and remembered

Fane and the wild longing for him which was not yet annihilated. Such moments as those must spoil all the pleasure of the day.

So the strange honeymoon continued. Yet another hard day's driving. Climbing up the steep winding road into Goschenen and through the St Gotthard Pass, which left Francesca dumb, almost pale with emotion. Here were dizzying heights and gorgeous views indeed, an ascent almost into the clouds. Over peaks on which they might feel gods, or, alternatively, mere pigmies – less than nothing in so vast a world.

They came to Lugano during the afternoon, and by sunset passed over the Italian frontier at Chiasso. As they drove down the Via Borgo Vico, Francesca clutched Julian's arm. He looked at her and saw that her eyes were shining and that she was as excited as a child.

'Well,' he said, 'here's your Italy. This is where Francesca comes into her own.'

'Marvellous!' she exclaimed.

When they reached Como her excitement was intense, and she had almost forgotten past tragedies. After the massive Alpine heights of Switzerland, this was all softer, more picturesque, and to Francesca her grandmother's birthplace had a peculiar emotional significance. She was enraptured by it.

The lake was pure jade green, clear as a

mirror under the vivid blue of the sky. The mountains were dotted with olive trees, and the slightest breath of wind made the leaves ripple to silver. The shore was a riot of insolent pink from the great clumps of azaleas fringing the lake for miles.

With shining eyes Francesca surveyed the white villas, the vineyards, the green palms, oranges and lemons, and those loveliest of trees, the cypresses. Slender, pointed, like sentinels, all the way along the lake they stood – dark and graceful against the aching blue of the sky.

She was never to forget that drive along the winding, curving white road which led them from Como to Cadenabbia. There they were met by a manservant in the service of the Donettis, Julian's friends, charming Italians who had sent their own motor-boat to take the bridal pair and their luggage across the shining lake to the Villa Barabella.

The sun was setting when they reached the villa. All her life Francesca remembered the exquisite vision which broke upon her sight as the motor-boat rounded the island on which the villa had been built for an Italian duc in the days of the Renaissance.

It was like a small palace, peach-tinted walls and jade-green shutters, white terraces, and a garden full of glorious flowers.

Julian gave Francesca a hand and helped her out on to the little landing-stage from which they climbed grey stone steps up to the carved balustrade where one tall cypress kept a proud, solitary guard.

The sun was setting, and the lake had become almost a violet colour. The air was warm and perfumed, and in the sky the first bright evening star already glittered.

'Well,' said Julian, 'do you like your Italy?'

She did not answer. Looking at her he saw that tears were raining down her cheeks. He took her arm and pressed it close to his side.

'My dear, are you unhappy?'

Then she whispered:

'No, but it's all so beautiful ... it's *my* Italy ... the lake just as my mother has described it to me ... and this place, this villa, is like a dream.'

'I'm glad you like my Barabella,' he said, 'I helped Signor Donetti restore it after he bought it a few years ago when it was going to ruin through neglect.'

'No wonder you love every stone of it,' she said.

A dark-eyed, pretty Italian maid, wearing a pink dress and white apron, and a grey-haired manservant with a face like a brown wrinkled nut welcomed them into the villa, where the lamps were already shining and a log fire had been lit in the big salon which had six windows overlooking the lake.

'These are two of Donetti's retainers, Maria and Guido, and old friends of mine,'

Julian told Francesca.

Francesca, with her usual charm of manner, greeted the servants, who responded effusively and wished the signora great happiness. Maria took her coat and hat, and Francesca stood a moment before the fire looking round the room while Julian attended to the luggage.

A beautiful room, full of lovely old furniture of the Renaissance period, soft rich brocaded curtains – rare tapestries – dark polished wood – and a ceiling that might have been painted by Michael Angelo.

Through the open windows she could see the waters of the lake, smooth and glistening. The velvet darkness was descending rapidly now. The sky was studded with stars. All along the shore there were twinkling lights from the little village. There was no sound save the rhythmic melody of bells on the water, bells attached to the fishermen's nets, drifting with the tide.

Francesca became suddenly conscious not only of the perfect beauty of the place, but of her own immense fatigue. The tears were trickling down her cheeks again as she sat back in a deep cushioned chair and shut her eyes. This was reaction, of course, after the excitement and strain of the long drive. They had done nearly seven hundred miles since they left France.

Then she opened her eyes and saw a grand

piano at the far end of the room. She had not noticed it when she first came in, but it stood out now from the other things in the salon.

She stared, growing suddenly cold and nervous. Fane sat there, playing those ivory keys. Fane with his fair, handsome head turned in her direction, smiling at her, beckoning to her to come and sing with him.

She put a hand to her throat, and a convulsive shudder went through her body.

'Fane,' she whispered under her breath.

Julian came in and found her lying in a half-fainting condition, too spent, too exhausted even to explain what had suddenly broken her down. He only knew that he loved her with all his soul as he saw her huddled there, her pale golden head so lovely against the high-backed Italian chair. He picked her up in his arms and carried her through the villa to her bedroom. He laid her down on the big gilt bed from which she could see the lake and all the soft beauty of the night.

'You're tired out, darling,' he said. Unconsciously he used that word which for so long he had reserved for his mother alone. 'Let Maria help you into bed. And now that you're here, you must stay in bed for a few days and get quite strong before you start doing anything else.'

She opened her eyes and looked at him

through the hot tears. Her thoughts were of him now, rather than herself.

'You've been so good to me,' she whispered. 'Don't think me ungrateful.'

'I don't, my dear, I couldn't do that. I know how much you've appreciated the trip.'

'You'll never know how much I love this Como. I shall be happy here. Wait and see.'

He took her hand and held it between his warm, strong fingers.

'That's all I ask – that you should be happy.'

'But why … what have I done to deserve all this…?'

She paused. Her throat hurt, ached so that she could scarcely get out the words.

And suddenly Julian lifted the little hand which he held in his, pressed it wordlessly to his lips, and walked from the room.

She knew intuitively, then, that he loved her. The knowledge came across her like a flash. It was not only friendship which made him do so much, give so much. *He loved her.* And it was real love that asked for nothing in return. Not the sort of love that tore a woman's heart out of her body only to break it and throw it back again.

Francesca lay very still, listening to the tinkling of the bells on the nets in the lake. The discovery of Julian's love did not frighten her, did not worry her. It filled her with an immense admiration for him when she remembered the incident in the Hôtel Joyeuse on their wedding night. It also filled her with an added sadness. If he loved her, then he would inevitably be hurt by her. Love can be so easily hurt when it is not returned.

'Maybe I am wrong,' she told herself. 'Maybe he just kissed my hand like that because he was sorry for me.'

But she knew in her heart of hearts that it was not so. She brooded over the thing until she was too tired to think any more.

When Julian came back to look at her she was asleep.

He tiptoed to the bed and stood a moment looking at her. When she was awake he was afraid to look too long, too deeply, into those eyes which held all the beauty which he had ever wanted to find. But now, when the long lashes were spread darkly against the pallor of her cheeks, he was able to look long and earnestly. He was unafraid of the passion which he knew must lie in his own eyes and betray him. He was able, in silence, to pour out his heart upon her and tell her how much he worshipped and wanted.

Yet the very sadness of her face in repose, the faint lines of suffering about the red flower of her mouth, warned him that his love was futile and hopeless. She suffered for that other man. She was still in love with Fane Braber. If she could lift those lashes this moment and see Fane standing beside her with outstretched arms, she would, perhaps, draw back in an instant's pride. But only an instant. Then she would reach up her arms to him. Julian could visualize their rapturous embrace and the wild relief in her heart.

God, what agony it was to love and to want in this way and know no release from the long pain!

He loved her so much that he knew while he stood there, watching her in the dim light of her beautiful Italian room, that he would go to any sacrifice to give her her heart's desire. Yes, he would even give her Fane if he could. He loved her as much as that.

He bent, touched her hair with his lips, then left her, went downstairs and walked out on to the terrace from which he could watch the moonlight spill its unearthly beauty into the lake.

He had known that this honeymoon would mean a battle with himself, but it was a harder fight than he had realized that it would be. And be began to wonder if, after all, he could bring any happiness to Francesca; or whether this marriage was a mistake which could only bring fresh misery to them both.

15

With morning some of the shadows seemed to lift in the hearts of these two who had come to the Villa Barabella.

A golden morning of sunlight. A sky blue as a gentian, and the lake bluer still, with the sheen of a mirror. The garden with its green cypress trees, its roses and azaleas, was like a little paradise, a small gem set in the vast jewel of the lake.

It was so lovely and joyous that Francesca, ever sensitive, responded to it and felt almost light-hearted when she came down from a long night's rest to join her husband, who had planned to take her out on the lake.

The Donettis were in Rome and had left their motorboat at Julian's disposal.

'You must see all the funny little villages along the lake,' Julian told Francesca, and then gave her a quick, searching glance which she met with a faint smile.

'Yes. I'm quite all right. Don't worry. I was only overtired last night.'

'And the throat?'

She made a moue.

'Not too bad.'

'It hurts still?'

'M'm. Not badly.'

Julian shook his head.

'We've got to have that put right. I'm going to write to a fellow who was at the Varsity with me. He's a doctor now and has done very well. He'll tell me what he thinks about this business, and if there is anybody who can cure you, he'll know.'

Francesca turned from Julian's grave scrutiny and looked through the window at the shining water.

'It's incurable, Julian. They've all said so.'

'"They" have been known to make mistakes before now.'

'Let's go out,' she said, as though the very conversation hurt her.

He followed her out of the villa, and the next moment they were in the white motor-boat, speeding through the blue waters in the sunlight away from the point of Barabella, past Cadenabbia and Bellaggio to the end of the lake.

Francesca, wearing a thin white silk dress and a white beret, leaned lazily against a red cushion, felt the warm sun beat upon her, and looked at the dark shadow of the mountains with enraptured eyes.

'It's all very beautiful,' she said.

Julian, sitting opposite her, nodded. He would like to have added that she, too, was very beautiful. But those were the things which must not be said because they were too intimate, too dangerous.

His manner was so friendly and ordinary that morning while he piloted her round the lake that she began to wonder if she had made a mistake last night. Perhaps he was not in love with her. It was just her imagination. He was only a friend – a rather marvellous friend. She talked to him and laughed with him and was happy. It was easy to be happy so long as she wasn't thinking; so long as the thought of Fane did not set a cloud over everything and make her feel that nothing, even this lovely Italy, meant anything at all since *he* was not here.

In one of the little villages at which they stopped for a rest and drink, Julian bought her a shawl.

'You mustn't be in Italy for twenty-four hours without a shawl,' he told her. 'And I know an old woman here who keeps beautiful ones – the genuine thing.'

The tiny shop, in a narrow cobbled street full of incredibly lovely archways and old buildings with shutters of turquoise blue and jade, was full of treasures. The owner, an aged woman with a brown peasant face and the beautiful dark eyes of her race, greeted Julian effusively.

'*Buon giorno, signor,*' she said in her high, thin voice, and burst into a torrent of Italian which Francesca could not attempt to follow but which Julian appeared to understand.

He translated some of it for her.

'Teresa is an old friend of mine and has sold me many things. She is full of excitement because I have told her you are my wife.'

Francesca immediately shook hands with the old woman, who broke into another torrent.

'What an old darling,' said Francesca. 'What does she say?'

Julian's grave face coloured like a boy's and he hesitated.

'Tell me,' said Francesca.

'Oh, a lot of flowery stuff,' he said. 'She says, quite rightly, that I have a very beautiful wife and she hopes we shall have great happiness – and many sons...' he ended with a self-conscious laugh.

Francesca flushed, too. But she did not laugh. Because she thought, suddenly:

'Of course he ought to have sons, this man. He's a fine person. And I believe in his heart he would like a real sort of home and wife and children. Why did he marry me?'

But Julian was not indulging in any emotional analysis. He was looking at the shawls which Teresa fetched for him. And so Francesca joined in the general excitement. She tried on one after another of the lovely, shimmering things which were spread for her inspection. Finally she chose one of fine black silk with a lovely long fringe and many coloured flowers embroidered upon it. It was not so heavy nor so luxurious as the bigger ones, Julian told her, which generally came from China or Spain. The little black one was of real Italian workmanship. He bought her that, and other things; a green, gilt-stamped blotter made of soft leather; an old gold ring which Teresa assured them had been worn by a lady of the court in the days of the Borgias.

Francesca had to stop Julian from buying.

'You're so much too generous,' she protested.

'I love to do it,' he said.

'I would like to give *you* something,' she said.

He answered:

'You've given me so much already.'

'Nothing,' she said in a helpless tone.

They went back to the motor-boat and continued their tour of the lake.

They returned to the villa for lunch, after which, Julian declared, they must both take the *siesta* of the country. It was too hot from noon onwards to do anything until four o'clock.

So Francesca read and dozed through the brooding, golden hours until she roused herself, bathed, put on a fresh white dress and went downstairs to the salon. Such inertia was delicious, but somehow she felt that it was wrong. She had led such a strenuous life during her career on the stage. Always flying from one rehearsal to another; to this party and that; and then the show last thing at night. Since her illness she had been devitalized, and now she could not quite accustom herself to the feeling that it was all right for her to do nothing. That is the way with people who have earned their own living for any length of time.

Julian was still in his own room, resting. The long, cool salon was deserted. Francesca walked about, looking at the tapestries, the many beautiful pieces of china, and the pictures which Signor Donetti collected and which, Julian had told her, were valuable.

This villa had a charm of its own. Francesca recognized it. The whole place charmed her. The Italian strain in her was responding to everything. And it all would have been so perfect if... That '*if*' seemed disloyal to Julian, and yet she could not stop it from leaping into her mind. *If* Fane had been here, too.

She remembered what Julian had said this morning about his doctor friend. Supposing he found somebody who *could* cure her throat? Supposing she could ever sing again? Supposing she became the old Francesca whom Fane had loved? He might want her back. Somehow she knew that he would and that Kay wouldn't mean anything more if *she* could sing again.

Francesca trembled from head to foot and put her face in her hands.

It was wrong to let such thoughts enter her mind. Wrong and humiliating. Hadn't Fane hurt her enough? How could she be so lacking in pride as to want this man who had left her when she was no longer any use to him?

'Idiot!' she said to herself passionately. 'Fool! Why even think about it? You couldn't sing if you tried. You'll never sing again.'

As if to prove this fact to herself she went to the piano and opened it. Cheeks hot, eyes glittering, she sat down and ran her hands over the keys. Instinctively she played that haunting refrain from *Gay Divorce* which she and Fane had sung together. Years ago, it seemed. But they had both adored it, and she could never like anything as much.

'Night and day, you are the one,
Only you beneath the moon and under the sun…
Night and day under the hide of me
There's oh! such a hungry yearning burning inside of me.
And this torment won't be through
Till you let me spend my life making love to you
Day and night, night and day…'

Where was her voice?

What was that ugly croaking ... that hoarse, discordant, cracking sound which was the travesty of a voice?

She felt a kind of horror descend upon her.

The keys jangled as she put her arms upon them, bowed her head and burst into tears.

"'And this torment won't be through...'" she sobbed the words aloud. *"Won't be through till..."* oh, Fane, *Fane!'*

Julian came into the salon. Julian, white under his tan, lips tense and eyes full of his own pain and pity for her. He had heard everything. Her heartbreak was his. Even if she could bear it, he felt that he could scarcely bear it for her. For he knew every inch of the path that leads from lost love into such a dark valley; knew that tortuous descent into despair, thence to indifference, to that state of mind in which there can be no more pain because the bitter cup has filled to overflowing, cracked and let some of the anguish away.

She had walked a long way, poor child, and she was still stumbling along as best she could. With all his soul he wanted to help her because he loved her so. If only the man she loved had been worth while it would have been easier for him. But it seemed intolerable to let her suffer like this for a mountebank, a cad who wasn't fit to lick her shoes.

He came up to her and put his arms

around her.

'Oh, my darling,' he said unconsciously using the endearment. 'Don't!'

She turned to him quite naturally and hid her face against his heart.

'Julian, I'm sorry. You must think me so ungrateful.'

'I don't. I understand.'

'It's so lovely here and I am happy ... I *am*.'

'You're trying to be. But I know how you really feel.'

'It's devilish, Julian. You know, don't you?'

'I know,' he said, and smiled wryly. Looking down at the fair silky head which was pressed against him, the thought of Irene was blank and meaningless. If only he could make Francesca understand that that was the way of things ... that wounds heal and that out of the ashes something new can be born. Like his love for her. A love which made the old pain seem futile, an utter waste of energy, of emotion, of everything.

'Help me,' Francesca was whispering while the tears still rained down her face.

'My dear, I'd do anything on earth for you. But what *can* I do?'

'I don't know.'

'You want your voice back. You want your lover back.'

'Your lover!' How bitterly he said that! Her tears ceased to flow and she lay mute and brooding against him, while his hand caressed her hair. And now her thought was of him. She was being utterly selfish. It could not be very pleasant for Julian to see her, his wife of a few days, making a little fool of herself like this over the man who had let her down.

She drew away from him and averted her face.

'Sorry. Don't take any notice of me.'

'You've no need to be sorry.'

She controlled herself, found her bag, took out mirror and powder-puff and hastily attended to her face.

'I won't let it happen again.'

He looked at her with melancholy.

'You mustn't be afraid to show me what you feel. It's bad to keep it all in.'

She put away her powder-puff, turned to him with outstretched hands.

'You're such a great dear. I have so much to thank you for.'

He was tempted to take her back into his arms, not as a friend and comforter, but as a lover who desired passionately to embrace her. And although he had the thing so well in control she could not fail to see what lay in his eyes. And once again she knew that this man was in love with her and she was suddenly afraid, not for herself but for him. It would be too awful if he, the kind, the generous, were to be hurt a second time.

He squeezed her hand tightly for an instant, then dropped it.

'Come and sit out on the terrace and have some tea. Afterwards I'll drive you into Como and you shall see your grandmother's birthplace. That will amuse you.'

She went with him, mutely, into the sunshine.

That same evening Julian came to a great resolve. No matter what he, personally, had to lose, he must try to give Francesca's lover back to her. He ought not to have married her. It had been crazy of him to imagine that his money, his companionship, anything that he could do, would compensate her for the loss of the man she loved. He must try to give Fane back to her. Yes! But first he must give her her voice. Without that, Fane would never come back. Fane didn't love her. He had only loved her beauty and her gifts; that golden, crooning voice which had stormed London.

Julian sat down and wrote a long letter to his friend, John Norris, who was a consultant-surgeon with a huge practice in Leeds.

It was a letter which put the whole of Francesca's case before him.

'For God's sake,' Julian wrote, 'if you know anybody in the world who you think would cure my wife's throat, send me his name and address.'

The answer from Leeds came a week later.

It seemed to both Francesca and Julian to have been a week of waiting – of curious expectancy ... with everything stationary – thoughts, emotions, hopes, agonies. A quiet week of uninterrupted sunshine during the day and silver moon and starlight at night. Of journeys by car up through the olive groves to the mountain tops, of excursions over the water, of rest and what Francesca termed 'real laziness.' And between them a kind of unspoken, undiscussed truce. It was as though that outburst of hers in the salon had spoiled things between them because they knew too much about each other.

He believed that his plan had failed and that she must be given back to the other man. And she believed that she had done him a great wrong in marrying him, because she knew now that he loved her and she could never give him what he wanted of her. But they did not discuss things. They were just friends sharing a mutual enjoyment of Italy and this exquisite villa in the centre of the lake. But it was all on the surface. It could not go on. They both knew it. They were both waiting. He for his answer from Leeds, and she ... for she knew not what.

There came with that post not only the letter from John Norris to his friend, but a letter for Francesca from Peggy Lawton.

Peggy's letter was full of news of the old circle and particularly of Fane.

What Peggy had to say about Fane was not particularly flattering. It made unpleasant reading for Francesca.

'Fane's a dirty dog, and you're well out of it, my dear,' wrote the candid friend. 'He's had a row with Kay, nobody quite knows why, except that everybody thinks he's sick of her, and although they still perform together, I don't think they see much of each other in private. Duffeyne told me the other day that he was sure that Fane would break the contract with Kay if he could find somebody he liked better. He certainly would if he could get *you* back! He as good as said so. That young man never thinks of anybody but himself and his own ends. He makes me tired. I'm glad you're married to Julian. And I do hope you're finding happiness out there.'

Francesca read that letter many times. Each time she read it, it hurt her. It was horrible to feel that this was what Peggy and the others must be thinking about Fane. He had let her down. Now he was going to let Kay down. He never thought of anybody but himself and his own ends, Peggy said. Well, that's what *she* had thought before she left London, before she had married Julian.

He was cruel and heartless. And yet she loved him. And other women loved him. But Julian, who was so generous and who would never let anybody down in this life, got nothing; had lost the only woman he had loved. Where was the justice of it all? What purpose had Fate in doing these things, in making such a muddle out of life and love?

Francesca crushed Peggy's letter up in her hand. She wished it hadn't come. It was like a little poisonous adder wriggling into a lovely garden. Her memories of Fane had been lovely ones, despite all the pain and bitterness. She did not want to be made to feel that he was despicable, and not worth a regret. Peggy said that she was lucky to be married to Julian. That was true. Perhaps she did not yet know how lucky. But she did know that the longer she lived under the same roof with Julian, the more she admired him and the more completely she could give him her trust.

Julian joined her on the terrace, where she had been sitting under the shade of a striped umbrella when the post came. In Julian's hand was an opened letter.

She smiled up at him. He looked down at her curiously and she saw now that there was an air of subdued excitement about him.

'What is it?' she said.

'I've heard from John Norris,' he said.

She caught her breath, and unconsciously

her hand went to her throat.

'Your doctor friend?'

'Yes.'

'What does he say?'

'I wrote and told him everything about you and asked him if he knew anybody who he thought could cure you.'

'Well?' she looked at him, wide-eyed, grown suddenly pale, her heart pounding.

'He says that he does know somebody who he thinks *could* cure you. He says that he knows a similar case to yours which this man cured.'

For an instant the blue, shining lake, the mountains, the dark cypresses and the whole of this lovely garden seemed to revolve in a haze about Francesca. Then she felt Julian's arm steadying her. She heard him say:

'Francesca, are you all right?'

'Yes. Tell me more. I don't believe it. It can't be true…'

'Read it,' he said, and thrust the letter in front of her.

She scanned the typed letter, excitement burning her up. It was true. This Dr Norris seemed quite certain of his facts. As certain as anybody could be about anything. This man, Norris said, whose name was Bernard Sanderson, was a brilliant surgeon, and a throat specialist. He had qualified at the Middlesex Hospital with Norris. In his time, although a young man, he had performed wonderful operations not only in England, but in Germany and in France.

'But why haven't I heard of him?' Francesca asked Julian piteously. 'They told me in town that I had seen everybody who was of any use.'

'You see what John says further on,' Julian told her. 'Sanderson no longer lives in London. He has a wife whom he adores, but whose health is bad. She's got T.B., poor woman, and for her sake he's thrown up his career in England and settled in Switzerland where she has some chance of living. He still practices, and Norris suggests that we get in touch with him. His home is in Chamonix.'

'I see,' said Francesca slowly.

'If John advises me to put you in Sanderson's hands, I know that there must be a big chance. I can rely entirely on what John says.'

Francesca shook her head.

'I can't believe that anybody can cure me now.'

'On the other hand, if there *is* a chance, you must take it.'

'Another operation...'

'And perhaps your voice will come back.'

She went scarlet and drew a deep breath.

'No, no, I can't believe that.'

'But it would mean everything to you.'

'Yes,' she began, then broke off and looked at him piteously. 'But why should I care whether I get my voice back or not? I've finished with the old life, and I'm married to you. I don't really want to sing any more.'

He looked at her steadily.

'I'm not so sure about that.'

'Don't let's bother about it now.'

'My dear child, do you think I asked John about this for nothing? If there's a chance on earth for you to recover your voice, I mean you to take it. I *want* you to.'

'But supposing...'

'Well, what?'

'Supposing this man did operate and cure me and I could sing again, and I...'

'And you went back to the stage?' he finished for her, and smiled. 'Well, what about it?'

'I don't want to go back to the stage,' she stammered.

Julian went on smiling. No, she had no great wish to return to the stage, but she wanted her voice back because of Fane, because she might find him again if that gate opened for her. He knew that it was in her mind and that, because she was loyal and generous, she was mortally afraid of telling him. He knew, too, that if he pressed her to take this chance and if Sanderson operated and was successful, he would be closing the gates of heaven upon himself. He would lose her. But that wouldn't matter if she was made happy again.

Suddenly, for the first time, he caught and held her close, kissed her with almost desperate passion on lips and eyes.

'Francesca! Oh, my darling!'

She gasped, flushed, trembling in his arms.

'Oh!'

'Forgive me,' he said unsteadily. 'Forget that I did that.'

He released her and turned away.

She looked after him, a choking sensation in her throat.

'What are you going to do?'

'Get into touch with Sanderson. I shall telephone to Switzerland tonight and talk to him, and we'll see if he can come here and see you. If not, I'll take you to him.'

'But, Julian…'

He turned and looked at her, a strange light in his eyes.

'Nothing matters, dear, except that you should get that throat of yours cured.'

He walked quickly away, leaving her there breathless, speechless, scarcely able to think. Her lips still stung from the kiss which he had imprinted upon them. And she was conscious not of anger or revulsion but of complete bewilderment. For if he loved her like that, how could he bear to risk losing her … to be, himself, instrumental in clearing the way for her … for Fane? … if such a thing were possible.

That was real love. In the face of it Francesca was suddenly ashamed. She had a sudden longing to call Julian back, to tell him that she thought him the finest person she had ever known in her life; to whisper to him:

'You're grand … a grand man…'

But she was much too embarrassed to do anything of the sort. She just stood there with her small fingers caressing that white slender throat which hurt and which he said must be cured … might be cured, and then…

Her thoughts carried her no farther.

16

There followed for Francesca what was probably the most exciting period of her life. A period during which most of her emotions came into play … hope, fear, doubt, even despair and then hope again. Vivid, aching memories of love and her lover. Gratitude and friendliness for Julian. And the one absorbing question of her throat and that voice which Bernard Sanderson believed he could cure.

Yes. Sanderson had not corroborated what all the others, the length and breadth of

England, had told her. He was optimistic. He was the first to infuse her with a confidence which she thought she had lost for ever and the belief that she was not a broken reed to be the object of pity, but still Somebody, with a wonderful gift which could bring the world back to her feet, *if* she wanted it there. But that remained to be seen.

There had been an unforgettable and stirring hour following upon Julian's telephone call to Chamonix. And that was in Sanderson's clinic in the mountains, to which she and Julian drove together.

A quiet, charming man, Bernard Sanderson, with a still boyish face and a boundless love of humanity. If he had remained in London he would undoubtedly have been one of the most eminent surgeons of the day. But nothing really counted except his wife, and for her sake he remained in Switzerland, and carried on a small practice here in his mountain home. That he cured many was certain, and it was singularly fortunate for those who came under his patronage.

John Norris had known what he was talking about when he advised Julian to take his wife to the clinic at Chamonix.

It seemed to Francesca much too good to be true when Sanderson's blue eyes smiled encouragingly at her after a careful examination, and he said:

'Why, yes ... I think we can restore that

singing voice of yours. I see nothing against it if you will come here and trust yourself to me and my nurses for a week or two.'

Francesca looked at him with wide eyes.

'But it can't be true! They said I was incurable.'

Sanderson smiled.

'None of us is infallible in our profession, Mrs Grey. Let me see, who operated on you? Ah yes, Trent-Conning ... and then you saw Sir Hugh Wynch ... both first-class men ... but I don't altogether agree with them. I'm not even sure that I agree with the original diagnosis. But I do think that there is a big chance, if all goes well, that I can put you right.'

'And I will be able to sing again?' she asked breathlessly.

'Yes.'

Francesca swallowed hard and turned to Julian. He, too, was smiling encouragingly. There was something about the grave tenderness on his face which roused an answering wave of tenderness in her. She gave him both her hands.

'Julian, *darling*, do you hear?'

The unusual endearment from her made his heart thrill. But he did not take advantage of it. He knew that she was excited and scarcely responsible for what she said or did. He just pressed the small hands tightly and said:

'It's fine … I can't tell you how glad I am, my dear. And you won't be afraid to let Mr Sanderson operate, will you? He says it isn't a long affair. You'll only be in the clinic a fortnight.'

'I don't mind anything if it's going to cure me.'

He kept her hands in his, looking down at her flushed, vivid little face. He felt a strange pang go through him. It meant so much to her, this cure! And what if 'The Girl with the Crooning Voice' came into existence again? What if he lost her? That was the risk that he was going to take, and it seemed to him a bigger risk than Francesca's operation. But it never entered his head to do anything save encourage her.

'Mr Sanderson advises that you should stay here tonight, and get the thing over at once. He can operate tomorrow morning.'

'And what of Italy and Barabella?' she asked ruefully.

'Barabella will be waiting for you. It will be ideal for your convalescence. The Donettis will be away for the next six months. When it gets too hot, I'll take you back to England.'

'Not a very jolly way of spending your honeymoon,' put in Sanderson. 'But we will make you comfortable, Mrs Grey, and if Mr Grey would like to stay with us in our chalet, we would be delighted. Any friend of

262

John Norris's is welcome.'

When it was time for Francesca to leave Julian and go to her room in the clinic – a lovely sunny room with an exquisite view of the mountains and wild flowers everywhere – she became suddenly very conscious that she did not want to be separated from him.

'I'm going to miss you,' she told him impulsively.

'It's worth a lot to me to know that,' he said.

'Thank you for everything that you've done ... that you're doing...'

'You know that there's nothing in the world that I wouldn't do for you.'

Her brown eyes suddenly dimmed with tears.

'You've been so much too good to me.'

He wanted to take her in his arms but dared not. He could not trust himself. He stood there looking out of her bedroom window through which the pure crisp air blew coolly from the mountain tops where lay the perpetual snows.

Then he glanced at the white bed which had been prepared for the new patient. He had a sudden uncomfortable vision of Francesca, with her throat bandaged, lying there white and still, instead of standing here, flushed and gay, rather like an excited child. An awful thought struck him:

'*God ... if she should die ... go out under the*

anaesthetic ... people do ... things go wrong even in minor operations ... with the best surgeons...'

If Francesca died there would be no future life for him. And if she lived and left him and went back to Fane ... would it not be worse than death?

Suddenly he felt her hand on his sleeve.

'Julian ... are you worried about something?'

He pulled himself together.

'About nothing except that you should get well quickly and that I should hear you sing to me. I've never heard you sing, you know.'

'I will! Mr Sanderson says I will.'

'God bless you, dear,' he said, pressed a swift kiss upon her hair and left her. At the door he turned back and added in a casual voice: 'I'll be allowed to see you tomorrow when you come round from the dope. Till then, good night and all my wishes for your good luck.'

He left her and she stood at the open window for a long time, her thoughts in confusion. A nurse, a cheerful English girl full of enthusiastic praise for Mr Sanderson and his wonderful work, came in and helped her prepare for bed. It was necessary that she should be quiet this evening and go to sleep early.

Francesca hardly heard what the nurse had to say. Her thoughts were too absorbing ...

curiously divided between two men – Fane and Julian. Fane whom she had loved so desperately; Julian to whom she was married and who loved her. She knew how much ... how wonderfully he loved ... to the exclusion of himself. She had felt a sudden desire to fling herself into his arms just now, hold on to him tightly and say:

'Take me away ... don't leave me ... let us stay together, you and I, just as I am. It doesn't matter about my throat. I don't want to sing again. I don't want to see Fane again.'

She knew, somewhere at the back of her mind, that if her voice was restored and Fane heard about it, he would come back to her, pursue her, never give her any rest until she belonged to him again. And that would be awful. She was Julian's wife, and she couldn't, wouldn't leave him for anybody. Even though they were not married in the accepted sense of the word – they were friends, bound legally, and she had made a contract which she must keep. Of course she *would* keep it. She wanted to. Julian was a dear. She liked him more every day, and she wasn't going to hand him out the sort of treatment that Irene had dealt him He was too good for that.

Oh why must she even remember Fane? Why take it for granted that he would come back to her life? It was just that she knew, somehow, that if she recovered he would want her. Then there would be all the bitterness of sending him away and going through the old agony.

But would it be such agony? Wasn't that pain diminishing ... a little more ... a little more with every twenty-four hours that passed ... just as Julian had said that it would? Julian had been so marvellous to her. She couldn't imagine herself leaving him now. She hadn't wanted to leave him this evening. She even felt an absurd pang of home-sickness once she was in bed in this strange white room up in the mountains. She wanted to find herself back in the big Italian bed overlooking the blue waters of Como ... and Julian in the warm, golden morning, sitting on the edge of the bed, drinking coffee with her, opening fresh ripe figs for her to eat. She adored figs.

She scarcely knew what she wanted. She felt a little crazy tonight. But she half regretted coming to Sanderson's clinic.

Of course she wanted that voice of hers back again. *Of course* she did! Yet she was afraid of the future.

She worked herself up into such a state of nerves that, later on, the nurse suggested to Mr Sanderson that little Mrs Grey might, perhaps, be all the better if her husband spent a few moments with her and calmed her down.

Sanderson smiled and nodded.

'He shall go up. We're dealing with the artistic temperament, nurse. Our young patient is, or was, a distinguished star before her illness, you know.'

Nurse knew. She had one of 'Fane and Francesca's' records, and she thought it was all very exciting ... having Francesca here in the clinic ... especially if Mr Sanderson restored that lost 'Crooning Voice.'

The doctor sent Julian up to his wife after dinner that night. Francesca was sitting up against her pillows looking out at an amazing sky full of dazzling stars, her thoughts in chaos and every nerve in her jangling.

When she saw Julian come into the room she greeted him with surprise. She had not expected him. But never had she been more glad to see that tall figure and the brown face which somehow always looked a little tired. The amazingly blue eyes were warm and vital and far from weary as he walked toward her.

'I've come to say good night,' he said. 'A special treat – for me.'

'And for me,' she said, with a funny little laugh.

He sat on the edge of the bed and took her hands in his. They were hot and dry. He could feel the slim little body shaking. Sanderson had warned him that she was in a highly nervous condition. He spoke to her soothingly.

'You're all right, aren't you, my dear? Quite comfortable ... had a nice supper?'

'I didn't want much.'

'Bed not too hard?'

'No, it's nice. It's all very comfortable, and the flowers are wonderful.' She looked round the room, which was dim because only the shaded lamp beside her bed was burning. Then she nodded at the open window. 'Aren't the stars glorious?'

'Yes, so is the whole place. I like the Swiss mountains in the summer.'

'But it's all a little frightening ... so high up ... and it's harder than my Italy. I prefer Como.'

'You shall go back.'

Suddenly she clasped both small feverish hands around one of his.

'Julian, promise that you *will* take me back.'

'But of course, dear. Why shouldn't I?'

'Oh, I don't know. There are all sorts of funny notions in my head tonight. I'm worried, and I don't know what about.'

He stroked the fair silky hair back from her forehead.

'You mustn't be. It's going to be a wonderful thing for you if Sanderson performs this miracle. He says he is going to make you exactly what you were in the old days ... an idol of the footlights, eh?' Julian smiled at her, the two lines which she liked to see cutting on either side of his mouth and chasing away the severity of his face.

'I don't know that I want to be an actress any more,' she said. Then added: 'And of course I *couldn't* be. I'm married to you.'

'My dear, if you wanted to go back...'

'But I don't think I do,' she broke in piteously.

'Then you shan't. Now don't worry any more. It's essential that you should be quiet tonight.'

Francesca looked up at him, a little pulse in her throat working. How quiet he was, how calm, how like a rock. And she had grown to lean on that rock. She would be lost without him. Fane had never made her feel that. Fane had brought her devastating passion, but never the feeling of security. And if one could combine the two it would be almost too much, unbearably much.

Did Julian love her in the way that Fane had once loved? With a man's desire? Or was his just the love of a brother, a friend? Was he suffering as *she* had suffered? Would her complete surrender make him happy in spite of what he had said on the first night of their honeymoon?

An emotion born not only of gratitude but of wholehearted admiration for this man surged through her tonight. He had done everything for her, and now, perhaps, he was going to be the means of restoring her voice and her health. For that alone she must show him that she was grateful ... she *must*.

She loosened her fingers from his and suddenly put an arm about his neck.

'Julian, darling Julian, I want to thank you ... for everything.'

The touch of her, and the nearness to that soft young breast which he could glimpse under the thin silk of the white pyjama suit which she was wearing, were intoxicants potent enough to break down even Julian's iron control. But he made an effort to master his feelings.

'My dear, you've nothing to thank me for, and besides, you've said "thank you" so many times already.'

But she clung to him.

'I want you to promise me something.'

'Anything.'

'That you'll always stay with me.'

'But you know I will.'

'And you'll take me back to Barabella.'

'You know I will,' he repeated, surprised and a little bewildered by her attitude.

'And you'll let us be alone ... you won't let anybody else come...'

'But of course if you want to be quiet, you shall be quiet.'

'It isn't only that...'

She broke off, helplessly. She scarcely knew what she wanted to tell him. She only knew that the thought of Fane was frightening her ... the thought of what she might feel if she saw Fane again.

Julian dimly guessed what lay in her mind. The moment held some bitterness for him – even now when her arm was about him and she was being unaccustomedly demonstrative, and utterly sweet to him, the shadow of Fane lay between them.

'You shall do exactly what you want,' he said, trying to reassure her. 'Now please, darling child, lie down and go to sleep and don't worry about anything any more.'

She lifted her face to his.

'Kiss me good night.'

The blood burned darkly under his tan. He drew back.

'Darling,' he protested. 'This isn't in our compact. It isn't quite fair...'

She knew then that his feeling for her was neither friendly nor fraternal alone. And somehow she was glad. Yes, she was feminine enough to be glad despite her own conflicting emotions. But it was in a wholly generous mood that she pulled his head down to hers and whispered:

'You shall kiss me – if you want to.'

'Want to,' he said thickly. 'My *God!*'

But only for a moment he allowed himself to hold the slim loveliness of her against him and feel his senses swim at the surrender of her soft mouth. The earth rocked a little for him and the stars seemed dizzily splendid but he would not let his passion for her altogether unbalance him. She must be kept quiet and she was in a condition of mind when she really was not responsible. She was just being sweet and kind and she was surely the most adorable person in the world, and he adored her. He heard himself telling her so a little wildly. He said:

'God knows I don't understand how any man on earth, having once kissed you, could keep away from you. My dear, please don't be too sweet to me. I can't stand it.'

She whispered:

'But I'm quite glad that you *want* to kiss me.'

'I don't think I understand…' he began.

'I don't understand myself tonight,' she broke in, her face flushed, her eyes melting. 'But I'm awfully fond of you, Julian – in my own way, and I want you to know it.'

'I do know it,' he said, although he winced a little at those words: 'my own way.' That wasn't the way that he really wanted. It was maddening to hold her so close and realise the gulf between them. Perhaps he did not give her credit for the real fervour with which she had offered that embrace. He laid her gently back on the pillows, smoothed the hair back from her forehead, and smiled down at her. She did not know how madly his heart was racing.

'You must go to sleep now, child.'

She gave a long sigh, put her arms behind her head and shut her eyes, then opened them and looked at him.

The knowledge that he loved her passionately seemed no cause for distress. It made her dimly proud. It made her feel close to him. She wanted to feel that way. She had felt so indescribably lonely and tormented until he came.

'Promise you'll come and see me tomorrow as soon as they allow you to.'

'Of course I will. What are you afraid of, dear?' He took her hand again and held it tightly.

'I don't know.'

'You mustn't worry, you know, otherwise Sanderson won't operate tomorrow.'

'I won't worry,' she said, sighing again.

'Then good night, and sleep well.'

Like a child she put both arms around his neck and now they kissed without passion. Julian trusted himself no further and went quickly from the room.

She switched out her lamp and lay there looking through the open window at the infinite stars which were like diamonds shining through the crystal clarity of the atmosphere. Her thoughts were still in confusion and she felt restless and unnerved. But after a while she fell asleep.

She dreamed that she was on the stage again – as 'The Girl with the Crooning

Voice.' Sitting in her old place on the piano with the white topper on the side of her head, singing one of the old songs.

Fane was at the piano playing for her. She was singing that haunting refrain from *Gay Divorce*.

'Night and day, you are the one,
Only you beneath the moon and under the sun...'

Then suddenly her voice cracked just as it had cracked at the end of the revue which had been her last performance. It cracked badly, and somebody in the audience tittered and she was filled with shame. She looked at the piano in horror and saw not Fane there but Julian. Julian's face was hard and cynical as it had been when she had first seen him at 'The Ivy' with his mother. His vivid blue eyes were full of disgust. He banged down the lid of the piano, rose and turned away.

'That finishes things with you,' he said.

She called after him in a panic:

'Julian! Julian, come back ... you didn't mean that – oh, Julian...'

But he vanished, and Fane stood there, handsome, gay, with his slightly superior, arrogant smile. He held out a hand and said:

'*I'm* here. What is it, Francesca?'

But she pushed him aside and all her agony was for Julian. She heard herself sobbing:

'I want Julian. Oh, Julian, darling, darling, come back to me.'

She awoke bathed in a cold sweat and sat up in bed for a long time, shivering, crying. More than ever this strange confusion of emotions destroyed her peace and balance. That dream had been so vivid, so poignant. She had dropped into a veritable abyss of despair because she had lost Julian. Fane hadn't mattered any more. Perhaps if he were here now she would find he wouldn't matter and that it was Julian, the strong, the faithful, the dependable, whom she dreaded to lose.

She could hear her own voice singing the words of *Night and Day*. A sudden thrill went through her and chased away the memory of her nightmare. Perhaps that was going to come true. Perhaps she *would* sing again. But if Mr Sanderson was going to operate she must be quiet and in a fitting condition to stand the ordeal tomorrow. After a while she slept again, and this time she did not dream, did not wake, until she opened her eyes to find the sun streaming into her room and a nurse waiting beside her.

17

Francesca was operated on at eleven o'clock that morning.

She took the anaesthetic calmly and seemed entirely devoid of nerves or strain, which was satisfactory to her doctors. Julian was the one who suffered during the half-hour that she was in the theatre.

He had been thinking about his wife all night, and had risen early and walked up the mountainside before breakfast. During her operation he refused to leave the clinic, and remained downstairs in the waiting-room, pacing up and down, smoking one cigarette after another. He had great faith in Bernard Sanderson, but that could not prevent tearing anxiety from consuming him while he waited for the surgeon to come down and tell him that the operation was over. He felt responsible. He had persuaded Francesca to go through this, and if the operation failed it would only weaken her for nothing and be a bitter disappointment. Above all, he wanted the thing to be a success for her sake. The ultimate issue need not be faced just now. Through the watches of the night he had lain awake in his room in Sanderson's chalet, listening to the mountain stream which gushed through their wooded garden, and remembered those few moments with Francesca when he had bidden her good night.

It had been heaven and hell combined when she had reached up her arms and drawn him down to her breast, and her lips had melted under his kiss. It had been like tasting forbidden fruit. Once having tasted it he was consumed with the desire for it again. But that had not been the real Francesca who regarded him as a friend and who had married him for friendship alone. That had been a generous emotional woman trying to show him her gratitude. He felt that he would be haunted all his life by the memory of so much sweetness. And he remembered it now while he paced the waiting-room, fearing, hoping, praying for her safety as he had not prayed since he was a child.

Once or twice the sweat broke out on his forehead and he felt frozen with fear at the idea that something untoward would happen and they would come down and tell him that all was not well. She might collapse … or she might have unexpected haemor-rhage… God, if only he could go through it all for her and know that she was safe and well!

Then Sanderson came down, still wearing his white coat. Julian's heart seemed to burst with relief when he saw that the surgeon was smiling.

'Well – is she all right?' he asked hoarsely.

'Quite,' said Sanderson. 'There's nothing to worry about.'

'Do you think it's going to be a success?'

'I hope and believe so.'

'Thank God.'

'What you want is a drink, my boy,' said Sanderson. 'Come along and have it.'

'Can't I see her?'

'She won't be conscious for a while yet. I'd see her later if I were you.'

Reluctantly, Julian followed the surgeon out of the clinic to the chalet which was at the other side of the grounds. And Bernard Sanderson thought:

'Poor devil! He's very much in love with this bride of his. She's a lovely thing, but I wish for his sake she hadn't called so frantically on the name of 'Fane' when she was going under the dope.'

'You think she'll be able to sing again?' Julian asked as they walked into the sunlight.

'That is my belief. But she won't be allowed to use that voice more than is necessary for a few weeks.'

'That doesn't matter if it will be all right in the end.'

'I think it will be.'

'That's all that matters,' said Julian.

278

When Francesca struggled back to consciousness and opened her eyes, still doped and drowsy, Julian was there beside her, holding on to her hand.

She felt calm and detached and quite safe – mainly because he was there. Vaguely her throat hurt. She put up a hand and touched the bandages. Her lips formed the name:

'Julian.'

'I'm here, darling,' he said, bending over her.

She muttered something unintelligible, closed her eyes and drifted back into the shadows.

She looked so marble white, so drained of colour, and so like a statue lying there, that his heart contracted. He had an uncomfortable recollection of the end of that book which they both loved. In *Farewell to Arms* Catherine's lover had seen her lying before him like a marble statue and she had been *dead*... He had gone out into the rain because he couldn't bear to look at her dead body.

Panic seized Julian.

'Is she all right?'

He turned to a nurse who was busy in the room with bowls and dressings on an enamel-wheeled table.

The nurse came and took Francesca's fragile wrist between her fingers.

'Absolutely. Doing well. No need to be

anxious, Mr Grey.'

'When will she wake again?'

'Not till later, I hope. We want her to sleep now.'

'Will you send for me if she wants me?'

'Indeed I will. I'll 'phone straight through to the chalet.'

Julian tiptoed to the door, took a last longing glance at the small, silver fair head which was all he could see above the rim of the white bedclothes.

The nurse smiled at him.

'That little wife of yours hasn't much thought for anybody but her husband, has she?'

He flushed red.

'Indeed?'

'Why yes,' said the nurse, and added in a confidential tone: 'Night-nurse heard her during the night. She must have had a bad dream that she'd lost you. She was calling out: "Darling, come back to me..." or something like that.'

Julian answered vaguely and walked out. His lips were set and his eyes had hardened.

She hadn't been calling for him. *'Darling come back to me'*... That had been for Fane ... *damn him!*

How pale, how still, how frail she looked lying there in her narrow bed with the bandages round her throat.

Perhaps he ought to send for Fane. She

might have a relapse and grow weak, never to recover voice or health, perhaps never recover life because she was eaten up with her desire for her lost lover. Perhaps he had better do the thing properly and put himself right out of the picture. At any rate, he ought to give Francesca every chance.

He acted more on the spur of the moment than was usual for Julian; himself a little unbalanced emotionally after the strain of the last few hours. What the nurse had repeated was the finishing touch. He could not know that she had been calling him, Julian; that her dream had been one in which she had lost him, wanted *him* rather than Fane.

He walked to the post office and sent a long wire to Francesca's former partner.

'Francesca's throat operated on this morning successfully. Every chance that she will recover voice. She wishes to see you. Can you come out. Wire me care of Bernard Sanderson, Chamonix – Julian Grey.'

That wire reached Fane Braber twenty-four hours after the revue *Stand By* ended and the Quality Theatre closed down for a month or two. Fane was preparing for a holiday prior to another production in which he would appear in the autumn. Not with Kay. He and Kay had quarrelled fiercely, and Kay, in a tantrum, had tossed her red curls and returned to America. Fane had found a new partner for the next show. A charming Viennese named Mitza, whose platinum blonde hair reminded him of Francesca's, and who had a willowy body and a haunting voice. He was full of enthusiasm about her and quite sure that her fascinating broken English would be an added attraction when she sang his songs.

He had every intention of spending a few weeks at Le Touquet, where the blonde Mitza would join him and they could rehearse together as well as enjoy the pleasures of Paris-Plage.

Julian Grey's wire, which was totally unexpected, flung him into a state of indecision. This was a bombshell and no mistake, and it was exploding at a very inconvenient moment. There were times when he had paused in his selfish, self-centred career to think about Francesca and feel remorse because of his treatment of her, times also when he wanted her back. Now, if she was going to recover her voice the memory of her held new attraction. On the other hand, there was Mitza for whom he entertained a secret passion and – there was Francesca's husband.

He seemed a queer sort of fellow … to wire for his wife's former lover. On the other hand, that line in the wire *She wishes to see you* troubled Fane. Perhaps Francesca was very ill and he ought to go to her for old time's sake. The drama of the idea appealed to him. He liked to be the centre of attraction. To have the spotlight turned on him. It would certainly be dramatic to arrive in Switzerland and have a touching scene at Francesca's bedside; flattering to know she had sent for him. He would save her life. He might even bring her back to England and waive Mitza if Francesca really recovered her voice. It would be a *beau geste* and grand publicity. He mentally drafted a wonderful paragraph for the papers:

'Fane saves life of former partner and brings the beautiful 'Girl with the Crooning Voice' back to life and the stage...'

He would compose a wonderful song for their reunion. That would be very popular and the box office would benefit. His prestige would go up with the receipts.

So attractive did this idea become in Fane's mind that he sent a wire to Chamonix which said:

'Tell her I will come to her at once.'

Julian received this answer, already regretting that he had sent the summons. He felt now that he had signed his own death-warrant. But having done it he must go through with it. More wires were exchanged. It was arranged that Julian would meet Fane's train and personally conduct him to the clinic.

'Of course I'm crazy,' Julian told himself, 'absolutely crazy. I'm wrecking my own honeymoon, such as it is, and probably wrecking my own happiness for good and all.'

But that was a secondary consideration to Francesca's happiness. He was quite certain that she wanted her lover back, and he was coming. The rest of things would work themselves out.

Meanwhile he decided not to tell Francesca that Fane was coming. It would be several days before the latter could arrive, and it was as well that Francesca should recover a little strength before being faced with any great emotion.

Francesca made rapid progress. There was more vitality and recuperative power in that slender body of hers than her doctors imagined. The third day after her operation her throat was well enough for her to take light nourishment, a little more than fluids. She was able to sit up, showing a tinge of pink in those cheeks which had looked so much too white when Julian had seen her directly after that operation.

She was not allowed to talk. Merely to whisper. There was to be no strain on her voice and she was not even to experiment with those vocal cords, Sanderson told her, until he gave her permission. As far as he could see, he had cleared up the trouble and she was cured. More than that he would not say, but it was enough to make Francesca's heart beat high with hope.

Strangely enough, after her operation, the thought of Fane receded farther and farther into the background, and it was upon her husband that her attention was concentrated. She looked forward to his visits. Missed him when he was not there beside her. Lay dozing and dreaming of the moment when he would take her back to her beloved Italy and the Villa Barabella. And there she was going to be a wife to him in every sense of the word. Yes, she had made up her mind to that. She knew indubitably that he was in love with her and she was not going to allow him to make any more sacrifices for her sake. If he wanted her in his arms, she would be ready and willing to surrender. She was going to make him happy; make up for all the misery that he had endured at the hands of Irene. And it wasn't going to be such sacrifice on her part, either. She was half fascinated by the idea of making Julian happy in every way. It was going to bring *her* happiness. In a secret, subtle way she was turning more and more to him; expanding under his love, just as a flower opens to the drenching sunlight.

But her feelings for him were too new and too delicate to express just yet. She was not sure of herself. She was going to let things take their natural course and meanwhile she was happier than she had been since the break with Fane.

Julian spoiled her. On that point she agreed with the nurses. Her bedroom was full of flowers, just as it had been at the nursing-home in London. All from Julian. He liked to shower people with things. She remembered how marvellous he had been to his old mother. More and more she understood why Mrs Grey had adored her son and less could she comprehend how Irene could have left him for an American millionaire.

One thing was brought very firmly before her notice. She could discuss Fane and the old life without being hurt by any of her memories. When one of her nurses produced a record for her, 'Fane and Francesca' singing *Broken Hearted,* she listened to it and lay against her pillow smiling. A queer, cynical little smile.

She was finished with heart-break. The reproduction of Fane's playing and his voice could no longer reduce her to a humiliating state of anguish. It seemed like an echo from another life which had been wiped out by the beauty of Julian's selfless devotion.

And to her own voice she could listen without grief.

Francesca touched her throat and smiled.

That would be wonderful … to be able to sing again. But it would be for Julian, Julian who had never heard her sing.

When he came to see her that afternoon, she had no idea of the wire which was in his coat pocket telling him that Fane Braber was leaving England for Chamonix tomorrow.

Julian meant to tell her. But his heart was heavy within him. He felt that this would be the end between him and Francesca. He would lose his wife. Friends they might remain, but Fane would come and take her away when she was well again. And she would go back to that other life in which he had never known her. The Villa Barabella, dreaming in its beautiful garden, surrounded on the shining lake, would know her no more. They would never be there together again. And even though he had not been her lover, he knew an aching longing for the old friendship, when he could be sure that she would hold out a hand and smile at him.

He was going to lose all that … he had thrown it away deliberately for her sake by sending for Fane.

How fair and lovely she looked, sitting up there with her little pink silk wrapper with pale pink swansdown hiding the still band-aged throat. She had put a touch of red on her lips today and nurse had combed the fair hair into sleek, golden waves. The dark eyes looked kindly upon him and made his heart ache all the worse, for her very kindness. It was one of her virtues and perhaps one of the rarest ... at least, so it seemed to him after the bitterness of life with Irene.

If only he could have kept her always ... just as she was ... without asking for more ... if only she had not loved Fane so utterly!

She whispered:

'I'm feeling so fine and well.'

'That's grand,' he said.

Her eyes danced.

'Am I a grand girl?'

'You bet you are, a fine girl!' he said and smiled back at her. She was such a child ... and never tired of quoting passages from Hemingway.

'What have you been doing?' she asked him.

'Wandering about Chamonix,' he told her. 'Just passing the time until I could come and see you.'

'It's so boring for you. Mr Sanderson won't let me speak properly for another two weeks.'

'Poor little Francesca. Fancy any woman not being allowed to speak for two whole weeks,' he teased her gently, trying not to show how his heart was aching within him.

Her dark eyes glowed up at him softly. Her kindliness made him miserable. Yes, it made things worse to have to give her back to her lover now, when she was being so charming and adorable to him.

He felt that he had better get the thing over. He put a hand in his pocket and took Fane's wire. With brows drawn together, he said:

'What would you like more than anything in the world, little Francesca?'

She looked at him questioningly.

'What do you mean?'

'Just what I asked. Tell me what you want more than anything else.'

Francesca deliberated. She imagined that Julian was playing a game; trying to amuse her. Indeed, she felt sure that in that generous way of his, which she had grown to appreciate so deeply, he would try to give her whatever she asked for.

She mused awhile. What *would* she like if she could make her choice? She had so much. Her voice was coming back; her health, Sanderson said, would completely recover now. She had money and position and every luxury as Julian's wife. She had Julian … kindest, dearest of men. *Dearest?* That was a word she had never really used before … it had never drifted into her mind as it did now. Today it entered her thoughts quite naturally. He *was* the dearest person in her life. That was a living truth. So what more could she ask?

She gave a little sigh and held a hand out

to him.

'I just want to hurry up and get fit and be able to sing to you – at Barabella,' she whispered.

Julian looked away from her. So much sweetness hurt him; made the part he had set himself to play well-nigh intolerable. Of course she was only being nice to him; she didn't *mean* that; she couldn't. He said almost curtly,

'You'd rather see Fane Braber more than anything in the world, wouldn't you, Francesca?'

She gasped, and her eyes seemed to darken and widen with amazement. This was utterly unexpected. It seemed to lash her across the face and cast a great ugly blot on her present contentment and happiness. Why, why should he have said that? Without pausing to think she answered:

'No … no … certainly not.'

'Ssh!' he said. He pressed her hand gently. She had spoken above a whisper in her sudden agitation. 'Don't use that poor voice.'

'Why ask me such a question?' she reproached him.

'Listen, dear,' he said. 'You may as well know that Braber is coming here … to see you… He is leaving tomorrow.'

Francesca lay still. The beautiful pink glow in her cheeks had quite gone; left them nearly as white as her pillows. Her eyes looked startled like a fawn's. She drew her hand away from her husband's and pressed her fingers tightly together over her heart. It was beating quickly and painfully. For a few seconds she could not speak. She had to digest that piece of information slowly ... with difficulty. Fane was coming here. *Fane*... coming to see her... She felt so dazed that she could scarcely think along normal lines. Then she spoke in a breathless, husky whisper:

'How do you know ... who said so ... and why ... *why* is he coming?'

'I have a wire from him in my pocket,' said Julian, feeling suddenly guilty ... as though he had done the wrong thing. The look in Francesca's eyes brought that sensation of guilt to him. There was none of the rapture, the joy in her demeanour that he had expected. He continued: 'I thought as you were ill and had called for him that it was my duty to send for him. Not only my duty – my – pleasure...' He stumbled over that word. 'I want you to be happy. I want you to see him if he ... still means so much to you. And he seems to want to see you, since he is coming out.' Francesca put a hand up to her forehead. It was damp and hot. She felt feverish; utterly unnerved and upset ... changed from the cool, peaceful, contented Francesca who had first received Julian this afternoon.

'You shouldn't have done this...'

'But if you want him with you...'

'I don't know that I do.'

'But my dear...'

'No, I don't know that I do,' she said in a wild little whispering voice. 'I'm *sure* that I don't. I don't *want* Fane here.'

'I felt sure that you did...' Julian was conscious now that he had made a blunder. But there was something so warm and exciting in that thought that he could not be wholly crushed by Francesca's obvious distress. Was it possible that her mad passion for Fane had died out? Or was it just that she was showing consideration for him, the man she had married; was too loyal to admit that she wanted Fane any more?

'Why, why did you send for him?' she kept asking.

'For your sake...'

'Not because you're fed up with me?'

'Francesca ... my *God!*...' That brought a passionate protest from him, and the blood leaping to his tanned face, pumped from a heart surcharged with almost desperate love for her.

She closed her eyes. Ah, no, it wasn't that. She had no right to imagine that for a single moment. He wasn't tired of her, but only giving her another proof of his limitless devotion. He loved her – for her sake he had sent for her lover. She had called for Fane, he said. When? She asked that, insisted on having an answer. Julian stammered the reply:

'In your sleep the night before the operation ... the night-nurse heard you calling for him. Darling, don't look like that, *please.* I don't blame you. My poor darling, don't I know what torments you've suffered and how brave you've been? I understand. I know you've wanted Fane, and if you are going to sing again, well ... there you are...' He broke off helplessly. His forehead was wet. He took out a silk handkerchief and wiped away the moisture.

She looked at him intently and nodded her head.

'I see. You're just trying to give me my heart's desire ... at any cost.'

'Yes.'

'But suppose it isn't my heart's desire, Julian?'

'Darling, don't deceive yourself ... just out of goodness to me.'

'I'm not doing that.'

'We agreed ... if either of us wanted to quit ... we'd get this marriage annulled ... or you could divorce me.'

She stayed silent a moment, her frantic heartbeats still hurting her breast. He'd do that ... go through the divorce courts for the second time in his life ... lose her ... admitting that he loved and needed her ... rather than that she should be unhappy. Truly he was a wonderful man, this Julian. There were not many people so unselfish in this world.

And what of Fane? She could scarcely credit the fact that he was actually coming here, to the clinic, *tomorrow*. Why? Why had he consented to come all this way? Why, unless he was finished with Kay, and anxious to re-open their affair? It was so like Fane to come just when the spirit moved him, regardless of Julian's feelings. Or was he being magnanimous and putting himself out to make the journey just because she was ill and Julian had asked him to come and see her?

She felt too confused to analyse the situation any more. In a helpless way she shook her head and put her fingertips against her eyelids.

'Oh, I don't know … I don't know…' she whispered.

'What don't you know?'

'Anything. It's all so unexpected. But I … don't want Fane to come.'

'Darling, in your heart you do.'

She shook her head mutely.

'He's on his way, Francesca. He'll be here tomorrow afternoon.'

'Need I see him, Julian?'

'Dearest, are you worrying because you're afraid the old feelings will revive? You needn't. I shan't stand in your way if you two … want to fix things up again.'

She could not speak. The tears were gushing from her eyes, falling thickly through her slender fingers. Then he was too distressed to do anything but kneel by the bed and gather her close to him and try his best to comfort her while he covered her hair with kisses.

'Darling child, don't cry. You mustn't, really! It won't do you any good … it'll do you harm and I shall get into such trouble with your doctor and nurses. Sweetheart, hush … there's nothing to cry for…'

She nodded her head vigorously against his shoulder.

She wanted to tell him that she was crying because of his marvellous goodness to her … that her tears were springing from her gratitude, but not only that … she realized how much he meant to her … how utterly impossible she found it to waive the thought of him and rejoice because Fane was coming tomorrow. She couldn't understand herself … or her emotions. She didn't try. She just knew that she did not really want Fane to come at all … and that she wanted Julian to go on holding her in his arms, kissing her hair, calling her 'sweetheart.' If only he understood that the night before her operation she had dreamed of *him* … that it had been *his* name she had called upon …

when he had seemed to turn from her ... desert her. Fane had not mattered in that nightmare. Fane did not matter now that she was awake and had all her faculties.

She was suddenly gloriously glad that she felt this way. The old grief had passed just as Julian had prophesied that it would. The fire had burnt itself out. It had been too fierce to last. She saw that now. Nothing was left but ashes. And they were cold. There is nothing so cold, so dead ... as the dead embers of passionate love.

She wanted to tell Julian all these things which were in her heart and somehow she could not. She could only lie in the blessed warmth and security of his arms and cry.

When those tears ceased to flow, she lay spent and white on her pillow, Julian's big handkerchief pressed to her eyes. She heard his anxious voice:

'Darling, I'll never forgive myself for upsetting you like this. Are you all right? Does the throat hurt?'

'No ... I'm all right...' she whispered.

'Have I done wrong? Don't you want to see Fane?'

'I'll see him.'

Yes, she had made up her mind to that. She would see him and prove for herself that love was dead between them. Prove it also to Julian.

Julian stood up with a great sigh. He himself felt emotionally exhausted; sick at heart at the thought that tomorrow, when she saw Fane, everything would revive between them and she would be lost to *him*. But that was what he had set himself out to achieve, so he went through with it.

'Tomorrow,' he said, 'I'll bring Braber along.'

Francesca nodded speechlessly.

'And you must swear that you won't worry; that you won't consider me or my feelings in the matter.'

She nodded again.

'Good,' he said, and moved toward the door.

Then she called him back.

'Tell me one thing … please…'

'Anything…'

'Would you mind very much if I … *did* leave you?'

He turned from her swiftly, smarting from the blow of that question … but not before she had seen his face contract.

'Naturally I'd mind,' he said, trying to speak lightly. 'I'm tremendously fond of you. But I want you to be happy. And if you are, then … I shall be happy. Just remember that.'

Her eyes filled with tears again. But she was answered. Her lips smiled a queer, tender, secret little smile which followed him as he walked out of her room.

18

Fane Braber did not reach Chamonix on the expected day. Neither did he get there at all. He had meant to go. He had quite looked forward to the little drama at Francesca's bedside and the subsequent reports in the newspapers. But at the last moment a minor, but somewhat obliterating, complaint seized him in the form of an influenza-cold caught at a theatrical ball when he foolishly sat out on a roof garden in the early hours. He was hot with dancing and then a chill followed. On the morning that he had meant to cross to France, he found himself in bed with a temperature. He wired to Francesca in person, expressing his regret, and assuring her that he would come at the first opportunity.

The effect of that wire upon Francesca baffled Julian. She did not appear to be in the least perturbed by it. She seemed even relieved. She said very little except:

'It's just as well he isn't able to come yet. I shall be able to cope with him so much better when I've got my voice back.'

That might have meant anything … everything. It left Julian worried and uncertain. Nevertheless, the main objective at the moment was Francesca's health, and perhaps it was all to the good, he thought, that she should not have to go through any emotional scenes before she was quite strong again.

He remained her unfailing friend and devotee. She, on her side, was almost shy of him. The thought of Fane was receding farther and farther into the background. But the more prominently Julian figured in her emotions and reactions, the more difficult she found it to be natural with him.

During the hours that he spent with her she became increasingly conscious not only of his admirable qualities of character but of that quiet charm which was essentially Julian. With that realization and the memory of those unguarded moments when he had held her in his arms and shown her that he was passionate lover as well as friend, it was not long before Francesca knew that there was something more than ordinary regard in her feelings for him.

She was altogether virginal, reticent. Almost as though there had never been another man in her life. She was all woman now, ready to be wooed and won. She felt almost ashamed of it. How was it possible that she should feel like this, when so recently she had been consumed with the agony of that other love? Then she told herself that it was only natural that on the rebound she should respond to this man who had proved to the uttermost his amazing love for her.

Gradually she ceased to be ashamed and gloried in her secret feelings. The time would come when she could tell him everything. But not yet. Not until she had seen Fane. She had made up her mind to that.

There was something very thrilling in that secret which she hugged to her heart. Sometimes when she caught Julian's vivid blue eyes fixed upon her with one of those revealing looks which proved that he was all lover, only repressing his passion because he imagined she would find it repellent, she was strongly inclined to throw herself into his arms. But she waited. She must be sure *this* time. She did not want to face another failure in love. Neither did she wish him to face one … he who had passed through the same annihilating fire as herself.

Meanwhile, she grew daily stronger and better. The throat healed with marvellous rapidity, and at the end of a fortnight she was allowed to use her speaking voice in full strength for the first time.

Sanderson was delighted with his patient. He pronounced her recovery to be complete.

'You will sing again,' he told her. 'I can't allow you to try it for another week, but I know that those vocal cords are all right.'

'"Oh, isn't it heavenly"…' She gave a joyous little laugh… 'I'll be able to sing *that* …

even if it *is* an old tune!'

He was glad for her. He had done something for her. He had been instrumental in this. But he imagined that half her rapture was because she believed that she would sing for and with Fane Braber again.

Undoubtedly the thing had been a success. Her speaking voice was clear as a bell. He had never known before what music lay in Francesca's voice. When he had first met her after that other operation all the clear beautiful timbre had vanished.

Sanderson pronounced her perfectly fit to leave the clinic if she wished. There seemed nothing that she wanted more than to get back to Italy, which thought eased some of the aching in Julian's heart. He liked to think that she wanted to return to their villa. He made immediate preparations to take her there.

'And what about Braber?' he asked her.

Francesca dropped her eyelids and said in a casual tone:

'I dare say he'll come to Barabella if he wants to see me.'

Evidently Fane did want to see her, because he wrote expressing his intention of visiting Como at the end of the week. He congratulated her warmly on the wonderful recovery of her voice, said that the one thing he longed to do was to hear her sing again, and asked her to book rooms for him at the

301

hotel nearest her villa.

Julian read this letter, his lips and eyes grim.

'Then *finita*,' he said to himself.

Francesca watched him, her own eyes glistening with the secret warmth of her new and stirring feeling for him, and thought:

'Oh, my darling, silly old Julian ... do you really think that I'm going to let Fane take me away from you now?'

They left Chamonix in the Bentley on a glorious summer's morning. It was arranged that she and Julian should return one day and stay at the chalet as the Sandersons' guests.

'You're one of my star patients,' the surgeon told Francesca, 'and when you come and stay with us we'll make you sing every day just to flatter me.'

As they drove away Francesca and Julian discussed the Sandersons.

'He's splendid, and his wife's a darling,' Francesca remarked, 'and I quite understand why he gave up his career in London just to live with her out here. After all, nothing is so important to him as her health, and she'll live here, whereas she might have died in England.'

'They're both of them dears,' Julian agreed.

'It's a change in these days to meet a couple who are so much in love with each other.'

Julian winced a little.

'Francesca the cynic.'

She laughed and snuggled down in the car beside him.

'Not so much of a cynic as you think, Julian. Not as cynical, for instance, as I was when we first drove through Switzerland to Italy.'

Julian Grey was silent. He took it for granted that she was happy because her lover was coming back to her. And it did not seem to him that she belonged to him even as much as she had done on their honeymoon trip, when there had been no idea of Fane ever entering her life again.

He was depressed and unlike himself by the time they reached Barabella. One of those fits of melancholy which had not settled upon him for months weighed him down despite his efforts to overcome it.

Francesca watched and was troubled by his gloom. Yet her heart leapt when she considered the significance of it. He was anticipating her departure from him. That was defeating him, with all his courage and selflessness. Dear, dear Julian! It seemed to her absurd that she should not tell him now, at once, that there was no need for him to be depressed; that she was never going to leave him again in this life. But still she shrank from making that revelation until she could give him undeniable proof.

They came back to Barabella late on a lovely warm afternoon when the first evening star was twinkling in a sky of heavenly blue, and the red and orange glow of the sunset was dipping into the ice water of the lake. As the motor-boat rounded the point now familiar to Francesca, the Villa Barabella appeared in its beautiful garden like a poem, a dream, mirrored in the smooth water.

For Julian it had lost much of its beauty, because it seemed to him that he had come back here to die another death ... a far worse one than that which he had endured when Irene had left him. But for Francesca it was a real home-coming and she looked upon the scene with rapt eyes.

'Oh, Julian, only one more week and I can stand out there by that cypress and sing to the very stars!'

'That will be wonderful,' he said, and squeezed the hand she thrust out to him.

Barabella meant nothing tonight, but the beauty of his young wife seemed to him to outline that of the stars. She looked so well, so young! He knew that when Fane Braber saw her, he was going to fall in love with her all over again.

'I hope to God the man comes soon and gets the thing over,' he told himself savagely.

Francesca, for quite another reason, hoped that Fane would come quickly, and 'get it over.'

It was a week before Fane arrived. He had recovered and gone down to the South of France with Mitza, and from there he came on to Como, curious to see the former partner whom he had so nearly married.

He was not at all sure that he meant to take her back. Mitza was very fascinating. But he would like to see Francesca. It would be interesting to hear her sing again. Everybody in Town in the old circle who had heard about the operation said that her recovery was a miracle.

On the day that Fane arrived at Como, Julian absented himself. He had no desire to see Braber or witness the reunion. He did not put it that way to his wife. When she informed him that Fane was coming, he announced quite casually that he would take that opportunity of going to Rome for a night.

'I want to look up Donetti. I owe him a visit. He's been so good, lending us the villa, and I'll be back some time tomorrow night.'

When Francesca said good-bye to him, she had an instant of paralyzing fear that he might not return to her. It brought her face to face with the knowledge that she was in love with this husband of hers and quite badly in love, if it came to that! She could not bear it if he got hurt in an accident, or deliberately left her for good and all, or anything of the kind. It flung her into such a panic that she almost gave herself away.

She seized his arm and made him swear that he would only be away for one night.

'Promise you'll come back,' she said.

He looked down at her in some surprise.

'But Braber will be here and...'

'That's nothing to do with it,' she broke in impatiently, 'I want you back.'

He thought:

'Yes, of course she'll need me. She looks upon me as a friend, and why not? I promised her friendship, and I promised her freedom if she ever wanted it. I've nothing to complain of. She'll want me to make arrangements...'

'I'll come back,' he told her quietly.

She let him go with a sigh of relief.

Leaning over the balustrade, she watched the white motor-boat take him away from her, and waved him goodbye. He waved back, smiling. But she knew that he had gone with a heart like lead. She felt angry with herself for sending him away like that – and almost angry with Fane who was the cause of the trouble. It amazed her that she should look at Julian's vanishing figure and feel such a wave of depression once he had gone, and scarcely a thrill in her body from the anticipation of Fane's arrival.

The meeting with Fane took place at the villa that morning. When Maria showed him into the salon, Francesca was sitting at the piano, singing for the first time. *That* was the real thrill of the day. To hear her own voice with all its former clarity and sweetness echoing through the big room. And she sang:

'Night and day, you are the one...'

But it was Julian's thin brown face with its intensely blue eyes, not Fane's, which figured in her imagination.

When Fane came with his light, graceful tread across the polished floor up to the piano, she let her hands fall from the keys and looked at him for a breathless moment. An intense, crucial moment. So many times in the past months she had hungered for this; tortured herself with the picture of him standing like this before her, holding out arms into which she would fling herself wildly, begging him never to leave her again.

Here he was, so very familiar, yet so different, Fane, a stranger. A man whom she saw coldly and without that old blind passion which had distorted her vision. He was handsome and *soignée* in his grey flannels, attractive, yes, that was undeniable. But the pointed brown suede shoes, the greenish silk shirt, and the glistening, rather long fair hair, all seemed just a shade too effeminate. Too studied. In the past it had never seemed to her that Fane had a touch of effeminacy about him. But perhaps now she was unconsciously drawing comparisons. She had grown used to Julian, who was big, so completely masculine.

Perhaps, too, she felt, now that she saw Fane again, an immense resentment against him for all the suffering that he had caused her. He had had no right to desert her in the first place. He had been callous, cruel. And she had been a little fool to let it hurt her so.

Why had he come now? Only because he knew that she was well, and could sing again. That made her once more attractive in his sight. But it was Julian who had taken her when she had been wrecked and lost and made her his wife. Did Fane imagine that he was going to come now and enjoy the success which she owed to somebody else?

It was Fane who spoke first.

'Francesca, my *sweet!*'

The old charming, insinuating voice. Francesca smiled a little as she rose from the piano stool and faced him. Once that voice had made the blood rush through her body, had enraptured or tormented her, as the case might be. Today it left her cold. How pleasant to feel like that about somebody who had once had the power to move her so! It was as though a great humiliation was lifted from her, and she could hold her head up high.

'Hullo, Fane,' she said, 'it's very nice of you to come all this way to see me.'

Her coolness was only an instant's setback. Fane thought her shy, gave a half-laugh, then drew close to her and took both her hands.

'Darling, you're lovelier than ever! And as for your voice... God, what a thrill to hear that again, and what a wonderful greeting for me as I came in!'

She drew her hands away gently and with a faint, cynical smile.

'Yes, the voice has come back.'

'And you, my sweet. You're going to come back too – to me ... to the world...'

He spoke impulsively, theatrically, and tried to take her in his arms.

'It will be so splendid for me and for everybody if we can go back to the old partnership... "Fane and Francesca" ... my sweet, it will thrill the public and Duffeyne will be crazy about it. There's nobody like you ... never has been. Kay could never hold a candle to you. There's something about you and your singing...'

He rambled on, ignoring the fact that her body was tense and unyielding in his embrace. He was filled with a sense of dramatic reunion and of his own wonderful generosity in giving her this chance. Yes, Mitza must fade out of it. He would have to make her a present of money, of course. It would be a great disappointment to her if he failed to sign that contract with her for the autumn.

But, really, Francesca was a proved public favourite and that was worth a lot to him. Added to which she appeared to him to have increased in beauty and attraction since he had last seen her. Of course she had been ill then, sickening for that wretched throat complaint.

Today she was entrancing in her white, sleeveless frock. She had a lovely little waist and knew how to wear the belts which were today's fashion. And he had never seen anything so dazzling as the brightness of Francesca's hair in the Italian sunshine, the fairness of her complexion in contrast to those dark, melting eyes. He'd be a fool to let her go again.

He tried to kiss her.

'My sweet! Do you still love your Fane a little?'

And then Francesca pushed him away and shook her head with a hard, cold smile curving her lips.

'I'm awfully sorry, Fane, but I'm afraid I don't love you at all!'

The bombshell exploded at Fane's feet and left him breathless. A look of stupefaction crossed his handsome face.

'You don't ... at all?'

'No. Why should I?'

'But ... you and I ... you swore you'd always...' he stammered and broke off. She was making him uncomfortable with that fixed smile of hers. Damn it, she wasn't at all the soft, yielding little thing that she used to be.

'Don't remind me of what I used to say, Fane,' came her chilling voice. 'I'm surprised at a man of your experience being so indiscreet.'

'Do you mean you don't care a damn about me any more?'

She answered without hesitation, and with the knowledge that she was able to speak with absolute sincerity:

'No, I don't love you any more. I don't say I hate you. I just feel quite indifferent. I'm sorry, but there it is, and I don't see how you can expect anything else.'

He went scarlet to the roots of his hair. She felt quite sorry for him. Knowing him as well as she did, she realised how badly his vanity was being hurt. She added, more kindly:

'I'm afraid you've come rather a long way for nothing, haven't you?'

Then Fane recovered himself.

He drew a gold case from his pocket, extracted a cigarette and snapped the case again. Francesca watched him. That case was familiar. She herself had given it to him a year ago. But it didn't even move her to see it or remember the old intimacy associated with it. Love was very dead, she reflected. It was as though it had never existed. As though this handsome, clever young man had never been her lover and she had never suffered an instant's pain through him.

'My dear Francesca,' he said, 'I must say your reception of me is a little astonishing.'

'I don't see why. You and I said good-bye for good and all many months ago.'

'But you sent for me.'

'I think my husband sent for you.'

'And why the devil, if...'

'I know,' she broke in, 'it was a little unnecessary dragging you out all this way, but I felt that I had to see you.'

He paused in the act of lighting his cigarette.

'Oh, then you *did* want to see me?'

'Yes, but not for the reasons which you apparently imagine. When I was operated on in Chamonix, Julian imagined that it was essential that I should see you. That was why he wired for you. And once I knew that you were coming I thought I'd better let you come. Just so that we should get things straight between us.'

'In what way get them straight?'

She looked away from him out of the window at the blue waters of the lake.

'It's all very difficult to explain. But briefly, Fane, this is the position; Julian's one wish is for me to be happy, even if it means his separation from me. He has taken it for granted that my only chance of happiness lies with you. He has gone to Rome today believing that I would slip back into the old partnership. I was practically certain in my mind that I wouldn't. But I thought it only fair to give the thing a chance. And I knew the moment I saw you that we could never begin again, you and I. That association is quite dead. And I don't quite see why you should imagine that you had only to come here and hold out a finger and that it would draw me back.'

'I thought your love for me was more lasting,' he said sullenly.

'Lasting!' she echoed. Her eyes flashed with sudden anger. 'How did you expect it to last when you did your best to kill it before I even married Julian? Besides, you seem to forget that I *am* married. Even if I wanted to renew our partnership, I think I'd have some compunction in leaving a man who has been so very good to me.'

'I see. So you've brought me out here just to tell me that you're in love with your husband?'

'You've put it into words, Fane. But I haven't said anything of the sort to him, yet. I tell you, he's gone to Rome imagining that he would come back to find me ready and waiting to quit ... with you.'

313

Fane gave a rather ugly laugh.

'I still don't see why you got me here.'

'Perhaps it was unfair of me. But I had to see you and make quite sure. I didn't want there to be a second tragedy.'

'Has there been a first?'

She drew a sudden breath and clenched her hands.

'I won't waste words telling you all that I went through when you first broke with me, Fane.'

He hunched his shoulders and began to walk up and down the long salon. She looked after him, her heart contracting. How familiar it was, that restless pacing of Fane's. But this sudden pain was remembrance of *her* pain, rather than of their love.

He stopped in front of her, the cigarette still unlighted between his fingers.

'Look here, Francesca, I seem to have been dragged out here for nothing and I think it's damnable. But I admit that I behaved damnably in the first place. We'll cry quits and I'll fade out of it, if you'll tell me the best and quickest way of getting back to Chiasso.'

'I didn't do this just for the pleasure for revenge,' she said, 'I just had to see you once more. That's all.'

'Thanks for the compliment. Having seen me, you're quite certain you love your husband, eh?' He gave a short laugh.

'Yes,' she said frankly.

'Delightful! Well! The whole thing's off. I was going to suggest a renewal of our contract, but of course...'

'Of course that *is* impossible,' she finished.

'I'm glad to find you so well and so happy,' he said stiffly.

She was half inclined to laugh now. Under the surface Fane was such a spoiled child. Always had been. Whatever he got out of life, he wanted more. And probably now he would want her because he couldn't get her.

She did not mean to be gratuitously unkind, but the woman in her found it impossible to resist putting one question to him.

'I wonder, Fane, if you would have come to take me back into your life if I was still an invalid without a voice?'

'I consider it a waste of time to prolong this discussion,' was his cold and evasive reply.

And it was at that juncture that they parted.

Francesca felt almost friendly toward Fane now that the crisis was past and she knew so definitely where she was. Her love and longing for Julian were bubbling within her like a strong, warm torrent waiting to be unloosed. She would have liked to communicate some of her happiness even to Fane.

'Why not have some lunch with me now

that you're here?' she asked him.

But Fane declined. He was bitterly offended. He was not used to being turned down. And he had been made to feel a fool. For that, alone, he would never forgive Francesca. In addition, he had a horrid little feeling that he had made a mistake. In losing Francesca he had lost something rare and beautiful which he was not likely to find again. That wasn't a pleasant thought. The sooner he got away from her the better. He must forget his ambition to put 'Fane and Francesca' before the public again. He would go back to Le Touquet, where he had left Mitza. That little devil would benefit by Francesca's unexpected withdrawal from the contest, anyhow. Not that she had ever meant to contest. He could see that now. Well, he wasn't going to worry too much. He had Mitza, thank heaven. He could not resist a dig at Julian Grey when he bade Francesca good-bye.

'I'm glad you've found your bear so attractive after all,' he said, just before the motor-boat took him back to the mainland. 'I must say he has a delightful lair.'

'Quite. But you know, my bear is really rather more like a lion,' said Francesca sweetly. 'Good-bye, Fane. Good luck. I've still got some of our records. It's quite amusing to listen to them.'

'I should smash them if I were you,' he

316

said savagely.

'Perhaps I will,' she said.

And she did, that same day. Those records which she had once treasured, wept over, she broke in half without a pang, and dropped the pieces into the deep waters of the lake.

'There lies love,' she thought ironically.

And went back into the villa, feeling so happy, so tremendously gay and relieved of all cares that she could have shouted her joy aloud to the sun.

That was the end of Fane, and the end of all doubts and misgivings, of inhibitions and repressions. The end, too, of Julian's troubles. She knew that he loved her. And she was going to make him happy now, knowing that there was no mistake.

She could not wait another night and day. That would be too much. She wired to him frantically. A wire which reached him at the Donettis' house in Rome that afternoon.

'Please come back at once – Francesca.'

Julian had only been at the Donettis' house in Rome for a few hours when that urgent wire reached him. Donetti, who was with his friend when he opened it, saw Julian change colour and said:

'Not bad news, I hope?'

'I don't know,' was Julian's reply, 'but I

317

think I must go straight back to the villa, if you will excuse me. My wife may be ill. I know she wouldn't wire for me unless it was serious.'

He caught the first train back from Rome to Chiasso. Donetti saw him off regretfully. He was a tremendous admirer of the Englishman and had looked forward to an evening with him. But it was obvious that he loved this newly-made wife of his very dearly. Naturally he would want to go to her if she wired for him. They had been married a very short time. But it left the Italian a little puzzled. He could not quite understand why Julian should have that tired, sad look in his eyes. True, he had always had a slightly melancholy air and the tragedy of his first marriage had altered him completely, but now that he was married to a girl with whom he was obviously very much in love, he should, in Donetti's opinion, look happier.

'I hope you will find everything all right, my dear fellow,' he said, when he bade Julian good-bye. 'Let us know.'

During the long, hot journey Julian remembered those words ironically.

He did not expect to find everything 'all right.' He could see only fresh trouble ahead. Perhaps Braber had changed his mind and not turned up, and Francesca had wired for him, Julian, frantic with disappointment. Or perhaps they had met and there had been no

318

reconciliation; Fane was a cad; it wouldn't surprise Julian to learn that he had hurt Francesca all over again.

These and half a dozen other explanations flitted through Julian's tired, harassed mind. But somehow never the right one. It never entered his head that Francesca should, of her own volition, have sent Fane away.

He was altogether weary and heavy-hearted when he came to the end of his journey, drove along the winding road which fringed the lake and completed his journey by boat to Barabella.

It was a perfect night; just such another of those radiant nights which he had spent at the villa with Francesca, racked with hopeless longing for her.

The clear blue sky was milky with stars and the lake was a silver pond, a mirror for that glittering canopy. The tall cypress which stood sentinel at the gateway of Barabella looked black, still, exquisitely outlined against the starlight. From one or two of the tall windows of the villa spilled the soft orange glow of lamplight. The air was fragrant with the scent of roses, drooping after the heat of the sunlight which had drenched them all through the long summer's day.

It was all so lovely and so meant for lovers. But Julian Grey almost felt at the end of patience and sacrifice as he walked up the stone steps on to the terrace. He couldn't stand very much more of this. He knew it. If he wasn't careful he was going to find himself in a worse state than the one which he had been in during his divorce from Irene.

Ricco, the boatman, saluted the English signor as he passed and said:

'*Buona sera.*'

Julian answered mechanically:

'*Buona notte.* Good night, Ricco.'

The Italian boy's soft voice followed him through the darkness:

'*Grazie, signor.*'

There seemed to Julian so much beauty and graciousness in this lovely villa, this lovely Italy, and so much sorrow. What a pity it was – more than that, it was a tragedy. Not only for himself, but for poor little Francesca. Things must have gone very wrong with her to send for him like this.

Then, like Fane Braber had done, earlier today, he stepped into the salon and heard Francesca singing.

He stopped on the threshold to listen, something gripping him by the heart. Whatever the fresh tragedy might be, here at least was the miracle which Sanderson had worked. Francesca had recovered her 'crooning' voice. Julian, although no musician, was sufficiently fond of music to appreciate the warm, sweet quality of that voice which he had never heard until now, save on a gramophone.

She sang gaily, not sadly, which struck him as being curious.

Then she saw Julian in the doorway and broke off abruptly.

'Oh, so you're here!' she exclaimed and stood up.

He came slowly toward her. He thought he had never seen anything so lovely as Francesca, the standard lamp by the piano shining softly upon her, making a halo of her blonde hair. She was wearing that parchment-satin frock with the long, tight sleeves and square neck which she had worn on their wedding night, and which had made her then seem to him as beautiful as a poem, and so much like a bride. There were white roses pinned to her shoulder-strap by the diamond and sapphire bar which he had given her that night at the Hôtel Joyeuse. The only other jewellery she wore were some pearl stud ear-rings which he had also given her and which had belonged to his mother.

Her cheeks were pink and her eyes were shining. There was a touch of excitement about the smile that she gave him which he failed to understand. Altogether he was baffled by her festive appearance and that look in her eyes. He spoke rather more curtly than he meant:

'What's the matter, Francesca? I got here as soon as I could. What's wrong?'

For an instant she found it difficult to reply. Her heart was beginning to race. All day her pulses had leapt and fluttered at the thought of his return. And all her life she seemed to have been waiting for this one moment. It was too good to be true. When Fane had come into this room this morning she had felt as cold and remote as the snow peaks on the mountains. But at the sight of Julian's tall figure, and thin, tired face, she was suffused with secret joy. She felt herself trembling like a very young girl in his presence.

He took a quick look round the salon, as though he half expected to see her lover lurking there in the shadows.

'What's happened? Why did you want me so urgently?' he asked with a touch of irritation.

That very irritability gave Francesca back the poise which she needed. It was so human, and the very sharpness of his voice made her tumble headlong into love with this husband of hers more completely than she had ever thought it possible to love any man. It was a more mature and profound way than that in which she had loved Fane Braber.

'Oh, Julian, darling Julian!' she stammered happily, and held out both hands to him.

Dazed and bewildered, he took them.

'Where's Braber?'

'Gone. He was only here ten minutes … quarter of an hour at the most.'

'But why?'

'Because I sent him away. At least I asked him to stay to lunch, but he was too annoyed with me to accept.'

Julian's eyes, bluer than ever with the intensity of his feelings, stared at his wife's flushed young face. He asked himself if she was mad … or if he himself was going mad.

She gave a low laugh and squeezed his fingers.

'Poor darling! You're all perplexed, aren't you?'

'I certainly don't understand…' he began.

'Of course you don't. But before I make any explanations, will you tell me something … on your word of honour, as children say?'

'Anything … what?'

'Do you love me?'

'For God's sake!' His voice was protesting.

'No, I'm not trying to tease you or just ask needless questions. I want to know. *Do* you love me?'

'You know I do. In the name of heaven, why do you even ask? Haven't you had enough proof?'

'Too much,' she answered, serious now and with her brown eyes melting. 'Much too much, darling Julian. You've been an absolute saint to me all the way through. Much better than I've deserved. I didn't realize that any man could be quite so wonderful. But I do realize it now, I assure you. And I want to try to be worthy of it all ... that is if you'll give me a chance ... to prove my love for you.'

He could only stare, but she felt his fingers dry and shaking in hers. Then he broke out:

'What do you mean ... *your* love for *me?* You don't love me.'

'Oh, but I do!'

'That's rot,' said Julian bluntly.

'But, darling, it isn't! I do love you. With all my heart. And much more than I can tell you. And that's why I sent Fane away, and that's why I wired for you. Because I wanted to tell you that. Because I knew I wouldn't sleep a wink tonight until I'd told you. Was it very mad of me? Ought I to have let you stay in Rome with your friends and leave it till tomorrow.'

The hot blood flamed into his face. The tired lines had vanished now. It was a boy's face, transfigured with a happiness which he could still scarcely credit. He gripped her hands so tightly that he hurt her.

'Good God, if this is true, I'd never have forgiven you if you hadn't sent for me ... it would have been terrible if you'd let another hour pass without telling me. But *is* it true? Francesca, I can't believe it. How is it possible? You've been in love with Braber all the way along...'

'I know that I *was* in love with him,' she said slowly, 'but it all seemed to die just before my operation. It just faded out. I knew then I didn't love him any more, and I'd been a fool to waste so much time. I felt that *you* meant much more to me. It may be difficult for you to realize, Julian, but you must try to believe what I say because it's the living truth.'

'Francesca,' he said, stammering her name, and pressed both her small hands together and covered them with kisses, *'Francesca!'*

She tilted her head and half shut her eyes, uttering a little sigh of ecstasy. Those kisses on her hands were amazingly satisfying to her. She had been half afraid that he might tell her that he didn't love her, that he didn't want her any more; half afraid that she had reached this wonderful conclusion on her part – too late.

'Perhaps I ought to have told you before,' she added, 'but I wanted to be sure. That's why I let Fane come. I didn't want to be too hasty until I'd seen him. I was so confused in my mind about the whole thing. But the moment he walked into the room this morning, I was quite certain that I didn't love him any more, and it was you who meant everything.'

He went on kissing her hands speechlessly, feverishly, like one intoxicated. This reception was so utterly different from any that he had imagined, so bewilderingly sweet, that he could not be rational. For once he was thrown entirely off his balance. But he stammered out a dozen questions which she answered:

'When did you first feel like this about me?'

'On the night before my operation, I think. I didn't want you to leave me. And then I dreamed that you didn't want me any more … a funny sort of dream all mixed up with Fane. Fane wanted me, but you walked away, and that seemed to break my heart. I called after you. The nurse heard me calling. She told you, didn't she?'

'Yes, yes, but I thought it was Braber you were calling for. And you were absolutely certain when you saw him today that the old feeling for him was quite dead?'

'Absolutely certain. He didn't mean anything. He offered me the old partnership. He was all ready to be my lover again. But it didn't move me. I was just angry with him for having hurt me in the past and with myself for wasting so much time over him. And angry, also, because I'd hurt you.'

'You never hurt me. You've been sweet to me.'

'No. I've taken everything and given nothing.'

'That isn't true.'

'But it is, Julian. You've spent so much

time trying to make me happy, and now it's your turn to be happy as well as me.'

He looked at her, his eyes burning blue, all his soul in them.

'Child, are you sure you aren't just being sorry for me? This isn't because you think you owe me something? You do really care for me a little?'

'More than a little, Julian. And I'm *not* sorry for you!' she said indignantly.

'Don't you understand how hard it is for me to believe all this?'

'But you must. Tell me that you do.'

'I will if you say so. If you'll really swear to me that you've sent Braber away because you love me now.'

'I do say so. I swear I sent Fane away because I love you!'

There was too much sincerity in her voice, in her eyes, to leave room for further doubt. He just took her in his arms and buried his lips soundlessly against her hair. She could feel his heart thumping against her breast. She was caught in the tide of his intoxication and swept along up to unimaginable heights. She whispered:

'Darling, darling ... my *darling* Julian...'

'You know I adore you,' he said, huskily. 'You know it...'

It seemed to them both that they touched the white-hot pinnacle of love, of fervent loving, during the long embrace, the long deep kiss that followed.

The white roses were crushed against her shoulder and the petals fluttered unheeded on to the rug. One shining strand of her hair was loosened, brushed against his face and stayed there like a little golden veil hiding the look of heaven in his eyes. But nothing could hide from her the happiness that was theirs in this revealing hour.

Afterwards, she lay in his arms on the wide sofa, the room in darkness and only the moonlit splendour of the lake visible to them, and came back to earth sufficiently to speak of mundane things.

'Julian, you haven't had anything to eat ... we must ring for some food...'

'I don't want any food, unless you do.'

'I've had mine. But you...'

'Later. Not now. Let's stay like this. Francesca, sweetheart, it's so new to me still, too incredible, I don't want to do anything but hold you, look at you, kiss you...'

Softly in the darkness her hand stroked the thickness of his hair.

'Darling lover...'

'Wonderful child, do you really love me?'

'I've told you that often enough. I'll make you conceited if I tell you any more.'

'No – go on telling me. I won't get conceited. I want all that you can give me ... life hasn't held anything like this for me before. And sometimes it's been very lonely...'

Then Francesca, woman-like, remembered that other wife, a little jealously.

'Can I make you as happy as *she* first made you?'

'Much, much happier, darling. You're so infinitely more my heart's desire than Irene ever was. I swear that. I love you a thousand times more than I ever loved her.'

'And I love you so much more than I loved Fane.'

'That's difficult to believe. I'm so dull, so different...'

'You're *my* heart's desire,' her soft voice whispered against his ear. 'But don't let's draw comparisons. Let's be happy like this ... always...'

'Always,' he echoed gravely, and drew her closer.

Through the open window there drifted the faint, musical tenor of a boy's voice singing an Italian song.

'Listen,' Francesca whispered.

'That's Ricco,' said Julian. 'He's singing a love song to his sweetheart somewhere out there on the lake.'

'I'll sing one to you.'

'You shall – many of them. Sweetheart, I never heard anything so beautiful as your voice when I first came home.'

'You gave it back to me, Julian.'

'No, Sanderson did that.'

'But it was really you. It's you who have

done everything for me.'

'And you've given me back life itself,' he told her.

'Darling!' she said, 'I'm so happy.'

'That's what I've always wanted you to be, Francesca.'

'And that's what I want *you* to be now. It's what your precious mother wanted, too. Julian darling, we didn't really deceive her after all. And if she knows ... if she can see us ... she'll be so glad.'

'I wish she could have lived to know this.'

'So do I. Do you remember that first day when you both came into "The Ivy," and saw me, and you looked at me with such a black scowl? You hated all women then ... and you didn't particularly like me.'

'That doesn't seem possible. But I suppose it was so. I seem to remember something of the kind.'

'I'm glad it's all worked out this way ... it's been worth all the pain, hasn't it?'

'I'd go through it all again for this,' he said, and brushed her hair and her eyelids with his lips.

'So would I. But, oh, Julian, aren't you glad we *don't* have to go through anything any more? Tonight we're beginning the whole of life again.'

He repeated what she said, knowing it to be a wonderful truth.

'The whole of life again... There never has

been another life … there never will be…
But only this one we shall lead together.'

'It's a happy ending as well as a beginning,
Julian. But endings aren't always happy.
What about our beloved *Farewell to Arms?*'

He hugged her jealously, poring over the
beauty of her face which was like a cameo in
the moonlight.

'No … it would have been too awful if
you'd died … if I had lost you like that
fellow lost Cat.'

'Let's always love each other like they
did… Hemingway understood love and
loving. I feel all that Cat felt about her man.
I feel that you're a fine boy … a grand
lover…'

'And you're a grand girl, darling.'

They laughed together and kissed. Then
there was silence except for the golden voice
of the young boatman on the lake, who went
on singing melodiously through the warm
Italian night.

The publishers hope that this book has given you enjoyable reading. Large Print Books are especially designed to be as easy to see and hold as possible. If you wish a complete list of our books please ask at your local library or write directly to:

Dales Large Print Books
Magna House, Long Preston,
Skipton, North Yorkshire.
BD23 4ND

This Large Print Book, for people
who cannot read normal print,
is published under the auspices of

THE ULVERSCROFT FOUNDATION